THE
WOLF DUKE

A VALOR OF VINEHILL NOVEL, VOLUME 2

K.J. JACKSON

First Edition: June 2019
ISBN: 978-1-940149-41-7

http://www.kjjackson.com

K.J. Jackson Books

Historical Romance:

Stone Devil Duke, *Hold Your Breath*
Unmasking the Marquess, *Hold Your Breath*
My Captain, My Earl, *Hold Your Breath*
Worth of a Duke, *Lords of Fate*
Earl of Destiny, *Lords of Fate*
Marquess of Fortune, *Lords of Fate*
Vow, *Lords of Action*
Promise, *Lords of Action*
Oath, *Lords of Action*
Of Valor & Vice, *Revelry's Tempest*
Of Sin & Sanctuary, *Revelry's Tempest*
Of Risk & Redemption, *Revelry's Tempest*
To Capture a Rogue, Logan's Legends, *Revelry's Tempest*
To Capture a Warrior, Logan's Legends, *Revelry's Tempest*
The Devil in the Duke, *Revelry's Tempest*
The Iron Earl, *Valor of Vinehill*
The Wolf Duke, *Valor of Vinehill*

Paranormal Romance:

Flame Moon
Triple Infinity, *Flame Moon #2*
Flux Flame, *Flame Moon #3*

Be sure to sign up for news of my next releases at
www.KJJackson.com

DEDICATION

– As Always,
For my favorite Ks

{ PROLOGUE }

"Torrie, we have to leave—the fire, smoke—the roof is coming down." Her voice screeching over the cracking of the inferno above their heads, Sloane lunged forward, grabbing her cousin's wrist as her eyes went frantic to the flames quickly eating the cottage roof.

Torrie didn't turn back to her, ripping her arm from Sloane's grasp. "I'm not leaving them." Desperate, but calm. Calm like she always was. Hell had just exploded around them and Torrie didn't so much as blink.

The smoke sank, surrounding Sloane, making every breath harder, thicker into her lungs than the last. She clawed her fingers around Torrie's arm again and wrenched her a step toward the door of the cottage. "The bloody roof is on fire, we have to get out of here now, Tor."

Torrie reversed course, yanking Sloane forward as she reached out and grabbed her mother's upper arm, her calmness quickly eroding. "Please, Mama. Please, come. Don't stay in here. Don't. Come with me—come with us."

Through the thickening smoke, flaming embers streaked down in front of Torrie's mother's face. Her mother looked to waver, glancing back at her husband and son.

"Torrie—"

"There isn't time, Mama. We have to get out now."

Sparks and flaming straw from the thatched roof rained down upon them, singeing Sloane's cheeks, the stench of her burning hair scorching her nostrils. She yanked Torrie back a step, screaming above the crackling filling her ears. "There isn't time, Torrie."

Wood splintered—angry—cracking above.

Blackness. Smoke becoming Sloane's world. Deafening her. Suffocating her.

But she was on her feet, not knocked to the ground. And her lock on Torrie was still solid.

An arm wrapped about her waist. Lifted her.

Jacob—her fool brother was keeping the blackguards outside at bay, but now he was inside this hell with them. Inside and picking her up.

Her left hand on Torrie's arm slipped off. She couldn't see through the wall of smoke, couldn't hear for the crash echoing in her ears. But at the last second before Jacob dragged her out of there, she swung out her right hand and—miracle—found Torrie's arm again.

She wasn't going to let go. She couldn't. Not of the one person who'd been her constant companion since she was three. Not of the only other person that she loved just as much as her brothers. For that was what Torrie was—her sister, even if they didn't share parents.

With Sloane tucked into his iron clamp about her waist, Jacob moved, turning to where she guessed the door was. She could feel Torrie's weight shift, her body dropping, dragging behind them.

She wasn't going to let go.

She wasn't.

Five steps of her brother's long stride, and he carried her out of the inferno of the fiery wreckage, while she dragged Torrie behind them.

Air. Air that wasn't smoke. Hazy daylight.

But flames still in front of her.

She twisted in Jacob's arms and he dropped her with a thud.

Torrie's face. Screaming. Flames devouring her.

Her skirts.

Sloane couldn't hear the screams, but every agonized contortion of Torrie's face sliced through her as her own pain. She had to put the flames out.

Crawling through the dirt, she reached Torrie writhing on the ground and started beating at the flames raging on her cousin's legs.

Her own flesh scorching, pain sliced into her left arm as the blazes sizzled through her skin. Pain that sent her nerves into spasms, but still she swung at the blazes.

The flames weren't going to win. They weren't going to take Torrie.

Not Torrie.

Not the best of them.

Blackness in front of her. Charred cloth. Seared skin. Her arm, Torrie's legs.

But the flames were out.

They were out.

Her head twisted.

Jacob. Where was Jacob?

She squinted through the flying embers and smoke.

No.

No, no, no.

He couldn't have gone back in.

"Jacob. Jacob!" She couldn't hear her own scream. Didn't know if her lungs made sound. She couldn't find her feet. Her head down, battling against the pain that threatened to flatten her to the ground, she dragged herself across the scorched earth toward the cottage.

She hadn't made it a foot before an explosion of spark and ash flashed in front of her, filling the air. The rest of the roof collapsed inward. A flaming hell searing everything to a crisp. To soot. To nothing.

Jacob. Torrie's mother, brother and father. All of them.

It didn't matter that she was still gasping for clean air. Didn't matter that her burnt left arm hung limply along her body. None of that stopped the raging pain searing through her veins.

She looked up at the corner of the cottage—the one corner that still stood and hadn't crashed inward with the roof. One of the blackguards that had set a flaming torch onto the cottage roof stood three steps from the flaming corner, watching her, a jeering sneer on his face.

The red that hit her eyes blinded her, blinded her to everything except for the bastard. Vicious fury surged through her limbs and she found her feet, picking up the dagger that Jacob had discarded to the ground.

She charged.

He had to pay.

Someone had to pay.

{ CHAPTER 1 }

Her toes butting up against the weathered grey stone, Sloane craned her neck, looking up at the wall looming before her, thick vines snaking their way upward.

She could do this. She'd done it hundreds of times growing up at Vinehill.

She reached out, her kidskin-gloved fingers wrapping about the hefty vine and tugging it.

Sturdy.

Sturdy enough for her weight.

A quick glance to her right and the soft glow of hundreds of torches lit on the grounds of Wolfbridge Castle flickered around the curve of the tall tower that marked the end of this wall. Between it and the three-quarter moon above, she could just discern the line she would need to take upward to be able to pop into the open window on the third level.

When Sloane and her maid, Milly, had weaved their horses through the thick woods on the northwest side of the hexagonal castle two days ago, scrutinizing the ancient ruddy tan stones, she'd known instantly this would be her best chance at getting into Wolfbridge unseen. The six sides of the structure were punctuated at each juncture with tall circular towers jutting into the sky, and they cloistered this side of the castle in darkness.

The castle had held a formidable seat of power once upon a time. Still so, if all the rumors she'd uncovered about the man living here were true.

She swallowed a deep breath and looked upward. The thickness of the vines tangling their way up the side of this wall was perfect. Combined with the house party the duke was throwing moving all attention for his guests to the front and south side gardens, the timing could not be better.

She could get up and into the castle. And then she could ruin the man.

The Duke of Wolfbridge—the Wolf Duke, a lone beast that was a cold and merciless scourge upon this earth—needed to pay for his sins and she was the one that would make him do so.

Shrugging off her short dark spencer jacket and tugging off the glove from her right hand, she bundled them together and set them on the ground, tucking them in between a fat root and the castle stone so they would be hidden were anyone to stroll by. She shoved the cap sleeves of her black dress high onto her shoulders. She couldn't afford to have the fabric cramping her movements if she was to do this as quickly as she hoped.

Adjusting the fine muslin of her dress between her legs, Sloane frowned. Breeches would have been preferable for climbing—as she would always steal her brothers' breeches when they were young—but she had no access to male clothing at the coaching inn where she'd left Milly. The dark dress, though not a full ball gown, would suffice if someone happened by her and inquired about her presence at Wolfbridge. She could easily claim she'd just arrived for the house party, a distant relative of the duke's. It would allow her enough margin of time to get to her horse tied beyond the tree line before the duke could verify she was an unknown.

The strains of the string ensemble playing outside from a balcony above the gardens floated into the warmth of the night air. For how cool the summer had been, steamy air had rushed the land in the last two days. With one last quick glance about her, Sloane set the toes of her boots onto the vines. Her hands searching through the leaves, she found trunk after trunk, quickly scaling up the side of the castle.

First level.

Only two more to go.

As she stretched up high with her right hand, her left hand slipped. Her muscles coiling, her right fingers snatched hard onto the nearest vine, the tips of her boots digging into the toeholds she'd found.

She stopped for one moment, her cheek resting on the cool green leaves as she stared at her left hand, shaking it.

She'd kept her left glove on but now regretted it. The leather was starting to slip with the night dew on the leaves.

Or was it her strength that failed her? As much as she'd tried to deny it, her left arm had never been as strong as it once was since the fire.

Damn her weak limb.

She flipped her head, setting her left cheek onto the leaves. She looked up, finding her line again in the shadows of the moon. She had to do this. Had to make it up there. She'd been planning this for too long for it to slip away because of a slippery glove.

A grimace set onto her lips and she clamped her left fingers hard around the vine they'd just slipped from.

Up. Only up.

Right toes solid. Arm up. Left toes solid. Arm up. Up. Up.

She was almost there. The vines were getting thin, but she was almost there. Two more hand clasps and she could wedge her foot onto the sill of the window.

She reached up with her right hand, stretching to her full length, lifting on the toes of her right foot. Risky, but she had to make it to the next vine.

The tingle started, sudden. Sudden and paralyzing, flooding her left arm.

Her left hand lost all feeling.

She grasped with her right. A clump of leaves.

Only leaves.

Their thin stems plucked—one tiny break after another—from the vine.

She slipped backward before she even knew what was happening.

Into the air.

The warm summer breeze cocooned her, almost comforting her as she fell.

Down.

Down.

Blackness.

~ ~ ~

"This had better be of life and death, Colton." Reiner Doran, Duke of Wolfbridge, trailed his butler, his long strides stuttered by the elderly servant's short, stooped steps.

Follow him. That was all Colton had told him, and he hadn't taken no for an answer. That Colton had even approached him in front of his guests conveyed the direness in his butler's mind on whatever had happened.

His household ran with nary a bump due to years of Colton's diligence, but his man could have at least waited until Reiner had extracted the next proposed runs of the ship, *The Nettled Ness*, from Lord Falsted.

Colton slowed, turning back to Reiner. "It is, your grace." He waved his wrinkled hand in the darkness. "Almost there."

Reiner looked out to the forest that abutted the clearing that surrounded Wolfbridge castle. Still. Still and thick, the air. Quiet with only the muted strains of the strings from the garden balcony in the night sky. A sound, almost like a horse nickering, floated through the air from the shadow of the trees. He shook his head.

A trick of the wind. What would a horse be doing in that thick of trees?

He looked forward. Colton was five steps ahead of him, walking around the curve of the tower anchoring this span of the castle.

The second he turned around the edge, he saw exactly why Colton had dragged him away from the party.

One of his footmen, Lawrence, stood waiting in the dark shadow of the castle. At his feet, a lump.

Reiner's steps sped and he passed Colton. He didn't stop until he reached the lump.

Except it wasn't a lump. It was a woman.

"We didn't move her, your grace." Colton hurried to catch up behind him. "Lawrence found her and retrieved me. I thought it best to retrieve you."

Reiner nodded, looking down at the woman. Dressed in black, that Lawrence had even noticed her in the deep shadow she was sprawled in was impressive.

"Is she alive?"

"Yes. Just dead to the world, your grace. Lawrence rolled her onto her back, but beyond that we didn't move her." Colton pointed up to the wall of the castle, his unfailingly steady voice not in the slightest vexed. "The best we can liken, she fell from the vines if that bump on her head is an indicator."

"Climbing…the vines? Whatever for?" Reiner looked up at the vines clambering up the stones of the ancient castle. A thick curtain of greenery, yes, but he doubted a person could use the creeper to climb upon. He reached out, his fingers stretching into the clumps of leaves. Finding a vine, he wrapped his hand around. Thick. He shook it. It didn't move.

It was possible. But why?

His eyes lifted and scanned the stone wall, straying to the right. An open window. An open window to his dressing room. He'd left it open himself not but four hours ago for the heat of the day.

But that was on the third level. No one would be foolish enough to climb that high on vines, of all things.

"A common thief?" Reiner whispered the possibility, even though he didn't quite believe it.

"It is what we imagine. What would you like to do with her, your grace?" Colton asked.

Reiner's look dropped to the woman. The top of her body caught what little light there was in the shadows. The blond hair about her temples was pulled back in a braid, but the rest of it was free from pins, spreading wide about her shoulders. The waist of her dark dress was high, just below the tight bodice, and the fabric spread from her torso with silky ease.

Reiner dropped to balance on his heels and picked up the hem of her skirt. Expensive, silk or extremely fine muslin. She was no ordinary thief.

"Why the black?" Reiner muttered more to himself than a question to his men.

"That's why we figured she was a thief," Lawrence said. "The black is all the better to hide in the shadows."

Reiner dropped the hem, grunting to himself. "Or she's in mourning."

He picked up her left wrist. The cream kidskin glove she wore stretched up past her elbow. She wore no glove on her right hand.

Still balancing on his heels, he looked up at Lawrence. "What did you find with her?"

"Just this jacket—her other glove was wrapped with it, though it's much shorter." Lawrence held up a bundle of items. "And this dagger from a sheath at her calf and her reticule strapped about her waist."

Reiner motioned for them. Lawrence handed him the items. He set the jacket on the ground, first looking inside the reticule. Coins, nothing else. He set it onto her jacket.

The knife he flipped around in his hand. Not ordinary. He ran the blade across his thumb. Honed sharp. The handle caught a shard of light from the moon, gold flashing. He squinted in the darkness. The smooth onyx handle was inlaid with strands of gold—a vine weaving, climbing toward the hilt.

This woman was no ordinary thief. She was of money, if nothing else. Her clothes, her coin, the smell of citrus and lavender lifting from her hair. Possibly even of a titled family.

But what would she be doing attempting to sneak into his home? On a vine of all things.

A shot of rage ran down his spine.

Lord Falsted.

The man would stoop to send just such a woman after him. After his secrets.

"Bring her to the Rose room."

"But, your grace, that is far too close to your chambers," Colton said. "There is still a room in the south wing available."

"I'll not have a possibly hazardous unknown locked into a room near the rest of our guests. Not until I know who she is and what she came here for."

"I can set her in the cellars."

"That is assuming she is here to do harm, Colton. We don't know what her business is here. She comes from money, judging by her dress. And if she is an innocent and connected to one of my guests—possibly injured or left for dead here, then I'll not have her waking in the cold dank of the undercrofts."

"But, your grace—"

"I can lock the door on the Rose room. We can lock the shutters." Reiner stood, looking at Colton. "She'll not escape the room if her intentions here are as we suspect."

Colton nodded. "As you wish, your grace." He motioned for Lawrence to pick up the woman.

Reiner turned, walking back the way he came.

He had a party to get back to.

{ CHAPTER 2 }

Reiner held the cup of water in his right hand, staring down at the young woman lying in the middle of the tester bed in the Rose room.

The night and day had come and gone and she hadn't roused. There hadn't been even a flutter of her lashes, but her breathing had remained steady.

His anger had not.

If this was what he suspected—and likely he was correct—that she'd been sent by Lord Falsted, then he planned to drag every modicum of information about who she was and what she was sent to do from her.

No matter what it took.

Her horse had been found just beyond the tree line this morning. The fine creature and the saddle just gave evidence to the fact that she had wealth behind her. Whose wealth was the current mystery. Not one of his guests made any mention that they were expecting a young woman to join them, nor did any act particularly guilty—as if they had just attacked an innocent woman and dumped her body behind the castle.

It would be exactly like Falsted to send a woman such as this to him to ruin him. The man's suspicions of Reiner knew no bounds. To his face, Falsted was nothing but congenial and accommodating. But Reiner knew the depths of the man's distrust.

In the dwindling evening rays of daylight streaming in through the slats of the locked shutters across the windows, he could see the woman's features plainly.

Blond hair with a slight curl to it. Rogue red strands weaved in with the deep honey color. Her bone structure delicate, her straight, perfectly proportioned nose tipped up a notch at the end, lending impishness to her face. Dark lashes fell long against her smooth white skin while her high cheekbones lent an air of grace to her face. Her flawless complexion was interrupted only by a feathery dusting of freckles across the bridge of her nose and the rather large bruised lump just above her left temple.

His look travelled down the length of her. Not short, not tall, she was proportioned well with nice curves along her svelte body. His gaze paused at the creamy skin rising above the bodice of her dress. Her breasts were tight against the dark fabric, rising up from her ribcage, perfect mounds to cup.

A beauty from head to toe.

Some bastard knew what he liked. Reiner had plenty of enemies—Falsted was just the most disgruntled at the moment. So he just had to find out which one of his enemies this chit worked for. How dangerous she was. He knew plenty of people would like to see him ruined—or dead.

Taking a long moment, his attention went down to his wrist and he folded back the fabric of his white lawn shirt to his mid-forearm. With the majority of his guests gone, he'd foregone his coat, opting for just a shirt and waistcoat for this confrontation. Changing the cup of water to his left hand, he repeated the process with his other sleeve. His fingers tightening around the glass, he stepped closer to her on the bed.

Without pause, he tossed the water into her face.

She jerked, curling onto her side in the bed, but didn't rouse.

At least she was moving.

Reiner went to the basin of water atop the chest of drawers and dipped the cup into it, filling the glass. He moved back to the bed, splashing the water full onto her face.

A brutal gasp and she sputtered, jolting upright in the bed, her arms flailing. Wiping the water from her lashes, she frantically looked around.

No sense of time or place in her eyes.

Her look landed on him.

Stark terror shot through her eyes. Blue eyes. Light blue eyes with the oddest rogue streak of golden amber that burst upward in her left iris. That one flaw in the unique color, as though Leonardo had mixed the color of her eyes from the seas, but then a speckle of gold paint had fallen into the creation.

Her head swung to the left side, searching. Searching. She gasped, pausing for a second as she saw the side table.

He'd set her dagger there on purpose, curious to see what she would do with it.

He didn't have to wait long.

In the next instant, her legs swung out from the bed and she popped onto her feet, snatching the knife and scurrying to the far corner of the room. A practiced hand, she held the onyx-handled blade deftly with seasoned grace.

One question answered.

She wasn't some innocent maiden dumped behind his castle.

Dagger high and pointed at him, she moved backward until she ran into the wall. Her gloved left hand flattened on the plaster for support as she eyed him. "Who are you?"

"Who am I?" Reiner turned from her, walking over to the chest of drawers to set the cup atop. He looked at her over his shoulder. "No I think the question is 'who are you?'"

Her head shook slightly. "No you—where am I and how did I get in here?"

Interesting—a Scottish lilt lined her words. He hadn't expected that. Reiner faced her fully, his arms crossing over his chest. "What were you doing trying to sneak into my home?"

She flicked the knife in the air. "I don't have a blasted idea where I am, sir, so I most certainly did not attempt to sneak into your home."

His eyebrow cocked. "No?"

"No." She shoved off from the wall, approaching him, the tip of the dagger high at his chest. "Now tell me where in the hell I am."

He didn't flinch. "You would like to play a game, then? Fine. You are at Wolfbridge Castle."

"Wolf…" Her look narrowed at him, confusion flickering across her eyes. "Wolfbridge…"

"Castle."

"What—where?" She shook her head and took another step toward him, the dagger within striking distance. "How did you get me here?"

"What's your name?"

She flicked the blade back and forth in the air. "Tell me how in the bloody hell you got me here."

"Tell me your name and I'll answer your question."

She paused for a moment, her lips pulling back tight. "Sloane." The word seethed from her mouth.

He offered a quick nod. "Sloane it is. I am Reiner. And I didn't get you anywhere. You got yourself to my grounds and I merely had the lump of you picked up from the dirt and set in here. But I'm pretty well convinced you already know that fact."

Confusion sank her gaze to slits, deep lines etching out from the edges of her eyes.

Reiner had to give her credit—she played it well, an actress of the highest order.

She gasped a deep breath, the air shaky into her lungs. "No. Impossible. I—I don't ken a Wolf—what is it?"

"Wolfbridge."

"No." Her look went hard. "No. I don't ken a Wolfbridge Castle." She flicked the blade higher. "Now let us try the truth, sir. Who are you?"

"I'm not the one telling lies, Sloane, if that is your true name." His left arm flicked up from the clamp across his chest and his finger circled around the room. "And you will be my guest—locked in here, of course, until you can remember who you are and what you planned to do once you broke into my home."

Her gaze flew about the room, pausing on one of the locked shutters across the windows. Her look travelled to each shutter. Two. Three. Four. All locked. Her head swiveled to the door. Closed.

Without warning, she lunged at him, dagger swiping wide. Reiner jumped a step backward just out of her reach.

A gargled squeak choked through her throat and her chest heaved in panic—in anger. His gaze dipped down.

Damn, the water had seeped onto the front of her dress, soaking it and turning the dark fabric almost transparent. Thin stays and an even thinner chemise matted to the fabric, leaving nothing to the imagination.

"What?" Her face scrunched in confusion for a second and then she followed his gaze, looking down.

Her stare flung up. "You bloody heathen." She lurched forward with the dagger high, swinging for him.

Reiner side-stepped her, dodging the flashing blade. He kept moving, forcing her to circle him. Swipe after swipe through the air, but she couldn't come close enough to nick skin.

They rounded each other four times.

"My brothers." Her voice screeched, the dagger swiping. "My brothers will come for you—they'll come for you with the force of a hundred men raging for blood."

"I doubt it." He dodged to the right, then stepped toward her and snatched her flailing wrist in midair.

She screamed and he twisted her back toward the bed, cracking the bones of her forearm across the left bottom bedpost. The dagger clattered to the wood floor.

He leaned in, his breath fuming as he set his face directly before hers. "Tell me who you work for."

Their eyes locked. For all his oversized menacing, she stared up at him with just as much raging defiance.

Five minutes with her and he'd lost his temper.

He never lost his temper.

The one tenet of his life. Always in control. Cold and in control.

He stood straight, tossing her wrist to the side, and bent to pick up the dagger. It had served its purpose.

Quick—a ghost wisping past him—she ran for the fireplace and picked up the iron poker.

Spinning fast, she swung it out. Swung it hard, the air whooshing around the metal.

She twisted on her feet, losing her balance and stumbling to the side. "My head." Her left hand went up, gripping at the lump at her temple. "Oh—hell—it hurts—it—" She fumbled another step to the left. "What—what did you do—it—"

She swayed in a wide circle, her face blanching white.

The fire poker fell from her hand, her eyelids flickering.

She dropped, collapsing straight down, her body crumpling onto itself.

Reiner stood, his breath still seething, staring at her inert form on the floor for a long minute. Waiting for her to move.

Surely she was playing at a ruse.

Another minute.

He set her dagger onto the top of the chest of drawers, far out of her reach, then approached her, kicking the fire poker away from her. He nudged her ribcage with his boot.

No reaction.

He dropped, balancing on his heels, and brushed back the moist blond hair from her face. Grabbing her chin, he shifted her head, turning her face to him. Dead weight.

Back to the sleeping angel.

Angel asleep. Demon awake.

He sighed and stood.

For a long moment he stared down at her.

Just as he was about to turn and walk out the door, his legs bent on their own accord and he slipped his left arm behind her back and his right under her knees. He lifted her, carrying her to the bed, and he set her on the rosy silk coverlet.

Fully intending to leave, he stepped away from the bed but then glanced at her one more time. Her left arm, still encased in the long kidskin glove, had landed unnaturally folded under her back.

That would eventually hurt.

With a sigh, he stepped back to the bed and settled her arm naturally alongside her torso, decidedly averting his gaze from her nipples peeking through the still wet fabric across her bodice.

With a sneer of disgust at his own action of mercy, he abruptly turned from her, grabbing the dagger off the chest and the iron poker from the floor before stalking to the door.

He'd be getting his answers from her soon enough.

One way or another.

{ CHAPTER 3 }

A dream.

A dream she was not at home in Vinehill. Somewhere far away. Indescribable. Anger coursing through her. Anger. Rage. And then a man out of nowhere. Jacob? Lachlan? No. Not her brothers.

The dark-haired man walked toward her, a dagger in his hand. Her dagger. How did he get her dagger?

Torrie's voice in her ear. Crying. Screaming. Begging her for help. Begging her to kill her. Sloane spun in a circle, searching for her cousin. Searching for a way to squelch her suffering.

A full circle and she again faced the man with her dagger morphing in and out of focus.

A dream slipping away.

She cracked her eyes open. Darkness. Darkness all around her. Stuffy air, almost suffocating.

Her eyes opened wider. No, not complete darkness. Slivers of moonlight eked in through the window. Coals glowed orange in a fireplace across the room.

Coals that should be on the opposite side of her.

She reached up, feeling the headboard above her. She wasn't upside down in bed.

Her head flipped on the pillows, her eyes seeking out the moonlight. The curtains weren't drawn, so why only slivers?

Slats—shutters. The windows in her bedroom didn't have shutters.

Where was she?

Her head weighing a thousand stones, she rolled to her side, lifting herself upright. The tips of her boots touched the floorboards. Why was she wearing boots in bed?

With a heave upward, she gained her feet and staggered toward the glowing coals in the fireplace. Onto her knees, and her fingers stumbled in the darkness until she found a chunk of wood sitting beside the fireplace on the marble hearth. She lifted it, pushing the edge of it into the glowing coals. The last thing the air in the room needed was more heat, but she couldn't see a thing.

The bark of the wood quickly caught flame and with the light she looked around at her surroundings. A bedroom—pretty with light colors decorating the room. White walls. Peach and rose-colored fabrics. A sturdy chest of drawers along the wall by the windows. A tester bed with thin, graceful lines. A plump wingback chair by the fireplace two feet away from her.

She was lucky she didn't stub her toe on the chair in the darkness.

Her eyes closed for a moment as her chin dipped to her chest.

She recognized this room. The room from her dream.

She sank backward, landing with a thud on her backside as her eyes opened.

The dream—not a dream. Reality. The man. The man that had been in this room demanding things from her—real. What had he demanded?

Her mind raced back hours.

Her name.

He wanted to know her name.

And she wanted to know where she was.

She'd been at Vinehill, safe in her bedroom, and now she was here. How could that be?

The man had told her—what was this place? Wolfbridge? A castle?

Her gut sank.

He was holding her captive in this room. He'd said so himself.

Why?

Who in the bloody hell did he think he was?

Her hand went to her forehead, rubbing it, trying to coax memories forward.

Reiner. He'd said his name was Reiner. And he wanted to know something from her. He wanted to know who she worked for. What she was doing there.

Surely she was still caught in a dream.

Her right hand dropped from her forehead and she went to pinch her left arm. Soft leather caught under her fingertips.

She looked down. Why would she be wearing a long kidskin glove so far up her left arm? That did nothing to help abate the heat in the room.

Flummoxed, she peeled the leather down her arm and off her hand.

She saw it instantly, but didn't recognize what it was.

Only that it was horrifying.

Her left hand shaking, she lifted it to the light of the fire to find strings of thick white skin wrapping, twisting around her forearm. The skin between it bright pink. Scars. Grotesque.

It wasn't her arm. Not her arm.

She screamed. Trying to brush it—scratch it—off her limb, trying to scrub the thick, tough scars from her skin. They didn't move.

"Get it off. Get it off. Get it off."

The screams came one after another, her fingernails digging into her scar tissue, trying to rip it from her body, rip it away. It wasn't hers. It wasn't her arm. Not her arm. Not her skin.

No matter how she dug into the mangled flesh, it didn't release. Her screams out of control, swallowing her whole, her look flew frantic to the flames.

Burn it away. She could burn it away.

On her hands and knees, screams still deafening and raw in her throat, she scrambled to the fire. Lifting her left arm, she thrust it out toward the blaze.

The tips of the hungry flames licked out and the instant before the heat singed her, she was slammed backward.

Hurled—sliding across the room until she hit the foot of the bedpost. Crumpled on the floor, she twisted, looking back toward the fireplace.

The man. The man from her dream. Reiner.

He stood between her and the flames, shirtless, only partially buttoned trousers covering his lower half. His arms curled out from his body, limbs of steel with his hands clasped into fists. His chest raged in heavy breaths. An angry Greek god of chiseled stone, except he was alive and breathing with flames of hell flashing behind him.

She looked down at her left arm. "It's still there." Shrieks she couldn't control flew from her mouth and she started clawing at her arm again.

A hand landed across her mouth, stifling her screams.

His other hand clamped down on her right wrist, yanking it from ripping away her own skin.

Her left hand found a target on his chest, connecting hard, and with a grunt, he sank down next to her, twisting her into his arms until she was on his lap, clamped to his body. He even wrapped a leg around hers to lock her into place.

She wasn't able to move and she knew it. But still she struggled, her body contorting against his chest, trying to free herself.

She struggled for minutes until she realized she wasn't going to be set free. Not under her own power.

She stilled. What would her brothers have her do?

Lachlan—he'd have her fight, fight with everything she had.

Except twice now, that hadn't worked.

Jacob—he'd have her stifle her rage and ask calm, common sense questions that gave no hint as to what she was thinking.

That, she hadn't tried.

Her gaze on the fire, her body stayed still as she tried to ignore the humiliation of being tangled in this heathen's arms.

A full minute passed before his hand dropped from her mouth and locked around her chest.

A slight cough to loosen the screams still lodged in her throat and she opened her mouth. "What did you do to me?"

His arms twitched and he tightened his hold. "Why do you insist I did all of this to you?"

"I was at Vinehill, and now I'm here. With a lump on my head that is shooting hot blades into my skull and an arm that is shredded and shriveled to monstrous proportions." Her head bowed, and she had to close her eyes against the swatch of mangled skin on her arm she could see peeking past his straining muscles. The breath she took stayed in her throat, not sinking into her lungs. "What happened to me?"

"That's exactly what I would like to know, Sloane."

"Why do you think I was trying to break into your home?"

"You were found just below the window to my chambers, unconscious. It appeared you were trying to climb vines to gain entrance into my castle."

"Climb vines?" Her muscles tensed. Climb vines— of course she would have no trouble climbing vines and storming a castle—she'd been doing that very thing at Vinehill since she was five. If she was trying to break into a home, that was exactly how she'd do it.

Information she had best keep to herself.

But she'd never heard of Wolfbridge Castle before, much less this man. There was no reason for it.

More information she wasn't about to share. From what little she could piece together, she'd lost time somehow.

Lost time and something drastic had happened. How else to explain her arm?

She tried twisting her head to look up at him, but could only catch a glimpse of his sharp jawline. "This castle—it is yours? You said 'my castle.'"

"Yes."

"And you think I was attempting to sneak into your chambers?"

"Yes."

"For what purpose?"

"That is what I'm waiting to hear from your lips."

"And you'll not let me go until you ken?"

"Correct."

With every word he spoke, his bare chest rumbled, vibrating behind her. Wholly indecent. Her look shifted forward and she stared at the flames for several long breaths.

At least Jacob's approach had orientated her to her current predicament. It didn't explain how she got there, or what had happened to her arm or her head. But it helped. Maybe her eldest brother truly was wise, as he always liked to remind her.

"Please let me go?" The request left her lips deflated, all fight gone from her body.

"Swear you won't try and attack me again?" His upper arms tensed, jutting into the outer edges of her shoulders.

She nodded.

"I need to hear it."

"I won't attack you. It's not like it would matter against this…" Her head shifted to the side and motioned to his body towering against hers. "This mass that you have."

He grunted—half of it an inordinately pleased chuckle—and his arms loosened their hold. Just as she was about to escape his grasp, his arms clamped around her again, locking her into place.

"Swear you also won't try and tear at your arm again— or burn it."

Her eyes closed, a long breath exhaling, and she nodded.

"I need to hear—"

"I swear I won't try and rip my arm off or burn it."

His hold lifted, setting her body free.

Disbelief that he released her so easily held her still and it took her an awkward moment to realize she needed to remove herself from his lap.

She scrambled off his legs, landing on the front edge of the marble hearth.

He pulled his legs up and rested both of his arms on the tips of his knees. His gaze locked onto her, hard, suspicious. For how dark his hair was, his eyes were light—brown but with light flecks of blue, maybe gold in them. It was hard to discern in the scant light of the fire. Hard to discern when his stare made her want to squirm.

She caught sight of the distorted flesh on her arm, and she lifted it, her eyes squinting as she looked at it in the light of the flames. Calm, or at least with eyes that weren't frantic, she could see the many cords of scar tissue running in long threads along her skin, as though her arm had been turned inside out, the tendons now dried and living on the outside instead of the inside. Her stomach rolled. "What—what is this?" She held her arm up to him.

"You don't know what did that to you?" His gaze caught on her eyes for a long breath before it dropped to her arm. "It looks like fire. Like your arm was burned to an extreme. It is what flesh looks like as it heals from a burn. You have no recollection?"

She shook her head, words unable to form as her gaze went down to her arm.

Fire? Burn?

How could she have suffered this and not remember?

He sighed, his left hand lifting to rub his eyes. "You are either the most skilled actress I have ever come across or it appears as though that lump on your head has knocked time and sense out of you." His fingers dropped from his eyes and his gaze skewered her. "Which is it?"

Sloane attempted to read his face, but there was nothing to discern. Just cold countenance.

She wasn't sure if he meant to attack her in the next breath or leave the room. And she wasn't sure which answer she spoke would produce which result.

Avoiding his hawk eyes, she looked down and flipped her left leg out from under her skirts. "I'm to be your captive?"

"Until you tell me who you work for and what you hoped to do—or steal—in my chambers, you are."

"And if I cannot remember?"

"I think you will. Whatever drove you here will not wait forever and I think you will break."

Averting her look as much as she could from her left arm, she loosened the laces on her left boot and pulled her toes free. She set the boot down with a clunk. "Then I may as well get comfortable in here since I don't have the answers you're seeking." She went to work on her right boot.

Both her feet free after tugging off her stockings, she wiggled her toes. Heaven. How long had she been wearing those? A day? Two?

Reiner gained his feet and stepped closer to her, his bare feet almost touching her skirt.

She dared a glance upward.

His face seethed with skepticism. "You'll find my patience will outweigh any game you are about to play here, Sloane."

"And I think you will find that I cannot confess to anything I cannot remember, Reiner." She set a sweet smile on her face. "Do you feed your captives, or do they wither away till death takes them?"

"It's the middle of the night. So they wither away until morning and a proper breakfast time has come." He turned from her, walking to the door.

Without another word, he exited the chamber.

The click of the lock echoed into the room.

Her chest fell, the air rushing out of her.

If she was going to be freed of this room, she would have to do much better than that.

{ CHAPTER 4 }

Two days.

Two days she'd been stuck in this stuffy, wretched room.

The insufferable man had delivered food—terribly delicious food, at that. Had a maid come in to empty the chamber pot. Made sure she had enough wood for the fireplace, not that the room needed any more heat stuffed into it. With the shutters locked against the windows, she hadn't had the slightest whiff of fresh air in days.

But beyond that, she hadn't caught the tiniest glimpse of this place she was captive in, save for the four walls surrounding her.

Her attention dropping from the shutters that were the current bane of her existence, Sloane looked down at her fingernails. The white slivers of her nails had been worn down to the skin, and now shocks of pain ran up her fingers every time the tips of them touched something.

She'd tried everything she could think of to unlock one of the shutters from its window. A splinter of wood that she'd whittled against the fireplace grate to gain a sharp point. It broke in the lock. Her own fingernails scraping along the wood holding the hinges. She'd barely made a scratch in the hard wood. The bottom of one of the side table's legs that she'd smashed apart and then tried to wedge for leverage along the lower edge of the shutter. That shaft of wood had splintered apart in her hands.

There was little to work with in the room. The drawers in the chest were empty except for linens for the bed and two washcloths. A silver-handled hair brush that did her no good. If only she'd had pins in her hair instead of a braid tied off with a ribbon. A pin would have at least allowed her the possibility of picking one of the locks on the shutters.

Not that she knew how to pick a lock. But she had nothing but time on her hands and she might just be able to figure it out.

All she'd been rewarded with for her efforts were bloody fingers and patience that was growing very, very weak.

Every time Reiner had entered the room during the past days, he'd coldly asked her if she had anything to tell him. Her answer was always the same. No.

Not unless she wanted to make up some fantastical tale about what she was after. But she didn't have the slightest clue as to who the man was, much less what he would have to steal that she would be willing to scale a castle in search of it.

For the cold brutality that emanated from him, she assumed an easily spotted lie from her lips would not be rewarded well.

A clink in the door lock drew her attention. Judging by the sunlight streaming in through the top cracks of the shutters, it was still in the middle of the day—far too early for Reiner to appear with an evening meal.

Maybe he'd figured it out—how she got here—the wicked twist of fate that had put her into his path. Maybe he was coming in to set her free. Apologize for the gross misunderstanding this all was.

The lock in the door turned and the door cracked open.

A head—a little head—peeked past the door into the room.

"Oh—you—you exist." A girl, not more than nine with dark curls framing her face and huge blue eyes, leaned in past the doorway, one foot sneaking into the room.

Sloane's jaw dropped. "I—who? Yes, I exist—who do you think I am?"

The girl's head turned as she glanced back over her shoulder into the hallway for a long moment. She looked to Sloane. "Are you the woman I heard screaming the other night? Uncle Reiner said you were in my imagination. A dream or a ghost, perhaps. But I have been hearing other sounds."

"You have?"

"I thought it was the guests—they like to scurry about the castle, find dark nooks to hide about in chasing games that seem quite silly. But they all left more than a day ago and I still heard the sounds."

"What sounds?"

"Scraping—scraping wood, perhaps. It is hard to figure it, though it is constant. I guessed it was in here." The girl scooted back slightly, hiding behind the door, only one eye visible. "Wait—you aren't going to harm me—you aren't truly a ghost—or a witch? Is that why he has you locked in here?"

This was it—her chance to escape.

Sloane shook her head, remaining very still in her spot across the room by the shutters. If she could entice the girl further into the room, she could push her aside and run.

"No. I'm not a witch or a ghost. I'm just being held here by your…uncle for reasons I do not exactly understand. But I wish you no ill will—what is your name?"

"Vicky."

"Vicky, then—I will not harm you. Your uncle, well, what I would like to do to him is an entirely different matter and directly because of his boorish behavior."

Visible relief flashed across the girl's blue eyes and she slipped fully into the room, closing the door behind her. "Thank goodness. I understand there are those that don't care for my uncle, some that even wish him harm from the whispers I hear. But you, you look too nice—too pretty to want to harm him."

Sloane's cheek drew up in a wry smile. "Do not be fooled by pretty—your uncle is handsome as well, but quite clearly the man has a heathen's heart."

The girl shrugged. "Maybe, though I wouldn't know. He is usually kind to me."

"Usually?"

"He does not pay me much mind."

Sloane nodded. Reiner didn't seem to have the disposition to afford much attention to a nine-year-old girl.

She looked past Vicky to the door. If she pushed the child just to the left, she could slip out the door and hopefully find a way out of this castle.

The girl's eyes widened and she took a step backward, her hands going behind her to grip the door handle. "Please, miss, don't run. Uncle Reiner would be very upset with me if he knew I was in here and I accidently freed you. I'm not sure what he would do to me."

The fear in the girl's eyes struck Sloane to her heart. Curiosity didn't deserve chastisement.

And the reality was that Sloane doubted she could get far. She didn't know anything of this castle, how to navigate the corridors, how many people were on staff, what the grounds were like.

Even if she could escape from the castle, she still had no idea where she was. Wolfbridge. A place she'd never heard of. She could be on the continent for all she knew. Or in the Americas, for the span of time her memory failed her—enough time for her to burn her arm and for it to heal—that was more than enough time to sail far across the seas. Anything was possible.

Her chances of immediate escape were not good. Not with what little she knew.

She set a kind smile on her face. "I'll not get you in trouble. I promise to not try to escape past you. How did you get in here? The door is locked."

"The key is in Uncle Reiner's chamber, sitting on his secretary. He does not bother hiding it."

"Well then, I'm surprised he lied to you about what was in this room—if he didn't want an inquisitive child to find the key and look in here, I would think he would hide it."

"Yes, that is exactly what I thought, miss." Vicky's head bobbed up and down and one of her dark curls fell in front of her left eye. She blew at it, then shoved it behind her ear. "You are Scottish?"

"Yes."

"You look like a lady—I thought it from the first."

"I do?"

Vicky pointed to Sloane's skirts. "Your dress is fine, even if it has wrinkles in it."

Sloane glanced down, her hand attempting to smooth the deep-set wrinkles from her ribcage downward. Her left hand and arm had gone back under the long glove—only twice had she stripped it off since discovering what had happened to her arm.

Both times had not gone well.

Sloane shrugged. "I suppose I am."

Vicky's eyes went wide. "Are you a duchess? Or a countess? Or a marchioness?"

Sloane chuckled. "No, no. I'm not married. My grandfather is a marquess."

"Oh. Well, that is still very exciting." Vicky stepped further into the room, her hand wrapping along the lower right post of the tester bed. "The usual ladies that show up at Wolfbridge don't like me. They wrinkle their noses and pretend I'm not here."

"The visitors to Wolfbridge are not the kindest people?"

Vicky sighed, leaning to the side and swaying back and forth, a pendulum swinging from the post. "I don't know. Maybe not. I know I am young and they don't care for young girls, but I have started to plan for when I am old enough."

Sloane moved to the bed, sitting on the foot of it as she watched Vicky. "How?"

"I have been learning French and German and Italian even though I hate Italian. Uncle Reiner insists upon it. I have been learning to dance, but my governess is old and stodgy. Miss Gregory refuses to teach me anything exciting—only the most boring steps of the minuet."

Sloane laughed. "You would like to learn to dance something else?"

Vicky's swaying stopped and she looked directly at Sloane, her eyes serious. "Oh yes, the quadrille and the cotillion and the reels and most of all, the waltz."

Sloane started. "You have seen people waltzing?"

"Oh yes." Vicky went back to swinging. "I watch all the parties from the alcoves looking down into the ballroom from the upper level. I have a chair and a blanket and everything. Sometimes I fall asleep watching the ladies and gentlemen dancing through the balusters."

A smile came to Sloane's lips. She remembered that feeling well, the fancy of youth when everything of the years ahead of her glittered in romantic possibilities. "I am surprised you've seen the waltz—I understand it is not at all proper in the most respectable establishments."

"I don't imagine Miss Gregory thinks Wolfbridge is at all respectable. She mutters it all the time when Uncle Reiner leaves the room. But it is hopeless—Miss Gregory will not have it."

"I could teach you all of those dances."

Vicky stopped her swinging, her jaw dropping. "You can?"

"Of course."

Vicky's eyes narrowed at her for a long second. A mirror image of the same suspicion that crinkled Reiner's eyes when he looked at her. "Why would you do that?"

"I am bored to tears in this room—is that a good enough reason?"

"I guess so." Vicky looked around the room and her nose scrunched. "I would be bored in here as well." The

distrust in her eyes slipped away as she looked at Sloane. "What did you say your name was?"

"Sloane."

A sweet smile, almost shy, lifted her plump cheeks. "Then I am most happy I snuck in here, Miss Sloane."

Night had settled and the door opened. For one brief second, Sloane hoped it was Vicky again. The girl was sweet, and they'd spent an hour going through the steps of the quadrille this afternoon. Real conversation with Vicky had been beyond welcome and it had kept her mind off her current predicament.

The second of hope passed.

She wasn't so lucky.

Reiner walked through the door with a tray of food balanced on one arm and he closed the door behind him. The aroma of seasoned grouse and roasted rosemary potatoes wafted into the room. She sat on the foot of the bed with her bare feet tucked under her and Reiner gave her only the quickest glance as he moved across the room to set the tray on the small round table in the corner by the fireplace.

"Did you have anything to admit to me this eve, Sloane?"

"Nothing new since you last asked this morn, Reiner."

Both his question and her answer deliberate and calm—cordial—as it always was.

He turned toward her, his gaze on her curious. "No? I understand you had a rogue visitor today."

His words sent a spike of fear through her heart—not for herself but for little Vicky.

But for once his golden brown eyes weren't weighed down with grim distrust as he looked at her. Suspicion still laced his gaze, but the cold irate glare had tempered.

"I did." She moved to the edge of the bed, straightening her skirts as she draped her legs off the side. "I do hope you do not blame Vicky. She was only curious—odd noises were coming from a locked room. It was actually quite brave of her to venture in here."

His eyebrow cocked. "Brave?"

Sloane nodded. "She had no inkling what she would find beyond the door, yet she entered anyway. That is brave."

Reiner offered a slight nod and moved to the center of the room, standing before her. "You did not try and escape past her. Why?"

"She's an innocent child. She didn't deserve to be blamed for my escape were I to push past her." Her look skewered him. "If I'm going to escape past anyone, it is to be past you, Reiner."

The smallest smile lifted the right side of his mouth. "Be that as it may, the guests that I have had here at Wolfbridge have departed and I have decided something."

She eyed him cautiously, gaining her feet. Her palm went to the front of her dark dress to smooth the impossibly wrinkled fabric. "Which is?"

"I have decided to let you out."

"You've decided to set me free? Tell me where I am so I can go home?"

A caustic chuckle left his lips. "That is not about to happen, Sloane. You know exactly what you need to tell me for that to happen. I merely meant I will let you free of this room."

She folded her arms in front of her. "So I can assume there are conditions?"

"Yes. You'll have two of my men shadowing you at all times. You cannot speak to the staff as to why you are here. You are welcome to the castle interior and to go on strolls in the south garden. That is the extent of your freedom until you tell me exactly who you are, who you work for, and what you were after in my room."

She had to stifle a sigh. Those same, constant demands he made of her grated on her nerves. But she wasn't a fool. She would trade almost anything for fresh air after days in the stifling room.

"Why now?"

"Simple. I was entertaining guests, as I'm sure you noticed when you snuck onto my grounds. I couldn't set you free in the castle without questions I'd rather not answer being asked by my guests."

"Such as why you'd decided to hold an innocent young woman captive?"

"Something akin to that." His shoulders lifted. "Though I doubt your presence here would have made anyone blink twice. The people I consort with know exactly who they are dealing with."

"So you're a well-known savage?"

"I'm a well-known cold-hearted knave." His look pinned her. "Take the offer, Sloane."

For as much as it riled her pride, she wasn't in a position to refuse. She nodded.

"Good. I'll have a bath and fresh garments brought up for you. You can wear them while your clothes are being cleaned, since it appears you are determined to stay here for a spell."

A kindness she didn't expect from him—even if her presence here was not by her choosing and he well knew that fact. She chose to not argue the point. "Thank you."

He inclined his head. "I will unlock the door in the morning." He moved to the doorway, pausing as his hand wrapped around the door handle. He looked back to her. "You should know that my niece has taken quite a liking to you."

"She has?"

His look dropped to the floor and he half nodded, half tilted his head to the side as though he wasn't quite sure what to make of his own statement. "I have not seen her this happy since…well…never. You can thank her for your freedom—she was most insistent on it."

"You consider this freedom?"

His look lifted to her, his golden-brown eyes amused. "Freedom from the shackles of this room, then. Do you wish to rescind your acceptance of the terms?"

"I would be a fool to do so."

"Or stubborn beyond reason." A small grin carved into the corners of his mouth. "I did consider your refusal of the offer a distinct possibility."

"Then this proves how very reasonable I can be—how very *honest* I can be."

His eyebrows cocked. "Honesty can be a most slippery line depending on who's casting it, Sloane. I don't trust. It's the only thing that's kept me alive and whole. And I don't intend to start."

He stepped out of the room, clicking the door closed behind him.

Sloane stared at the door.

Insufferable. Truly insufferable.

{ CHAPTER 5 }

Sloane hid a smile as Miss Gregory left the spacious library.

Vicky was right. The woman did have the sourest disposition.

She held in her grin until Miss Gregory's footsteps echoed away along the stone corridor, the sound disappearing as she withdrew up the stairs to her chamber.

They'd been dancing—rather, practicing the steps to the dances Sloane was teaching Vicky. Miss Gregory had been disapproving, but willing to woodenly supply the music for the dances on the pianoforte with a chastising gleam in her eye. That was until Vicky had insisted it was time to learn how to waltz.

That, Miss Gregory could not stand for. With a condemning grunt, she'd exited the room to retire for the evening.

The last three days had been delightful—if she could consider being held prisoner in a far-too-large castle delightful. It was the prisoner part that rankled all her sensibilities. Beyond that, the days had been inordinately pleasant—the food the cook made was extraordinary and the castle had been thoroughly modernized as far as she'd seen. So very different from Vinehill, with its twisty stone corridors and drafty nooks. There wasn't a spot in the Wolfbridge that she hadn't felt the warm embrace of comfort.

It was unnerving, almost, this much opulence surrounding her. The duke was beyond wealthy. That much was obvious. Her home at Vinehill Castle in Stirlingshire was grand—but grand in the way only a six hundred year old castle could be. Ancient stones. A labyrinth of hallways. Cold that could sneak up upon her and freeze her to the bone. Her grandfather had rebuilt much of the castle, but it still held tight to ghosts of the past.

The governess's footsteps long since faded, Sloane finally looked at Vicky and could not help the laughter bubbling up from her throat. Vicky looked like a cat that had just eaten a canary—the only thing missing was froth foaming from her mouth.

"Do not look so pleased with yourself. Poor Miss Gregory is in serious straits over worrying on your immortal soul," Sloane said.

"She can worry on her own soul—she has no say in mine." Vicky walked away from the area in the middle of the library where they had rolled the rug up and cleared the furniture to make room for dancing. She stopped next to the pianoforte, picking up the sheet music she'd pulled and set in front of Miss Gregory. "I thought I could get her to play it before she realized what it was."

"She's a prude, not a lackwit, Vicky. I had a governess or two which were the exact same way."

"You did?"

"Yes. My brothers and I used to play a particular game—Valor of Vinehill—that would drive them each batty."

"Valor of Vinehill? That sounds exciting, how did you play it?"

"It involved climbing the vines that ran up the side of our grandfather's castle and then storming in through the windows. The one that could climb the fastest and quickest would win. And we had at least—"she paused, counting on her fingers—"six of our governesses quit after not being able to get us down from the wall. We were quite terrible rascals now that I reflect upon it."

Vicky giggled. "Terrible, maybe—though it does sound exciting—I wish I had brothers." Vicky set the sheet music back onto the pianoforte.

"Yes, I didn't ken it when I was younger—they thought I was a pest and I thought they were mean for not always including me—but now I would move heaven and earth for either of them."

"They sound like princes—are they handsome?"

Sloane chuckled. "I suppose some ladies are enamored with them—I've been looking at their faces for far too many years to be able to tell if they're handsome. Though if it feeds the fantasy of them, they are both big men— warriors." Her eyes darkened for a moment. "Warriors that will be out for blood once they discover I've been held captive here."

Vicky's eyes expanded to saucers. "They won't hurt Uncle Reiner, will they?"

"I don't ken what they'll do, Vicky."

"Well, then he should let you go. And apologize. That will stop them, won't it?"

"Possibly. I do agree with you—he should let me go." Her lips puckered into a frown. That was too much to hope for at the moment.

Claude and Lawrence—the two guards Reiner had ordered to follow her every step—sat just outside the library in the corridor. It'd been that way since the morning she'd found her door open when she awoke. They were always just outside the door—just ten steps behind her. It was clear Reiner had no intention of letting her go until he got answers.

Answers she wished she had for herself.

The most important answers she needed being what had happened to her arm and then, how did she get here?

Wiping the sourness from her face, Sloane clapped her hands and motioned for Vicky to come to her. "But let us not dwell on that, for it is something we cannot change at the moment. Let us start on the waltz—from what I can remember of it. Since we have no music I can hum a tune, if it will help."

"I thought you said you knew how to dance it." Vicky walked toward her.

"I do, but only from seeing it afar at a country ball and with an imaginary partner in my arms as I copied the steps. As I said, my governesses and chaperones were staunch protectors of my virtue and in London I was whisked away from any ballroom the moment the word 'waltz' was whispered. My grandfather had high, high standards of the poor women meant to keep my reputation impeccable." She chuckled to herself. "If it wasn't climbing vines, it was my penchant for being drawn to scandal at parties that did them in. I fear I owe all of them apology after apology."

Vicky grinned. "And I fear I will be much like you, Miss Sloane."

"Why? Is Miss Gregory not your first governess? How many have you gone through?"

The mischievous smile widened on Vicky's face. "She's my third."

Sloane chuckled. "Your third? My, you do put them through the paces, don't you? I always had my brothers to blame for the governesses throwing up their hands and leaving. It is unfortunate you don't have someone else to condemn as I did—it is entirely convenient to do so, whether they deserve the blame or not."

Sloane studied the girl for a long moment. Her thick dark hair and dark lashes set off the spark of her blue eyes. "You will be something to behold when you join the marriage mart in London in a number of years. So we best get to perfecting those steps. By the time you arrive in London, the waltz will be very proper, I imagine."

Vicky nodded, stepping in front of her.

"I will try and lead, though I never imagined myself in the role." Sloane set her right hand around Vicky's torso, just below her lower shoulder blade. "Your left hand will rest above my arm, just wrapping the outer tip of my shoulder." Vicky's hand went in place. "And then we clasp our other hands. I do believe they are held rather high."

Sloane centered their bodies and looked at Vicky. "It is three steps. You will go backward and I will go forward. One step, one to the side, and close the feet. Then we repeat starting with the other foot."

Vicky nodded. "It sounds simple."

Sloane cleared her throat, then a lilting hum bubbled from her throat. With a nod at Vicky, she started forward.

Her knee instantly bumped into Vicky's thigh. Vicky giggled.

"Apologies. We'll start again." Sloane reset her feet and started the tune once more. Another nod, and she stepped with her left foot toward Vicky. Her right foot went out to the side and her left foot closed the gap as she dragged Vicky with her. The girl hopped a step to catch up to Sloane just as she started forward with her right foot. Sloane banged into Vicky, tumbling atop her.

Hopping and tumbling were definitely not a part of the waltz.

Their arms tangled awkwardly and set Vicky into a fit of laughter. Sloane could do nothing but join in. "That is definitely not how it is done. It is hard to hum and think about my feet at the same time, much less consider where your feet are."

"Perhaps I could assist in that."

Sloane's gaze snapped to the library entrance.

Reiner filled the doorway, the width of his shoulders almost touching both sides of the wooden casing.

"Oh, yes, Uncle Reiner. Please do. We tried to convince Miss Gregory to play the pianoforte for the music, but she would have nothing to do with it. If you could play it, Miss Sloane could concentrate better on her feet."

A half smile lifted his cheek as he looked from Vicky to Sloane. "Shall I give it a go?"

Sloane's head tilted toward the pianoforte. "It may help."

"Then I am happy to oblige."

He strode across the room, passing Sloane and Vicky on the makeshift dance floor, and settled himself in front of the pianoforte.

After shifting the sheets of music in front of him, he studied them for a moment. His thick fingers spread atop the keys and without the slightest hesitation he worked through the first sheet in perfect tempo.

Thick fingers that had no business being that light upon the keys.

He paused and looked up at her and his niece. "Are you to begin?"

She jumped from her stare, and spun to Vicky. "Same as before—you are backward and I am forward." She set her hand onto Vicky's back and grabbed her hand. "Ready?"

"Yes."

Sloane nodded to Reiner.

He started playing again and after several beats, Sloane started forth. Left foot. Slide with right. Close. Right foot forward. Slide with left. Close. Left foot forward.

On that beat, Vicky went back with her left foot as well, and they collided. Vicky hopped back on her right foot.

With both of their heads bowed to concentrate on their feet, they went through the steps five more times, bumping into each other every other step.

The music ended with a chuckle coming from Reiner as Vicky bumped into Sloane once more.

She stepped away from Vicky with a sigh. "It would seem I am not as adept at leading as I had hoped. In my mind it went much better than that." She looked to Reiner. "Am I not doing it correctly? I do feel as though I have it down, but I do not lead very well—I cannot guide her into the next step as I should."

A grin set onto his lips. "No, it does lack some... finesse."

"Finesse?"

"The kind only a man well-versed in the dance could bring to the steps."

Vicky bounded over to the pianoforte, her fingers tapping on the rosewood. "You should show her, Uncle Reiner, so she can show me. I will play the music—I have been practicing the sheets for it."

His eyebrows lifted. "You've been practicing? Willingly?"

"Yes. I can do it."

Reiner edged his way off the bench and motioned Vicky to the open spot. "If it will get you to willingly practice, then I am a fool to say no."

Vicky quickly sank down onto the bench, arranging the sheets of music in front of her. She played a couple of bars, speeding up as she went until she was at the pace Reiner played at.

He walked across the room to Sloane and held out his left hand to her. "Shall we?"

She hesitated for one second, staring up at the man. She'd never imagined the first time she truly danced the waltz it was to be with a man she wasn't in love with— and of all things, the man that was currently holding her captive.

She glanced at Vicky. The girl was looking at her—her wide blue eyes pleading as she nodded her head.

Wrong. This was wrong for so many reasons.

But she lifted her right hand and set it in his.

His free hand slid around her side, settling just below her shoulder blade, and he pulled her a step closer than she ever would have dared to be near the man on her own.

Her head bowed, looking at the scant slice of floor between them.

"No, your eyes must be up," Reiner said. "Watching in my face where I am to lead you next—not staring at my feet. By the time my feet are moving it's too late. You have to see it in my eyes."

Of course. Of course he'd have her looking at him. All the better to pin his cold skeptical stare on her.

Her gloved left hand moved to sit along his shoulder and Sloane lifted her look to meet his.

His light brown eyes weren't the slightest bit wary. Warm even, the brown turning into a warm golden honey. Nothing like she'd seen in him before and it gave her pause—sent suspicion deep into *her* look.

"Flip it in your mind. You're going backwards now." He looked to Vicky. "You can begin."

He let Vicky get through four measures before his look centered on Sloane and he started forth.

The first steps went fine, but at the point she was to switch starting feet, her gaze dropped between them.

"Up. Eyes up."

The order made her jump and her gaze lifted and locked onto his.

She moved into the steps, letting his grip along her back guide her body, his hand covering hers dictate direction. One, two, three. One, two, three.

He shifted her around the cleared space of the floor three times before it felt natural, before she could read in his eyes exactly what his intention was for the direction of the steps.

His eyes had relaxed even more. Golden brown eyes. She studied them. Almost amber in the warm light of the library. Yet still eyes that would unnerve her if she wasn't so intent on concentrating where her feet were moving.

She was waltzing. For the first time in her life, she was sweeping across the floor in the scandalous, beautiful dance.

She cleared her throat as he shifted her around a turn. "You dance well."

"You expected I could not?"

"You aren't married, so I assumed you hadn't yet gone through your paces in the marriage mart, which would have honed your prowess on your feet."

His lips pursed for a moment. "Who said I wasn't married?"

Her head snapped back. "But Vicky said—you are?"

"No. I'm not." A grin came to his lips. "I was just curious how you get your information."

Her fingers on his shoulder lifted and she tapped him. "That was unfair."

"Convenient." The grin didn't leave his face. "To be honest, I haven't participated in the marriage mart because it's tedious and I have no need to go trolling for an heiress."

"Don't you have to produce an heir?"

His shoulders lifted slightly. "Eventually. Though it's not a priority for me."

Sloane nodded, a smile playing about the corners of her lips. "So you will just order a random, irreproachable lady from London when it comes to it?"

"I hadn't considered that, but it does sound like a palatable option."

A chuckle escaped her lips. "At least you will be able to woo the lass with your dancing skills."

"I don't imagine the wife I have will lower herself to waltzing, of all things."

"No?"

"No. Virtuous and of good birthing lines, as that would be her purpose. Not dancing."

She shook her head, averting her eyes from him.

"You think otherwise?"

Sloane met his look. "It sounds like you want a horse. What woman would willingly accept that in a marriage?"

"Anyone that married me."

Her fingers on his shoulder flipped up into the air. "Posh. Not when there is so much more to life than birthing heirs to a title."

His eyes flipped far too fast into frosty cold. "You are an expert on what women want in a marriage?"

"I am at least of the same gender—so that makes me more of an expert than you."

"I think you overestimate the women that would trade anything away to be a duchess."

She shrugged. "You're correct. I am not an expert in those women. I've frankly never understood them."

"I'm going to create scandal and spin you."

No time to prepare, the words were out of his mouth the exact moment he flung her out from his hold, spinning her under his high left hand.

The gasp in her throat ended just as his right arm clamped back about her body.

Laughter bubbled up from her chest. "That—that is what I would take over a title any day."

His eyebrow cocked. "A dance and a spin?"

"Yes." Her head nodded. "Aye. Absolutely. This is what I'll wait for. Thank goodness I've been able to avoid the trap of chasing an almighty title."

Reiner set them back into even steps and Sloane became acutely aware that their bodies were closer than before. Too close. The tips of her breasts grazing his chest with every step. His hold around her back clamping her more fully than before. Her neck craning her head upward just to keep eye contact with him.

This was why this dance was dangerous. Why her governess had scurried her away so quickly from it. The speed, the closeness, the spin. It sent blood pumping fast through her veins and wicked thoughts into her head. Wicked thoughts of the devilishly handsome man that was holding her captive.

The very offense of that thought hit her hard.

She shouldn't be enjoying this—shouldn't have laughter falling from her lips. Her gaze dipped to stare at his chest, at the cut just above his dark waistcoat and below where his cravat was tucked neatly in place.

"How many brothers do you have?"

Her head snapped backward at the question. She blinked hard, her look lifting to skewer him. "You were eavesdropping?"

He offered a slight shrug. "I heard the music stop and I was walking by to see if everyone had retired for the evening."

"So you stopped outside the door and listened in on a private conversation? That is the very definition of eavesdropping."

He stopped all motion, his hands abruptly dropping from her. "Vicky, you can stop."

Vicky looked up from the music, her fingers trailing on the last few keys. "What? Why?"

He turned fully toward his niece. "We are done for the evening. Could you please retire to your rooms?"

Vicky's hand waved toward the cleared area of the floor. "But I would like to try the dance again, now that I've seen it done properly. I know Miss Sloane could teach me now."

"She will have to do it another evening." His cool voice held no room for disobedience.

With an exaggerated sigh that dragged out as only a nine-year-old could accomplish, Vicky stood from the bench and stomped across the room and out the door.

Sloane started to follow Vicky, but Reiner stepped in front of her, shaking his head and pointing to the floor next to her feet. A silent order. She was not to move.

Reiner went to the door of the library and closed it.

He turned around and strode across the room to her. Stopping far too close, he glared down at her. "There is no such thing as a private conversation with my niece. I need

to know every word everyone says to her, and you, of all people, are not immune to that."

Sloane looked up at him, meeting his glare with her own. "You sound like a tyrant."

"I sound like an uncle that swore no harm would ever come to his niece." The vehemence in the rumble of his voice made her pause.

Pause and take a step back. Her look fell to the smooth wooden planks of the floor between them. She had to remember he believed she was there to harm him—that she was an enemy.

But she couldn't possibly be there to harm Vicky. Could she?

What in the blasted world could have happened to her to make her want to harm him or his niece?

But she knew herself. Knew what she was and was not capable of doing, no matter what had happened to her in the void of the past weeks or months. Steady, her gaze rose to him. "I would never harm that girl, Reiner. She's an innocent."

"Yes, and there's no better way to harm me than through her."

She shook her head. "I don't ken what has made you so spiteful that you distrust everyone—to the extent that you would keep me—another innocent—captive here. And for what? Out of fear of what I could possibly do to you? You found me—I have no idea what I'm doing here or how I got here—and you won't help me figure it out. You want answers, Reiner, well, I want them as well. I want them more than you do." Her voice started to shake. "But if there is one thing that I ken about myself, it's that I would never hurt an innocent child. Never. That you would even insinuate it sends a rage through my belly."

His hand flipped up in the air. "What would you like me to do, Sloane? While there are things you don't remember, there are clearly things that you do recall and are refusing to tell me. The fact that you have brothers? That your grandfather is a marquess?"

Vicky must have told him that fact, for she'd kept her mouth clamped tight against him learning the slightest thing about her. Her arms clamped in front of her chest. "And I could say the exact same of you. You are refusing to tell me anything that would help me solve the mystery of why I'm here."

He inclined his head slightly, pinning her with his brown eyes that swirled in the crossroads between cold and warm. "Yes, so how about I propose a deal?"

Her eyes narrowed at him. "A deal consisting of what?"

"For every piece of information you give me, I give you one back of equal importance."

Her jaw shifted back and forth as she tried to read him. Tried to discern if the man was even worthy of the trust it would take for a deal like that.

A deep breath, and she exhaled it in a long sigh. "I will agree." She held up her hand. "As long as we agree first upon the questions that equate importance."

"Agreed." He nodded. "Your grandfather is a marquess—I want to know his name."

"And I want to ken exactly where I am right now—by the accents of everyone in this castle, I cannot imagine we are in Scotland?"

He pierced her with his stark amber-hued eyes. "You'll answer mine if I answer yours?"

She nodded.

"You're in England at Wolfbridge Castle in Lincolnshire, thirty miles northeast of Lincoln."

She stumbled a step backward, her arm clasping across her belly. Lincolnshire? What was she doing weeks away from Vinehill—from her home?

"The—the nearest village?" She managed to mumble the words out.

"Binbrook. An hour ride away."

Her hand lifted, rubbing her forehead. Lincolnshire. In the middle of nowhere.

"My turn, Sloane."

Her look jerked up to him. It took her three gasps of breath before she could force air across her tongue. Her look dropped to the flames in the fireplace just behind Reiner. She'd made the deal, now she had to live by it. "My—my grandfather is the Marquess of Vinehill and…"

"And?"

Slowly, her look lifted to him, defiant. "And he will send warriors for me once he knows where I am."

{ CHAPTER 6 }

The Marquess of Vinehill.

Her grandfather was a marquess he'd only heard of once. And at that, he'd had to tease out from vague recollections who the man was. He wasn't an enemy—at least not one that Reiner knew of.

Reiner leaned toward the third level open window in his chamber as his fingers worked his cravat. Walking into the castle from his morning ride an hour ago, he saw Sloane and Vicky escaping into the expansive gardens that unfurled out from the south side of the castle.

His look trailed along the top rows of the evergreen hedges until he spotted a flash of pink. It disappeared, then reappeared a row away. A flash of blue. Disappeared. Flitting into view again two rows away.

Were his niece and Sloane running?

In her pink dress, Vicky appeared on the far edge of the rows, just outside the east border of the gardens. He saw the blue dress, saw Sloane sneaking up on her before Vicky knew what was approaching. An arm's length away, Sloane lunged, catching Vicky around the waist.

Vicky squealed and then hysterical laughter floated up through the air to him.

Playing. They were chasing each other.

He scanned the outer edges of the garden. Claude stood on the far edge of the evergreen rows, kicking at rocks, a bored look on his face. Closer to the castle,

Lawrence had moved around the side of the hedges to watch Sloane catch Vicky.

Sloane released Vicky and darted back into the hedgerows. With another squeal, Vicky dove in, chasing.

Reiner shook his head. The woman had constant mischief about her and was corrupting his niece. Vicky should be inside practicing her sheets of music. He looked at the mirror next to the window, crisping the lines of his cravat.

A screaming laugh shrieked into the air. Laughter that unsettled him.

He stepped to the right, searching the rows of greenery. Vicky must have caught Sloane, though he couldn't see them past the tops of the hedges.

His bottom lip jutted up. In just the few days Sloane had been at the castle, Vicky was growing far too attached to their guest. And why not? The woman had a constant spark in her eye—she was clearly accustomed to having the world as her own grand park—hunting out the fun in any situation with uncommon enthusiasm. Enthusiasm that was infectious if one was in the orb of it.

Even knowing she was captive on his estate hadn't curtailed her spirits—only when she looked at him. When she looked at him, sharp, incredibly pointy daggers surfaced in her eyes with one aim. Him.

Sloane and Vicky emerged from the lines of hedgerows and walked to the Butterfly Pond that ran lengthwise along the greenery. They sat on the granite stone ledge that lined the east end of the pond. Vicky was telling a story, her hands animated and flying through the air. A wide smile lit up Sloane's face and she nodded constantly as Vicky talked.

He'd never seen his niece talk so much. To anyone. It was as though Vicky had been living in a clam-shell and Sloane had come along and cracked it open, setting her free.

He shook his head, the scowl deepening on his face.

Far, far too attached.

It was aggravating how much happiness seemed to swirl about Sloane. As if her only thought in life was what would make her happy in the next moment.

Happiness he wanted gone before it could corrupt Vicky.

His spine stiffened.

The woman was only here until Reiner could get answers about her purpose for trying to sneak into Wolfbridge. Once he got the answers, she'd be gone, one way or another.

It'd been four days since she'd told him who her grandfather was, and he'd had to rethink the whole idea of keeping her captive until she broke and confessed all. It would not do, holding the granddaughter of a marquess against her will.

But he still needed answers before he could set her free. He'd sent Simmons to London to discreetly gather as much information about the marquess as possible, and he was more than irate his solicitor hadn't returned yet.

The short message that Simmons had sent back about her grandfather was perplexing. Her family was not destitute, as far as Simmons had been able to discern. So she would not be one that was bound by the debts of her family—willing to break into his home in order to pay them off. Instead, her grandfather owned an impressive swath of land in Stirlingshire. Sloane had been raised a lady, groomed to marry a peer—and while she had attended one short season in London two years past, nothing had come of it.

Reiner stared at Sloane, watching her pick up pebbles at her feet and plunk them into the pond. The cerulean dress he'd had a maid procure for her fit her well, though tight in the chest. She still wore the long glove on her left arm, even in the warmth of the day. Her right hand was bare. Pinned into a soft chignon, her hair that he'd originally thought was blond showed streaks of red in the sunlight, casting a warm, rosy glow to the color of her hair. She sat utterly relaxed with Vicky, a smile radiant on her face.

He shook his head. The likelihood of her trying to sneak into his room to do him harm was less a possibility than he'd originally thought. But it still didn't answer the question of what she was doing there.

Until he had that, he was stuck. For too much was at stake for him to let her go without those very answers.

~ ~ ~

They trailed through the beds of late summer roses and asters, Vicky stopping every other foot and plucking fresh blooms to add to the quickly expanding bouquet in her hand. Bending over deep purple asters, she looked back over her shoulder at Sloane, wrinkling her nose.

"I just don't see the purpose in practicing my French as it concerns flowers."

"Well, one, we promised Miss Gregory we would practice your French as we took in a breath of fresh air,"

Sloane said. "And two, you never ken when some fine French gentleman will want to discuss with you the intricacies of the flora in France."

Vicky snorted, standing up as she tucked an aster stem into her hand. "I don't think I would ever like to discuss with a man any sort of flora. Especially in French."

"You might be surprised what will pass as fascinating conversation at dinner parties." Sloane gave a visible shudder. "But I think we've run through enough French for the day. Tomorrow we'll tackle the best ways to enrich soil in French. I think you'll find that conversation fascinating."

"Yes. Oh please, yes, let us be done for the day." Vicky sighed out the words. Far too dramatic, but it still brought a chuckle to Sloane's lips.

The girl pointed to the evergreen hedgerows several hundred paces away with her bouquet of flowers. "Shall we play Catch the Cat again? That was so much fun."

"First we must put the flowers in water, lest they wilt away."

"Claude could do it for us." Before Sloane could stop her, Vicky bounded over to Claude where he stood with Lawrence at the gravel pathway that led from the yew labyrinth to the symmetrical rows of raised flower beds. "Claude, could you please bring these into Mrs. Flurten and ask her for a vase?"

A burly man with dark curly hair skimming his eyebrows and leathery skin, Claude cringed at the request. "I'm not a cursed housemaid, young miss."

Vicky didn't blink at his gruffness. "Please?" She held up the bouquet to him.

His face scrunched in horrified indignation. But he grumbled nonsensical words and took the bouquet from her, turning and walking toward the castle.

Vicky spun back to Sloane, an impish grin on her face.

Sloane shook her head at her and the right side of her face lifted in a crooked smile. While what Vicky had just done reeked of prerogative, Sloane hadn't minded that one of her constant, dour shadows had been sent off to deliver a frilly bundle of flowers. "You will drive your suitors in London into madness in ten years' time, you scamp."

Vicky giggled and shrugged.

They started walking across the wide expanse of lawn toward the hedgerows.

"What is it that you think Uncle Reiner wants from you?"

Sloane's look lifted to the clear blue sky above them, dotted with only sparse, puffy clouds. For several steps, she didn't say a word.

"I wish I knew. I wish I knew exactly what I was doing behind the castle—if I truly was trying to climb the vines and get into his room. I wish I knew what happened to my arm." She lifted her left hand. "I wish I knew why I would travel so far from home."

Several steps passed before Vicky looked up at her. "Can I tell you a secret?"

"Of course."

"I hope you never remember. I hope you have to stay here with us. You are the only fun thing that has happened here at Wolfbridge in four years."

"Your uncle is not fun?" Sloane chuckled to herself. "Strike that question, for I ken very well how cold and sour your uncle is."

"You do not like him?"

Sloane's steps hiccupped and her eyebrows drew together.

Did she like him? Regard him as anything other than an ogre holding her captive? She walked a few more steps, her head tilting to the side.

"Miss Sloane, you do not care for my uncle?" Worry wrinkled Vicky's brow.

She grabbed the girl's hand. "Do not fret. I apologize for my words. I absolutely despise his actions. But as for the actual man…" She shook her head and then looked down to Vicky. "It is just that your uncle is entirely aggravating."

"Oh yes." Vicky nodded her head, her eyes going wide. "I know all about it."

"You do?"

"Yes. My mama left me a letter speaking to that very regard."

"She did?"

"She died, but she left me a letter first." Vicky tugged her hand from Sloane's grip and she pulled up the small rectangular metal box that she always had strung about her waist. She opened the top flap and tucked inside was a neatly folded paper—it looked like two sheets with ink covering every free speck of white space. "See? I keep it in here."

Sloane had thought the delicately painted metal box an odd adornment, but this made sense. No wonder Vicky wore it every day dangling from her waist.

Vicky snapped the top of the box closed, flipping the wire down over the tiny nub to latch it. "Uncle Reiner is arrogant, bossy, and aggravating in how he has to control everything about him—a duke to his bones, my mama said. That he is prickly and will not regard me with much favor at times. But she also told me he is kind to his core, he likes to laugh, and he is terribly lonely."

"Lonely?" Sloane frowned. "But you said he has parties all the time."

"Yes, but I do not think the people that come are his friends. They are not nice people. They treat the servants horribly when they are not in front of him and I do not care for it." The edges of her eyes crinkled in indignation. "Reiner always demands I treat them with respect—he says my station calls for it—but he apparently cannot control his guests."

"That is…interesting."

Vicky reached out and plucked a sprig of green leaves from the tall, sculpted boxwoods they passed and she spun it in her fingers. "Yes. And my mama also said Uncle Reiner would love me dearly. But I think she was wrong about that."

"Why do you say that?"

Her wide blue eyes lifted to Sloane. "He does not pay me any mind—not much at all. It has been quite lonely here."

"But your life had more joy in it four years ago?"

"Before Mrs. Kean died, yes. Mrs. Kean was my mama's maid and closest friend, I think. She was happy and she spent all her time with me. She taught me all the songs that my mama used to sing." Vicky's chin tilted up oddly in

an attempt to not let sadness take hold. Sloane knew that
look. Knew it well.

"Do you have your mother's voice?"

Vicky shrugged. "Possibly—I am not sure. Mrs. Kean
always said she could hear my mama in me. And whenever
Miss Gregory has me practice songs and Uncle Reiner
hears, he gets a sad look on his face and leaves the room. I
think it's because I sound like her." She shrugged. "Or I am
dreadful at singing and the screech of it brings tears to his
eyes—that is the other possibility."

Sloane wrapped her arm around the girl's shoulders
and squeezed her. "I would venture that is not the case, as
your voice is very sweet. You must sing for me tonight after
dinner. And if we can get your uncle into the room, I will
watch him very closely to see if he is cringing or merely
melancholy."

Vicky giggled. "Maybe he will join us. He never
bothers with me much, but with you here…" Her shoulders
lifted under Sloane's arm. "He's been different ever since he
sent me in to you."

Sloane jerked to a stop. "What do you mean he sent
you in to me?"

Vicky took two more steps, but Sloane caught her arm,
twisting Vicky to face her. The girl's cheeks turned red, her
eyes darting about, squirrelly to escape Sloane.

Sloane grabbed her other arm, bending at the waist so
she was eye level with the girl. "Tell me, Vicky."

"Into your room—when you were locked in there. He
wanted me to ask you who you were." Vicky hopped from
one foot to the other, her arms squirming under Sloane's
grip. "He didn't know and he couldn't get you to tell him."

Sloane's eyes went wide, stunned, and then her head snapped back. "He used you? He sent you into my room to ask me questions?"

Vicky's lips pulled inward, her mouth clamping shut.

Her fingers dug into the girl's arms. "Tell me right now, Vicky. Tell me if he used you to get to me."

Her cherub face crumbling, Vicky nodded. "I'm sorry, Sloane—but I didn't know you and I didn't know how nice you were and Uncle Reiner wanted me to help him. He never needs my help, never thinks on me, and he asked me to do it. So I did. He didn't know if you were dangerous or not."

"He didn't know if I was dangerous?" Her voice went into full screech. "So he sent a little girl in to talk to me?"

Tears started to brim in Vicky's eyes. "I'm so sorry, Sloane. I didn't think it would hurt anything and after he let you out I was just so happy to have someone to talk to that I didn't think it mattered."

Sloane's head dropped forward as she seethed in a breath of rage. Releasing Vicky's arms, her head jerked up and she wiped a thumb across Vicky's cheek, swiping away a fat tear. "Don't you worry on it, Vicky. This isn't your fault at all. That responsibility lies solely with your uncle." She clasped her hands onto Vicky's cheeks. "Do you understand? This isn't your fault. I am mad at your uncle, not you. Tell me you understand that."

Vicky nodded, the distraught tears in her eyes somewhat mollified.

"Good." She pulled Vicky into a quick hug. "Now you will have to excuse me for a few minutes."

Without waiting for Vicky to reply, Sloane spun from her and charged toward the castle.

She made it into the interior and was stalking down the main corridor that ran the length of the first level before Lawrence's boots clomped onto the floor a distance behind her, quickly catching up. She stopped at the door to the study just down the hall from the library.

Her look whipped back to the guard, her words a hiss. "Leave me be, Lawrence."

"But, miss, you cannot disturb his grace." The words came out between heaving breaths that sent his whole body jerking with every gasp. He must have run up the hill after her.

Her hand went onto the door handle. "But nothing—you think his grace cannot manage a wee woman like me?" Before Lawrence could jump in front of her, she pushed her way into the room and slammed the door behind her.

Behind his desk, Reiner jumped at the intrusion.

She didn't give him a moment to breathe and was across the room in six strides, her rising voice filling the wide expanse. "How could you do that to poor Vicky—do you ken how distraught she is right now? Having to keep your blasted secrets?"

Reiner watched her approach, a glacial look registering on his face. "Secrets? Slo—"

Her arm flew wide, not letting him interrupt her tirade. "All she wants is for you to notice her—notice her just a little. And when you finally do it is only because you want to use her."

Belying the cold countenance on his face, a vein in his forehead started to throb. He stood, his hands splaying wide on the smooth surface of his desk. "I beg you not to barge into my study and scold me."

"You sent a child—a child—in to ask me questions when you couldn't get answers yourself. You didn't ken if I was dangerous—I could have hurt her."

Recognition sparked in his brown eyes. "You are speaking of when Vicky first went into your room?"

"Of course that's what I'm speaking of." Her words hissed. "You sent an innocent child into a dangerous situation."

His head shook. "I was just outside the door, Sloane. I would have stopped you before you could do any damage to her."

"You would have stopped me?" Her right hand flew up and thumped down onto the desk. She leaned forward, her eyes skewering him. "You blasted idiot. Do you ken how long it takes to hurt someone—to kill someone? Seconds. Seconds it would have taken me to harm her—and you— you put her in that danger. What kind of a man are you?"

The rage that flew across his face was palpable, spiking the very air around him. "You're standing incredibly close to me when you rightly know it would take me only seconds to reach out and injure or kill you."

"So now you're threatening me?" Her eyebrows went impossibly high and she straightened, pulling her shoulders back. "Although, that's much more admirable than tossing your innocent niece in front of danger."

A growl bubbled from his throat and he stalked around the desk, stopping when he was only a breath away. His look sliced into her. "You are in no position to judge how I run my household, Sloane."

"I am in no position?" Her hand slapped onto her chest as she turned to fully face him. "Of course I'm in no position to do so—I'm a bloody captive here—so who better to tell you that you're being a miserable uncle?"

He leaned over her, a snarl on his lips. "Don't force me to lock you up in your room again—for I will do so and throw away the blasted key."

"If that's what it takes to get you to see what an ogre you're being to your niece, then it's bloody well worth it." She stepped in closer, her chest brushing against his as she craned her neck to keep her eyes locked on him. "Do you ken how belittling that is—to not be seen as anything other than a means to an end? To be given no regard except for how she can serve your needs?"

Her hands folded into fists at her sides. "She's a real person, Reiner. A little person that needs to be seen as valuable just because she is who she is. She needs to matter aside from whatever blasted plans you have for her. Do you even ken anything about her? Do you ken that she has incredible wit? That she loves to run but is never allowed to? That she speaks French so flawlessly at this point you could send her to the French court and not a person would blink an eye?"

Her lip curled up and she shook her head, taking a step backward. "Yet all you see her for is her studies. How to mold her so that you can marry her off the first chance you get. Or are you to make an alliance with her marriage—that seems much more your style. Use those under your thumb for your own purp—"

His hand around her back was as quick as a descending hawk and he yanked her into him, his lips covering hers.

The words bubbling in her throat fizzled into nothingness against the hardness of his lips, the whole of him consuming her.

His heated breath on her cheek. The slight dark grizzle on his face pinpricks against her skin. His hand moving up her back, his fingers digging into her hair as he tilted her head for better access.

Lost.

She fell into a chasm of instinct that swallowed her whole—all thoughts abandoning her head except for the feel of his lips, his body long against hers, his tongue slipping past her teeth, carnal in how he explored her.

She'd never been kissed like this. Not to this extent. Not this thoroughly. Not with such wanton resolve that the core of her began to vibrate, hum with insistence for things she'd never explored with a man.

Entirely right.

Every speck of her body felt right. Hot. Craving more.

Entirely wrong.

She was his captive. Being held here against her will. A pleasant prison. But a prison nonetheless.

Her head snapped back, her hands wedging between them and she shoved backward with all her might.

She stumbled three steps, catching herself on the desk.

Her gloved hand went to her swollen lips, wiping the taste of him from her mouth. The taste she was thirsty for not but a moment ago.

Wrong.

Wrong and she had to remember that fact.

She shook her head, trying to right her askew equilibrium.

For how much she'd just enjoyed that kiss, it was wrong.

It had to be wrong.

No matter how right it had just felt to her body.

"What—what was that for?" She spit out the words through heavy breaths, refusing to meet his eyes.

"To cease your tirade." His hand lifted, running along the back of his neck in an uncharacteristic fidget. His crisp gaze pierced her, scrutinizing her.

He was just as shaken as she was.

Her fingers fell from her lips. "You could have closed my mouth in a thousand different ways."

He shrugged, his hand dropping from his neck, and he tapped his fingers along the edge of the desk. "Then it was you." A deep breath lifted his chest. "You. You come in here to yell at me about—of all things—how I'm failing my niece."

"You are failing her."

He exhaled a long sigh. "It is not my intention." His left eyebrow cocked. "If I may be so bold in suggesting it, it sounds like you are acutely familiar with how she feels."

"I...I..." Her lips drew inward for a long moment. She hadn't intended this to be about her, but he had just succinctly hit the mark. "If you knew my grandfather, you would understand quite well how familiar I am with how Vicky feels at being a pawn."

"You were raised to make the finest match?"

"If by that you mean the most advantageous match for the Vinehill estate, then aye. I was."

"Yet that has not happened as of yet?"

"I have been…resisting my grandfather's machinations. I went to London for a spell to placate him. It bought me some time."

"There were no gentlemen to your liking?"

"None that didn't attempt to hide their paramours from the scandal sheets and the gossips. I was not about to harness myself with such a man. I found much of the season distasteful—the common acceptance of mistresses. Growing up in Scotland, I am mostly accustomed to matches that are at the very least, founded upon mutual respect. There is often genuine love, which negates the need of affairs with whores."

An odd smile curled the corners of his lips. "There are no affairs in Scotland?"

She flitted her fingers in the air. "I am not a prude—of course there are plenty of husbands that stray. I ken it well. That does not mean I will be accepting of such a man for myself."

Reiner nodded, the odd grin gone from his face.

She wasn't sure if he was placating her or if he truly understood her desire for a match of mutual desire and affection. Regardless, he was sidetracking her from her purpose in his study. Jacob liked to do that when she was in a fit—change the topic until she was no longer railing.

"But this is not about me, this is about your niece—about you sending her in to try and extract information from me. It is about you using her."

"I do think you overstep your judgement," he said. "You have only spent several days with her."

"And that is all it has taken. You're the one that allowed me near her, Reiner. And I, for one, am not about to let an innocent fall to the mercy of an overbearing ogre if I can help it."

Her intended barb hit as intended.

His hand on the desk curled into a fist. "If you were innocent, Sloane, you would have long since told me what you're truly doing here."

Her mouth clamped closed.

The blasted man still didn't believe her.

Still didn't believe she had no clue as to how she got to Wolfbridge and what she had intended to do there.

With a strained nod, she spun from him and went to the door.

He didn't attempt to stop her.

{ CHAPTER 7 }

He'd managed to avoid her for two days.

Reiner opened the door of his study, glancing down the main hallway. Shadows hugged the corridor with only a few sconces lit so one didn't stumble—beyond that, it was silent, not a soul nearby.

He opened the door fully with a shake of his head. What had he sunk to? Hiding in his own house.

But he wasn't ready to see the exasperating woman again. Not after that kiss.

A kiss that had seared him with a fiery blade straight through his chest. A kiss that had too quickly sent his blood to boiling, his cock straining.

The scorn that she'd walked into the study with—that she'd blasted at him—should have sent him into a wrathful fury. Instead, it had sent his lips onto hers. His body aching to touch her.

And it wasn't just because she was beautiful—he was a master at avoiding the snares of beautiful women. Or at least he had been once.

No, it was her bloody outrage at the injustice of what he'd done to his niece. Outrage on behalf of the one person that mattered to him in this life.

Sloane had raged into his study, defender of the innocent.

The worst part about it was that the blasted woman was right. He had used Vicky for his own purposes. An imbecilic plan.

Reiner stepped into the hallway, peering into the shadows at the far end of the corridor.

He didn't want to risk another encounter with her tonight. Not when it was late and he was exhausted.

He couldn't afford to fall into her snare again. He had let his guard down once before—let a beautiful woman prey on his cock. It'd been four months since the witch, Madeline, had snaked her way into his bed and nearly cost him everything. And she hadn't been half as beautiful as Sloane.

Sloane needed to be off limits, no matter what his cock insisted upon. No matter that he found himself staring at her from afar, longing to be touching her body, basking in her laughter.

Off limits, for the destruction she could cause.

That was assuming Falsted had sent her as his next spy.

The irksome thought popped into his head. The thought he'd been ignoring ever since he saw her lying prone on the ground below the vines.

What if Falsted or one of his other enemies hadn't sent her? What if she wasn't there to ruin everything—ruin him?

What then?

For his actions against Sloane had been grievous, in the least. Absolutely barbaric in the worst.

Locking her in a room.

Keeping her here against her will.

Kissing her when she was his captive.

He had all the power and she had none, and he well knew that fact.

Never mind that she'd kissed him back. That her body had pressed into his. That soft mewls had escaped from her throat.

Disgust at himself curled his lip and he started down the hallway.

Halfway to the main staircase a grumble echoed into the hallway from behind him. He spun and retraced his steps toward the sound.

Another grumble and then a small squeak—almost as though a scream was cut off.

Reiner opened the door to the library.

The rug was still rolled up from the dancing Sloane was practicing with Vicky. The furniture askew throughout the room—chairs against walls, tables pushed to the edges, and the settee had been dragged over to sit in front of the hearth.

Low flames still flickered in the fireplace and in their shadows Reiner spied two lumps on the settee. He stepped fully into the room.

Sloane and Vicky had both fallen asleep with Vicky curled into Sloane's side. A book sat on Sloane's lap, open with a few pages fanning upwards.

He looked about the library. Where were Claude and Lawrence? Neither one had been in the hallway, keeping guard like they had been ordered to do.

His gaze dropped back to the settee. His niece looked content, a small smile even turning up the corners of her mouth as she slept.

It was Sloane that grumbled, soft moans raw in her throat, almost as though she was in a bad dream she couldn't escape from.

With a sigh, he moved around the settee and jiggled Vicky's arm. She didn't awaken.

Not wanting to scare her awake, he slipped his hands between Vicky and Sloane and picked his niece up. She curled into him, her face tucking into his neck. Just like she'd done when he'd picked her up as a tiny child.

He carried her up to her bed, tucking her tight under the covers. Probably too tight, but he wanted her to feel like she was still curled up with someone.

Clicking the door to Vicky's room closed, Reiner paused. He should just turn toward his room and retire himself. Leave Sloane to her slumber down in the library.

Two steps toward his chambers and he heard Sloane scream. A real scream this time—not the muffled agony escaping from her throat earlier.

Within seconds he was down the stairs and to the library.

For the hundreds of possibilities that scattered through his mind as he flew down the stairs, he didn't expect to find Sloane still on the settee, still dead to the world.

But now her body thrashed, screams ripping from her throat every other breath.

"Sloane." Reiner set his hand on her shoulder, gripping tight and shaking her. "Sloane."

A scream choked off as she jerked upright, her eyes flying open.

She sat stupefied, blinking, her eyes going from the fire to Reiner as she tried to orientate herself to the world around her.

Reiner was afraid to release his grip on her shoulder for fear she would slip back into whatever dream had a death hold on her.

His hand still on her shoulder, he sank to balance on his heels, his eyes level with hers. "What was that? Your dream? You were screaming."

"Dream? I was screaming? I…" She blinked hard, her eyes closing as she tried to conjure the memory. A shiver ran through her and she shook her head. "I…I don't ken. I cannot see…but it was awful—the most brutal pain in my chest—as though my heart was being ripped out."

Her eyes opened to him, a flush of pink filling her cheeks. "I—please excuse me." She pushed up from the settee, her shoulder dipping so his hand fell off her, and she moved around him to gain her feet. The book fell from her lap and thudded to the ground.

She made motion to pick it up, but then gasped, falling backward and landing hard on the settee. She glanced at him, her blue eyes bewildered. "It seems to have taken my legs out from under me."

Reiner nodded, standing straight. "It appears to have done a little more than take your legs out from you. It terrorized you, full and through."

"It did?"

"The way your body was just thrashing about—yes."

"I was thrashing?"

He nodded. "And screaming."

"Oh." Her gaze, still stupefied, went to the fire. The blush that tinged her cheeks deepened.

"Did you remember something?"

She shook her head. "No…I thought…no."

Reiner went across the room to the mahogany sideboard and he picked up the thick-cut glass decanter of brandy. Into a tumbler went several healthy swallows of the amber liquid. He brought it back to Sloane and held it out to her. "Promise me something."

"What?"

"When you do remember, you come to me first."

Her gaze lifted to meet his and, her hand shaking, she took the glass from him. Her look dropped to the fire. One sip. Two. Three.

Half the brandy gone and she'd not even flinched at the strength of it.

But she hadn't answered him.

Her gaze remained on the flames. "Vicky wants to sing for you, but she's afraid to do so."

He blinked hard at the odd shift in topic. "She is? Why? She has a lovely voice."

"She thinks it makes you sad." Sloane's blue eyes lifted to him. "And she doesn't want to make you sad."

His bottom lip jutted up in a frown.

"So it does make you sad?"

Reiner shrugged. He should leave the room. Cease this conversation now.

In spite of the rational thoughts in his head, his blasted mouth opened. "I killed my sister just as surely as I had sent a blade into her heart."

"What? No."

He exhaled a long breath. "Corentine, my sister, was staying here at Wolfbridge when she gave birth to Vicky and then died a day after. It was after she and her husband had both left for India to visit lands he acquired. My sister realized a month after they departed she was with child, so she came back directly to Wolfbridge to stay, as neither of them wanted the child born anywhere but in England. My brother-in-law was supposed to follow her back in three months' time. He never did."

"Why not?"

"I don't know. I don't know what delayed him. I don't know why he stopped returning Corentine's letters. We feared his death, but never heard word of what happened to him. I sent missives to him of Corentine's death and Vicky's birth, but I'm not positive he received any of them. The only thing I discovered was that the last ship he was seen on was lost in a storm." Reiner ran a hand through this dark hair. "Had he been here—Corentine may still be alive."

Sloane shook her head. "How can you say that—the danger of birthing a child does not discriminate between who is in the room."

"Ah, but it does. If he had been here, they would have been in London near her midwife. Corentine knew her babe was turned wrong inside of her—the midwife had told her that and was to flip the babe before she came. Corentine asked me to have her midwife brought from London, but I didn't do it soon enough. If I had sent for the midwife even a day earlier…everything would be different. The midwife wouldn't have…" His head tilted back and he shook it, trying to clear the memories.

It took several breaths for his gaze to drop to Sloane. "The midwife would have made it here in time. She would have turned the babe. But instead all I had to offer Corentine was a decrepit old midwife and an inept doctor that had no business birthing babies. Corentine died sixteen hours after Vicky was born. My fault."

"You don't know what would have happened if her midwife had made it here."

"Exactly. Corentine could have lived. Vicky could have her mother." His words stopped, his lips pulling inward for a long moment. "Vicky looks just like my sister. Sounds just like her."

Sloane twisted the tumbler of brandy in her hands, staring at it for a long moment. Her look lifted to him. "Do you ken she carries about a letter from her mother?"

"What do you know of it?"

"You've seen it?"

"I wrote it."

"You did?"

"I had to. Corentine was dying and she wanted to leave Vicky with something of her—something of her mind, words of hers. But she couldn't lift her hand because she was so weak at the end."

"So you wrote those words about how cantankerous you are?"

A sad smile lifted the right side of his face. "I could not refuse her. I'd never seen my sister so happy as when that child was born. Those few minutes she had with her daughter—they were everything to her. Her life well lived for those few, precious seconds when she could hold her babe. Vicky was everything to her." He nodded. "So she dictated the letter. I wrote the words as she spoke them. Though she did manage to sign it."

"You loved her deeply, didn't you?"

"Yes. It was always just my sister and I until she married and left Wolfbridge."

"That explains why Vicky's singing makes you sad."

He turned from Sloane and walked over to the sideboard, then poured himself a tumbler of brandy. "Maybe it does. She sings exactly like her mother. My sister was only a year younger than me—there wasn't a time she wasn't with me. Corentine was always singing—always—and she had the most beautiful voice. She was the one bright light in my life."

He took a healthy swallow of the brandy before walking across the room to Sloane and stopping by the fireplace. "I was devastated when she left for marriage, even though I knew it had to happen. But I would get letters from her telling me how much she missed me and England—she never wanted to be away."

"What of your parents?"

He turned to her. "My mother died when I was three. We rarely saw our father. He died when I was sixteen."

"Why did you not see him?"

"He enjoyed life in London far more than here at Wolfbridge." He dropped his gaze to the fire for a long moment, thinking he could cease the conversation. Again, his mouth opened on its own accord. "He was a cold man. Any time that we did spend together he was grooming me for the future. 'Crush those that cross you. A man of your stature needs no one. Emotion is weakness.' Dictums that were drilled into my head ever since I could understand

words. But then I had Corentine and she buffered all of what he was."

With a slight shake of his head, he looked to her. "And your mother and father?"

She shrugged. "They died of consumption when I was three. I don't remember them. Jacob and Lachlan—my brothers—raised me. And my cousin Torrie is the same age as I and always lived with us, and we raised each other. She's my sister for all purposes. Those three, they are my family."

"Not your grandfather?"

Her lips drew inward for a breath. "My grandfather is…difficult. Demanding. He has always been so. But it has been easiest for me. I wasn't the heir or the bothersome spare. I have been useful as a pawn for alliances—that is all."

A frown set into his face. "He sounds much like my father."

Sloane took a sip from her tumbler, her canny blue eyes contemplating him. "The more I know of you, the more of a mystery you are. I cannot place you—place your kindness when you choose to show it."

"I'm not the ogre you think I am?"

Her shoulders lifted in a slight shrug. "I don't know what you are. If I could remember how I got here—why I'm here—maybe all of this would make sense. But you—you I cannot unravel. You don't make sense."

His eyebrows slanted inward. "In what way?"

"You hold me captive, but give me free rein of everything here—including access to your niece. If you truly thought I was a threat, you would still have me locked up in that chamber next to yours."

"True."

"So why continue to hold me here?"

You're mine to protect.

The rogue thought flew through his head, gnawing with razor sharp teeth hard into his mind. A thought that didn't make it to his lips.

He'd been fighting it, fighting it since the first seconds he'd wrapped his arms around her when she was screaming in her room.

She was his to protect.

And that she'd added a spark to his life where there was none. That he was lonely and he hadn't realized it until the very moment she smiled at him after they had danced. That her smiles and laughter infected everyone around her—lightened everyone around her. That her outrageous tales of brave Scottish warriors and their outlandish antics entertained them during dinners—so much so they would often forget to eat. That her mischievous grin when she was conspiring with Vicky to escape his niece's lessons made him chuckle instead of groan. That he wanted her—her body, her mind.

He said none of that. *Couldn't* say any of it. Not yet. Maybe never.

So he stared at her silently for a long moment. Her blue eyes never wavered from his.

Reiner cleared his throat. "Maybe you need to stop thinking of this as being held captive. Maybe I will make more sense if you shift your thinking. You're my guest, being encouraged to stay until you can recall what you hoped to accomplish here. You remember and we both win."

"Is that what you think this is?"

He shrugged. "It makes it more palatable for me."

She snorted a laugh. "Call it what you wish, Reiner. I'm your prisoner."

He stifled a sigh and moved to sit down on the far side of the settee. He couldn't argue with her truth. His elbow propped on the curve of the carved mahogany arm of the settee and he angled his body toward her. "It is an unfortunate happenstance. But I cannot let you go until I know the truth. Too much is at stake. The safety of my niece is at stake."

Her eyes flew wide in alarm. "Vicky is in danger?"

"I don't know. But I'm not about to take that chance."

Sloane nodded, her forefinger rubbing along the top rim of her glass. Her gaze fell onto the fire and her lips parted. "I'll tell you one thing if you tell me one thing."

"Something of importance?"

She nodded.

"I am willing if you are."

Her stare remained on the flames of the fire. "I can climb. Climb really well."

His head tilted to the side. "Climb what?"

"Climb the types of vines that grow on castles." She looked to him, her voice just above a whisper as though she were revealing her greatest secret. "The castle I grew up in had ancient vines growing up along the south wall. My brothers and Torrie and I, we would all play a game. Valor of Vinehill—where we would storm the castle. The game included climbing the vines to gain access to the upper floors. I spent summer after summer climbing vines three, four, five stories high."

"You're saying—"

"As unlikely as it is"—she rushed on, her face scrunching with her words—"it's entirely possible I was trying to gain access to your chamber by climbing up the vines if that's where they led to."

"So…"

"It is possible that you are right. That I am here to ruin you. Or do something to you. But I do not ken what that thing is. It may very well be happenstance that I was walking by your castle and stumbled and hit my head."

"People don't just happen to walk by Wolfbridge, Sloane. They have to travel here. Travel here on purpose."

"I have gathered that." Her attention swung back to the fire, the tumbler going to her lips.

It wasn't an admission of guilt.

No, something very different. An admission of being lost.

Lost with no guiding light as to what led her here. The constant spark in her blue eyes dimmed, sadness taking root. Sadness he didn't want to see.

"My turn."

Her look swung back to him.

"You were right. I never should have used Vicky like that—sending her in to question you."

Sloane's head snapped back, her blue eyes shocked. "I did not imagine you would consider my point on the matter."

"Was I just to ignore your outrage on my niece's behalf?" He cocked an eyebrow, looking at her over the rim of his glass as he took a sip. "I'm not a stupid man, Sloane. I can recognize when I am wrong. And I will have to beg for your assistance in how I can ask forgiveness from her."

An odd smile came to her face, the spark relighting in her eyes. "I don't think you need to. She worships you. Have you not realized that? She doesn't think there is anyone stronger or smarter than you. I fear for her when she goes to London one day and discovers men like you are few and far between."

"Men like me?"

Her hand flittered in the air between them. "I mean as she sees you. Smart and strong and handsome."

"You didn't mention handsome before."

"I didn't? Surely—"

Without thought, he leaned forward across the expanse of the settee, his lips on hers cutting off her words.

Lips that were instantly responsive. Breath that quivered under the crush of him. Hell, she felt so good. So soft. So pliable.

His hand went to her neck, digging through her blond hair that hung free down her back and he found the base of her neck, his fingers teasing the bumps up along her spine. Her skin instantly prickled under his touch. Responsive to the slightest nudge of his fingertips.

Her lips parted under his and he pressed forth, his tongue slipping past the edge of her mouth, exploring the taste of her.

Warm honey and brandy.

And lust. She tasted like lust. Like she would draw him in and be the death of him.

His hand slipped up to cup the back of her head and he tilted it, deepening the kiss.

A soft purr rumbled from her throat and she pulled slightly away, breaking the kiss.

She was stopping this.

Stopping this before it went too far. He should let it be—but hell, every fiber of his being wanted to pull her back to him. Set her body next to his.

She heaved a breath as her eyes opened to him.

His hand went to her temple, his thumb running over the spot that had been a wicked lump days ago. "You can't deny this. What this is between us."

She remained only a feather's width away. So close her breath was almost his own.

She shook her head. "No. I can't. But—"

"But you want to deny it?"

"No. No, I don't. But I cannot accept it when—"

"You can leave. Leave Wolfbridge anytime you want, Sloane." He leaned past her and set his glass on the side table next to the settee, then wedged the tumbler she had clasped in front of her from her hands. He set that glass next to his and then his focus went solely onto her, his words guttural in their honesty. "You say it, and I will have a horse saddled for you. Have my carriage readied. You say it and you can leave. You can leave this instant. You're not my prisoner, Sloane."

"You are"—she pulled back slightly from him, her eyes searching his face—"you are serious?"

"Dead serious."

She stared at him for a long moment. The gold mark in her left iris sparked, almost like fire against the ocean blue of her eye. "Then I'll not deny it."

All the invitation he needed. He leaned forward, his lips finding hers again. Parting them. Possessing the full skin, the flick of her tongue against his, the taste of her.

Her hands lifted, sliding up his arms and curling about his neck. The bare fingers of her right hand went upward to bury into his hair as she pulled her body forward. Pulled her body into him.

Heaven help him. Her body, her breasts pressing into him.

His mouth dropped from her lips and trailed down her neck. She didn't stop him, didn't move away, didn't say a word.

If anything, her breath sped, her hold along the back of his head tightening.

He moved his hand along her side upward, his thumb brushing the side of her breast.

An exhale. A soft moan at the caress.

His hand drifted downward, and before he could slip it around to the small of her back, her left hand moved down, grasping his wrist and bringing it back upward to her breast.

He smiled into the skin in the crook of her neck. She wasn't afraid to tell him what she liked. Refreshing. And aggravating to any last strains of decorum he possessed.

Teasing along the bare skin above her bodice, his thumb slid beneath the lace edging of the fabric. He tugged the muslin downward, the shift, the stays, as his lips trailed a path to her breast. Just as the fabric cleared her nipple, he set his lips about the pink nub, his tongue caressing the tip of it.

"Aaaa." Part gasp, part carnal exhale from her throat.

"You enjoy that?" he asked, his mouth still tangled with her breast.

"Yes. From your lips—" She paused, drawing a trembling breath. "Yes, I do."

The taste of her skin sweet citrus, intoxicating, he could have set his lips onto her breast and not looked up for days.

He shifted her closer, dragging her left leg over his lap to pull her closer and his hand caught her calf just under the bottom hem of her skirt. His hand trailed upward. Past the silk stocking. Past the ribbon that held the stocking in place. Bare skin. Her inner thigh. Soft, supple, and tensing, prickling under his touch.

"Yes—that—your hand higher." Breathless words stuttered from her lungs in between gasps for breath.

Words that sent him into a maelstrom of his own making that he no longer had control of.

Damn his bloody limbs and fingers. He wasn't able to stop this—resist her. His fingers trailed higher, reaching the core of her.

A soft groan raw in her throat urged him on.

He slipped his forefinger into her folds.

A guttural growl left her lips and nearly undid him. "Yes."

She wanted more.

And damn if he wasn't strong enough to deny her.

He slipped another finger into her folds, finding her nubbin. His ring finger found way, and he started long circular strokes about it. Enough to tease. Enough to draw out the pleasure he was watching flash across her face.

Yet she wasn't about to be teased, her grip around his neck tightening, her nails digging into his skin. "Reiner, more—" A gasp cut off her words.

He collapsed his circle, tightening it around her nubbin, flicking, caressing until she was taut and straining, her hips taking on movement of their own against his touch.

It took several gasps before sound passed her lips again, her chest rising hard against the onslaught of his tongue. "Yes. Yes."

He took her nipple in his lips, slipping his teeth around it. Pressing ever so slightly.

He sent her into a frenzy.

Her body arching against him, her nails clawing at his back, he sped his fingers at her core, pulling her, pushing her over the edge.

She came with a jolt, every limb straining, her full lips wide and heaving for breath. A scream escaped from her throat and he lifted his head from her breast, collapsing his mouth against hers to smother the sound.

Her scream wavering, he pulled up slightly to watch her. Heaven help him, she was gorgeous. Transfixed, he wanted nothing more than to sink himself into her. To bury his shaft deep into her wet folds, feel her body clench around him, not giving him up. But not before she rode this—not before the pleasure that was seizing her body had its due.

He hovered above her, drawing out the pleasure from her core for as long as her body reacted to his touch.

Her blue eyes opened to him, wonderment and pleasure flushing her face. "What was that?"

Her words cut him to the core. Cut any thoughts he had of driving into her. "Something I wasn't prepared for." He blinked hard, his hand dropping from the folds of her skirt, his head moving backward. Moving away from her.

The naiveté in her eyes, the ragged way her body responded to him. She was an innocent of the highest order.

Or a very skilled actress.

The last thought wedged into his head, refusing to lift away. The last time a courtesan of remarkable skill had been sent to ensnare him. So why not an innocent this time?

He stood from the settee, the fabric of his trousers stretched tight against his engorged, raging member.

He'd been down this path before. Let a woman so far into his life that it could have ruined everything. Let his cock put everything he'd worked for in danger.

"My apologies, Sloane." He inclined his head to her. "I shouldn't have taken advantage of you as I just did. Please, retire to your chamber and know I will not force myself upon you again."

She sat up straight, shoving her skirts down off her lap. "You didn't force anything, Reiner."

"You are kind. But my actions are unforgivable." He motioned to the door. "Please retire, I will put down the fire."

Her forehead crinkled as she gained her feet. The slight flush in her cheeks from earlier was turning decidedly pink. Her mouth opened for one moment, then clamped closed. With a quick glance at him, she turned to the door and walked stiffly from the room.

Her embarrassment only added to the excruciating moments of awkwardness.

He prayed to hell he was right about her reasons for being at Wolfbridge. That she had been sent here to harm him.

For if that wasn't the case, it had been one odious action after another from him. Not a one she deserved.

And he would pay dearly for it.

That he was sure of.

{ CHAPTER 8 }

Sloane stared at the stable boy—gangly and just a few years older than Vicky—scurrying about the stall in front of her, readying a mare for her to ride.

The boy walked past her, disappeared into a stall on the opposite wall, and then emerged with a sidesaddle, the leather polished to such a shine she wondered if it had ever been ridden. He heaved it over the front half wall of the stall, leaving it draped there while he shook out the numnah to be spread on the speckled brown mare's back.

The toes of her boots dug into the dirt. She'd changed into the black clothes that she'd arrived at Wolfbridge in after she'd said good eve to Vicky. Her hand twisted along the folds of her dark skirt into the deep pocket, making sure her dagger was in place in the folds of the fabric. Her blade had reappeared days ago, sitting on top of the chest of drawers in her room. Reiner hadn't mentioned it, but she knew it was an offering of trust that he would give it back. How hard it was for him to do, she wasn't sure.

She hadn't had the heart to tell Vicky what she was about to do. What she *needed* to do.

She had to leave Wolfbridge.

Reiner had said she could leave and she was about to lose more than her memories if she stayed in this place.

It'd been a full day since he kissed her late at night in the library and she was still mortified by her own actions. She hadn't put up the slightest resistance to his touch. To his

lips. No. She had encouraged every single second of his lips wandering on her body. Where his hands had travelled.

And for how he'd asked her to leave the library the previous night, it was as though he was asking her to leave Wolfbridge.

Maybe she had misunderstood everything last night. How his lips felt on hers. How his hands had trailed over her skin, hungry. How he had smiled when he'd had to swallow her scream with a searing kiss. Her body had never reacted like that to a man's touch before. To a man's kiss. To his caresses.

But he had turned her into a common trollop within minutes of his attentions on her body.

Maybe now he was done with her. Maybe that was all he wanted. To prove he could make her writhe under him.

Her look averted from the stable boy as a blush travelled up her neck, heating it to uncomfortable proportions. If the boy merely glanced in her direction, he'd absolutely be able to tell where her mind had just wandered. What she had done.

But daylight had come this morning, and with it, a level head. She'd been caught in the shadows of the night, the possibilities of pleasure she'd never experienced. It had been too easy. Too easy to talk to Reiner. Too easy to study his every movement. Too easy to say yes to him, as denying his touch had been the last thing on her mind.

The man was infuriating. And kind. And handsome. And caring. And in rare, sparkling moments when he let his guard down, funny. And the heat in his eyes when he looked at her sparked to life the core of her—the tingling throbbing between her legs that begged for everything his golden brown eyes promised.

He wasn't the cold duke she'd thought him to be.

The exact opposite, in fact.

And a man like that was far more dangerous than a frigid duke in a lonely castle. It'd been embarrassing how quickly she'd been swept into the moment. In what she'd allowed.

She needed to leave. Leave before another encounter with him that would prove to be her downfall, for she didn't think she was capable of saying no to the man. Not when she wanted exactly what he was offering.

Weakness, but she could only manage to leave when she was levelheaded. Not in the heat of the night.

"Sloane."

Reiner's low voice boomed along the main corridor of the stable.

Sloane jumped, spinning to him as horses nickered at the disturbance.

He strode toward her, stopping an arm's length away as he surveyed the stable boy setting the numnah in place.

"Leave us, John."

The boy stepped away from the mare. "Yes, your grace." With a quick bow of his head he slipped past Sloane and walked out the front of the stable.

Reiner watched him until he was clear of the building. He turned to Sloane, his gaze piercing her. "What are you doing?"

"Leaving. You said I could go, so I am."

His mouth opened for a moment, a harsh exhale escaping. Just when he looked to bombard her with orders, his mouth clamped closed.

His gaze drifted off of her for a long breath, his look concentrating on the open rear entrance of the stables. "It is almost twilight." He looked to her. "You cannot travel in darkness."

"The moon is already out and it is clear. It will be enough to get me into the nearest village."

"And then what? What do you do there? Where do you go? You cannot think to seriously do this."

"Were you serious when you said I could leave?"

His jaw twitched, shifting to the left. "I was. You can go if it is truly your wish."

Her right eyebrow lifted. "You aren't stopping me?"

He shook his head, even as his chest lifted in an exasperated inhale. "No." The word came out long and drawn in clear battle against himself.

She glanced at the mare to her left. "Then saddle my horse."

His left fingers rolled inward for a moment, uncurling as he inclined his head toward her and moved to the sidesaddle. Silently, he lifted it and set it on the horse, tightening the girth. The saddle secure, he stood straight, his hand going to the long neck of the horse. He set the bridle in place, attaching it, then grabbed the reins and led the horse to the block outside the stall.

Her breath held, Sloane stepped up on the block and mounted the horse.

Avoiding Reiner's sharp stare, she fiddled with her skirts, arranging them about her legs.

He led the horse two steps toward the opening of the stable, but then stopped abruptly, turning around to her. "You don't know what you're doing, Sloane. The trouble you have involved yourself in. You still don't remember anything and you have no idea what awaits you out there. It's not safe. You—"

"I ken what I'm doing, Reiner. What I have to do."

"Do you?" He shook his head, but shifted the reins about the mare's neck and handed them up to her.

She took them, settling the leather in her hands.

His hand drifted downward, landing on her thigh. "You don't have to do anything, Sloane. Not here. Not for me." His hand slipped off her leg and he took a step backward.

She stared down at him, her gaze caught in his. The breath in her chest froze in place, her lungs tightening until her chest started to hurt. He was letting her go. Giving her the freedom she was so desperate for.

She had to leave. She *had* to.

But her hands were frozen on the reins. Her legs still.

"Why aren't you leaving, Sloane?"

She couldn't look away from him. "I don't know."

"You don't?"

She shook her head, her eyes still locked with his.

He took a step forward, his fingers lifting to rest on her knee. Holding her in place or touching her one last time she wasn't sure. He cleared his throat. "Can I wager a guess?"

"If you wish."

"You feel safe here. Safe with me. And that—" He pointed to her left arm. "Whatever happened to cause that was not safe. It was horrific. And you know in your gut you

don't want to retreat to that place. Don't want to have to face whatever it was that happened to you."

Her lips pulled in for a long moment before she exhaled. "Maybe."

"So stay." The words left him, raw and guttural.

Slowly, his hand lifted from her knee and he held his palm up to her.

For all his golden brown eyes swore that she was safe here—she felt it from him, felt it in her bones—she feared she was making a horrid mistake.

But everything Reiner had done for her—aside from those first days of holding her captive in a room—had proven him honorable. He'd treated her with respect, welcomed her in his home, at his table, with his niece. He wasn't a monster. Wasn't about to cause her harm. If anything, he was a harbor. A harbor against the turmoil of not remembering. Against the sobering reality of her mangled arm.

She drew a breath deep into her lungs, her voice shaking as she exhaled. Her gaze dropped to his upturned palm. "I don't want to want to stay."

"I know."

Her fingers lifted and she grabbed his hand, slowly sliding down from the saddle.

Her boots thudded to the ground and she lifted her gaze to him, afraid that she'd just given up all that she was.

His brown eyes swept across her face. Relief. Desire. But most clearly, resolve shined in his eyes. He was going to keep her safe. Of that she was certain.

She hadn't lost a thing of herself.

"We will figure this out together." His right hand reached up, sliding behind her neck and he leaned forward, his lips finding hers in a kiss that started gentle, but expanded, swallowing her, searing her to the bone. Emblazoning his mark on her soul.

He broke the kiss, his fingers moving along the hair aside her temple as his forehead dipped to meet hers. "You didn't answer me last night, but I need this from you, Sloane. I need you to swear to me that you'll tell me if you remember. If your memories come back, you come to me first. Don't leave. You need to tell me." The fire in his look warmed the gold in his eyes. Warmed them to the space where all coldness had vanished, only concern left in the wake.

Her eyes closed against him for a long breath. "I don't ken if I can promise that."

"You can."

She nodded, her forehead moving against his.

But she couldn't bring herself to say the words.

~ ~ ~

Just as Vicky turned about a rounded tower corner of the castle in front of her, a waft of smoke from a fire by the stables blew in front of Sloane and the thick air sent her eyelids closing against the sting.

The acerbic air singed her nostrils, the unyielding destruction of smoke and embers filling her head. It instantly sent her mind into a whirlwind of blackness. Lost to another world.

A world she couldn't touch, but was drowning in just the same.

Ash, smoke all around her. Suffocating. Screams. Pain. Pain that gripped onto her soul and dragged her into a hell of flames and suffering.

"Sloane."

Her eyes popped open and it took her several blinks to focus on Vicky in front of her.

"Are you coming, Sloane?"

She nodded, the terror that had just snaked around her chest easing.

The blasted dream.

She'd had it twice now. The first time, she'd mostly forgotten it, though stray remnants of the terror had stuck in her chest for days. The second time she hadn't forgotten so quickly. The horror of it, the snippets of a building crashing around her, smoke smothering her, screams, her hand stretching out, reaching for an arm in the blackness.

Those moments of the dream had wedged into her mind, real and visceral, the raw terror not dissipating with her open eyes as it had the first time.

She exhaled through her nose, trying to clear the smoke from clinging inside her nostrils. With a quick shake of her head, she started forth again, following Vicky. It was a beautiful day, the cool wetness from the past few days easing into sunny, dry skies.

Sloane kicked a rock with her toe, sending it careening into the stone at the base of the castle. Vicky glanced over her shoulder at her and with a smile, picked up her steps around the outer southwestern wall of the castle.

For the thousandth time that week, she was asking herself why she wasn't already sixty miles from Wolfbridge. Reiner had given her permission six days ago. Saddled a horse for her.

Say the word and she could leave.

So why wasn't she already gone?

The wily scoundrel. He'd given her free rein to leave—but now she wanted to know what she was doing here just as much as he did. There were too many questions for her to just leave and never look back. Questions that needed answers she wasn't sure she could find anywhere else.

Not to mention the fact that in her heart, if she was honest with herself, she didn't want to leave Vicky. Didn't want to leave Reiner.

He'd been nothing but a gentleman the past days, even managing to keep all their interactions within the respectability of being in front of Vicky or the staff. Even as he was still wary of her intentions at Wolfbridge, he was wooing her, in his own peculiar way.

Not with kisses and promises of Eden, but with his wit and charm, and with his reluctant, but good-natured willingness to play the same songs again and again on the pianoforte as Vicky learned the dances.

Sloane picked up her stride as she realized she wasn't keeping up with Vicky's spry steps, but still glanced over her shoulder to see if any more smoke was headed in her direction. From this angle of the castle, she could still see the far edge of the evergreen hedge lining the southern gardens. Her gaze swept the landscape, forest, landscape, garden, then back again. The smoke had moved off and Claude and Lawrence were nowhere in sight.

They hadn't been anywhere near her in days. Not since Reiner had kissed her in the stable.

He hadn't been lying. She was free to go. Free to point her toes to the left and walk directly into the woods and disappear. He wasn't going to have her stopped. Wasn't going to drag her back into the castle.

Freedom that made her want to stay all the more.

"Sloane, hurry—it's just on the backside of the castle." Vicky peeked her head back around the upcoming curve of stones. The girl had remembered a few minutes ago the thicket of raspberries growing along the edge of the forest at the rear of the castle and was now determined to get there with haste.

Sloane smiled and hurried her legs.

Raspberries did sound good. Maybe if she ate enough of them she would fall asleep in a berry-induced stupor that would tell her what to do next. Leave or stay?

Sloane rounded the corner and watched with a grin as Vicky darted across the long expanse of lawn to the far woods, her pail swinging wildly on her arm. If it was possible, the girl had more energy than she did.

Vicky had already picked half a pail full of the berries by the time Sloane made it to the thicket. She plucked one off the vine and popped it into her mouth. Perfectly ripe.

Her smile spread wide. "Why haven't we been out here before?"

"They weren't ripe three weeks ago, and I was checking them every day and was being disappointed every day, so I just gave up. Then you appeared here and I didn't remember them until just now." Red drops of the berries stained the outer edges of her mouth.

Sloane nodded. "Thank goodness you did. It would have been horrible to miss these." She looked into Vicky's pail. "Have you eaten as many as you've plucked?"

"Probably more." Vicky laughed.

Sloane's fingers went busy, plucking the berries from their stems. Following Vicky's lead, half went into her mouth, the other half into the pail.

Her mouth full, she turned around and took in this area of the estate. Vicky had never brought her back here. The castle wasn't as elaborate from this side, more form than function. If she transplanted in her mind what she knew of the interior of the castle, she had to be looking at the outside wall of the great hall. Three stories high, the hall was as grand as it had to have been when it was first constructed. There were several small, wide windows high in the stone wall that she recognized from inside the hall. To the right of them, a row of four tall vertical windows lined the rest of this span of the castle.

Just below the tall windows, a wide expanse of heavy vines grew up along the outside wall, curving between the windows when they reached to that height.

Vines that would be perfect for climbing.

Without a word to Vicky, she walked toward the vines, throbs of foreboding heartbeats thundering in her head.

This was it. This was the very spot where she had been found.

Why had she not made her way back here before?

Her steps quickened.

She slid to a stop in front of the base of the vines spurting upward from the ground—gnarled roots

determined not to live underground, but to burst toward the sky.

Her neck craning, she looked straight up. Vines that were made for climbing. Her gaze moved across the vines and leaves, finding the sturdy spots amongst the weak. The zigzagging line upward. Upward and leading directly to an open window.

Her throat collapsing, she reached out with her gloved left hand and touched the thick vine in front of her, her fingers sliding along the bark. Her eyes closed.

Instant.

Devastating.

It took less than a breath for all of it to come to her.

The monstrosity of the last six months slammed into her chest. Taking her breath away. Crushing her soul.

She stumbled backward, falling onto her backside. But her feet kept moving, her hands clawing the dirt and pushing her away from the vines—away from the memories filling her head. One moment after another smashed into her skull, rattling about in ferocious mayhem.

"Sloane." A bucket clunked to the ground behind her. "Sloane. What happened? What happened?"

Shaking. Her shoulder was shaking.

She looked at it, her head moving slow, so slow it was as if the world had stopped.

Vicky.

Vicky terrified.

Vicky on her knees and shaking her. Shaking her shoulder.

"Sloane—what is it? What has happened? Tell me—tell me and I will go get Uncle Reiner. He will help—he will help with whatever just happened."

Sloane clamped a hand onto Vicky's wrist, her words fighting through the boulders of memories lodging into her brain. "No—no. Not Reiner."

Her fingers tightened around Vicky's wrist until the girl squealed and tried to yank her arm away.

Sloane's fingers flew wide. She didn't mean to hurt Vicky. Didn't mean to send such terror into her eyes.

Her head fell forward as she drew her knees upward. For a long moment, she curled into herself, closing her eyes and drawing several deep breaths.

"Sloane?"

Her head snapped up and she found Vicky's wide eyes. "I'm sorry, Vicky. I didn't mean to scare you. It is nothing. I stumbled backward and landed on my tailbone and it took my breath away. I am fine now. My breathing has recovered."

The furrow across Vicky's brow stayed in place. "You are positive you are well?"

"I am. I am sorry I frightened you." Sloane glanced over her shoulder. The metal bucket of raspberries lay on its side, squashed red juices of the berries spilling onto the grass. "Oh, no. Not the berries."

Vicky scooted across the ground to scoop up the salvageable berries into the bucket.

Sloane pushed herself onto her quivering legs. "I do feel as though I should go inside and rest, though, probably lie down in my room."

Vicky nodded and grabbed her hand, squeezing it. Leave it to the sweet child to try and comfort her. "I can still fetch Uncle Reiner if it will make you feel better?"

"No. A few minutes of rest and I will be well. I am sure of it." Averting her gaze from the vines, Sloane started walking toward the far corner of the castle.

Within minutes she was in her room, alone after sending Vicky to work on her lessons with Miss Gregory.

She clicked the door closed, her legs stiff as she walked to the bed and sat down on the edge.

Her right hand shaking, she reached to her left elbow and slipped her forefinger under the top edge of her glove.

Peeling down the kidskin, she lifted her mangled bare skin to the daylight.

For long seconds she stared at the twisted, ravaged skin that had once been smooth.

Her eyes had to flip away. Even now she couldn't bear to look at it.

So she set her eyes on her dagger atop the chest across the room. Stared at it for minutes where she let all she'd just remembered sink fully into her consciousness.

Bloody hell. Not Reiner.

Her heart thudded in her ribcage, an invisible vise clamping down about her chest.

Not Reiner. Not him.

Not when she had begun to believe he wasn't the devil himself—not when she had damn well started to like the man.

Much more than like.

Damn him. Damn him to hell.

With a gasp, her head snapped up, her eyes on the back
of the door.

She had to leave Wolfbridge.

And she had to take what she came here for.

~ ~ ~

Sloane waited until the stable boy slipped out the back
of the center stable and found himself a sturdy tree to lean
against for a midafternoon snooze.

She'd seen him do it twice before on the days she and
Vicky were outside in the afternoon sun. His habit was her
opportunity.

Reiner had said she could leave Wolfbridge at any time,
but she wasn't about to test his words. Not now when she
remembered exactly what she was doing at the castle.

She slipped into the stable, looking along the stalls
for Biscuit. Four stalls from the back entrance, she heard
a whinny she recognized. Biscuit smelled her before she
found her mare. Sloane glanced around. Her sidesaddle was
hanging across from the stall.

She shoved the satchel she'd found and strapped across
her body to her backside, and a sharp corner of the book
inside jabbed into her spine. As fast as her hands would
allow, she saddled Biscuit and led her horse out of the rear
of the stable.

A quick glance to the trees at her left verified the stable
boy was still snoozing. She tugged on Biscuit's reins, leading
her onto the trail that veered into the woods at the north
side of the stable. With any luck, it would meet up with the
trail she'd originally taken into Wolfbridge.

Five minutes and she found the main trail and mounted her horse. She waited not a breath to send Biscuit thundering down the path.

Setting her gaze forward, she didn't dare to give the castle a backward glance. She couldn't afford to. Not if she was to escape now.

Two hours later she was dragging her maid out of the coaching inn in Caistor. Milly had waited in place as instructed, especially after she had learned from a passing Wolfbridge servant that a woman of Sloane's description was now in residence at the castle.

Sloane hated to set Milly on a horse with her fear of riding, but her maid would have to suffer it until they reached Doncaster where she could arrange travel north.

With the bundles of the few items that had come to Caistor with them now secured on the back of the horses, Sloane looked at the sky just outside the village. There had to be enough daylight to reach Doncaster. She would have to push the horses, but they could make it. Make it and then she could book passage on the first coach she could find. Post chaise. Mail coach. Stagecoach. She didn't care. Just as long as they disappeared amongst the travelers moving north.

They had to get lost.

For if they didn't and Reiner found her…

She cringed.

No. She couldn't think on that possibility. Couldn't think on what would be his rage.

She set Biscuit into a manageable trot, refusing to glance over her shoulder for fear he was already on her tail with vengeance in his eyes and descending on her like a demon from hell.

If he found her…if he caught her. She didn't want to see it coming. She wanted it quick. Painless.

She managed to keep her gaze forward.

A mistake.

For if she had, she would have noticed two rough brutes quickly saddling their horses at the livery stable on the edge of the village, their hooded eyes watching her and Milly ride from town.

{ CHAPTER 9 }

"Dom, I need to get in and out without my grandfather or Lachlan knowing."

"Curse me bally, lass. I should have known not to trust that stable boy dragging me out here." Two full heads taller than her, Domnall, the brawniest Scotsman Sloane knew, glanced over her head, searching in the dark shadows of the main stable. "Where's Milly?" The low rumble of his voice seeped into the cool night air, echoing in the furthest crevices of the stalls.

"At a coaching inn. I didn't want to bring her and get her involved if my brother finds me here." The Deerhound next to Domnall's leg approached her, nose twitching, and she held her palm under its snout. One sniff and it nudged her, looking for a scratch. Sloane obliged, sinking her fingers into the fur behind its ears. "This is a new one?"

"Just started training her a month ago. By far the smartest one I've ever worked with."

Sloane's fingers sank into the wiry hair along the dog's neck. "She's also a pretty one. Proud."

"Full of herself, that is her one downfall. But also strong-willed and a protector to the last. She's been dubbed Theodora."

Sloane chuckled. "Fitting."

He cleared his throat. "Lach's not going to like this, you sneaking into the castle." His thumbs tucked into the top of his trousers as he eyed her. "What are ye doing here, lass? They think you're still in London."

She looked to Vinehill castle looming behind Domnall, the strong, tall walls outlined in the moonlight. "Which is exactly why I need you to get me in and out of the castle without Lach or any of the staff aware. I don't want my brother to have the slightest inkling that I was here."

"Which means you'll be leaving again after ye get into the castle? What's this about? You're not in trouble, are you?"

"No, Dom, I'm fine—I just need to see Torrie without Lachlan or my grandfather trapping me into staying."

"Ye need to see Torrie?"

She nodded.

His eyes went hooded. "These have been dark days for her."

"She hasn't been healing?"

"Her body, aye, as painful as it's been. Her mind is a different matter."

Sloane's bottom lip drew inward, her look drifting off to the tower that held Torrie's chamber. "I had thought my leaving would be better for her. So she wouldn't feel the need to repeat the minutia of the fire every day, every hour with me. How it could have been different. How we failed. What it cost her—cost us."

Domnall shrugged. "I think it was better for you. Torrie—I don't ken. She keeps all that to herself now. Except for the outbursts."

"There are still outbursts?"

Domnall nodded.

Sloane drew in a deep breath. "Still, I need to see her."

He pointed to her shoulder. "Then pull your cloak up to cover your head and I'll get you up to Torrie's room through the north tower. And then I never saw ye. If Lachlan discovers I ken you stepped foot in the castle without seeing him, he'll have my bloody bollocks cut off."

Sloane smiled. Domnall had never curbed his tongue about her, just the same as her brothers. She'd always appreciated that about him. She tugged the hood of her dark cloak over her head. "Thank you, Dom."

"Where are ye sleeping, lass?"

They started up to the castle through the shadows, Sloane following the large Scotsman.

"In Buchlyvie."

"Hell and damnation, Sloane—that's a two—three hour ride in the dark."

"I made it here without trouble."

"No. I'll not have ye in the woods by yourself. I'll be waiting with your horse at the stable when ye are done to see ye back to Buchlyvie."

"It's not necessary, Dom."

He looked over his shoulder at her, his booming voice rising above a whisper. "Bugger that. I may help sneak ye in and out of the castle, but I'll not be taking chances with your well-being, lass." He turned forward, keeping his pace. "And I'll nae argue the matter with ye."

Sloane smiled at his back. She'd had two big brothers by birth. And one additional big brother by luck. "Aye, I will gladly take the company back to Buchlyvie, Dom. Thank you."

Five minutes later she was trudging up the northern tower's steep circular staircase behind Domnall and his candle, questioning with every step her motives for coming to Vinehill to visit with Torrie.

Questioning everything she'd done in the last five days.

She hadn't gone to Lord Falsted like she was supposed to with the book she'd stolen from Reiner's room. Falsted was a bane upon the lands around Vinehill—setting far too many clearings into motion, destroying too many lives— but he'd been the one to show her the evidence. Evidence that meant Reiner had to pay. Evidence she couldn't dispute.

It would be so much easier if she didn't believe Falsted. If he hadn't encouraged her to go after Reiner and ruin him. For now she didn't know if she could do that.

So she had travelled north instead. Away from Reiner. Away from Lord Falsted.

And it had taken days to admit to herself why.

She didn't want to see Reiner ruined and that's what the book would do.

Somewhere during her time at Wolfbridge, she'd become conflicted. Lost her thirst for vengeance.

Reiner needed to pay for all that he had taken from her. For all that he had destroyed. For all of that he needed to fall.

Yet she couldn't destroy him. Couldn't be the cause of it.

She couldn't watch the man she'd come to know be ruined. Especially by her hand.

It was so much easier when he was a target. A cold, mythical demon she was determined to see pay for his sins.

Except he wasn't mythical. He wasn't a demon.

He was just a man. A flesh and blood man that looked at her with such heat in his eyes it seared her to her toes. A man that had held her, pulling her from the throes of terror-filled dreams. A man that had played silly tunes on the pianoforte for Vicky because she wanted to dance. A man that had held her far too close when he'd danced with her. A man that had kissed her and sent her body into undeniable pleasure.

He wasn't the monster she had wanted to destroy.

He'd abused that sliver of time when she couldn't remember what he was and he'd wormed his way into her every thought.

Just as the devil himself would have.

She needed Reiner to be the monster again. He had to be if she was to execute the vengeance he was due.

And Torrie could do that for her. Torrie could make him into the monster again.

Domnall stopped in front of Torrie's door and turned to Sloane. "I'll have your horse waiting for ye at the stables, lass." He set the candle on the half-round table just to the left of Torrie's door. "I ken ye can make your way through the castle in the dark, but take the candle with ye. I don't want ye to break your neck on the stairs on the way out."

"Thank you, Dom." She went to her toes to kiss his cheek, then turned to the heavy oak door.

She needed this. Needed Torrie to remind her of what she must do. To remove the conflict of every thought warring in her head. To reset the blaze for vengeance.

Straightening her spine, Sloane set her chin down and went into Torrie's room.

"You are awake."

Sloane's cousin lay on her bed, a sheet bunched and draped over her stomach, her legs sticking out, bare to

the air. Her eyes open, she stared at the peach upholstery draped above her from the ends of the tester bed.

Torrie didn't react to the intrusion into her room. Only a blink.

Sloane moved to her bedside, looking down at her cousin—her sister for all purposes, for they had been raised together here at Vinehill.

Her gaze fixed on Torrie's face, not venturing downward. Torrie's pretty features looked far more aged than she remembered from when she left Vinehill months ago with their plot for vengeance firmly in her head.

"You are awake," Sloane repeated softly, not sure how to break Torrie from her reverie.

"And you've returned." Torrie's head shifted slightly on the pillow and she looked at Sloane.

"I have. At least for these few minutes." Sloane reached out and stroked strands of Torrie's dark hair along her temple that had escaped the simple braid that caught her locks. Her hair had always held such lustrous majesty. How long had it been since it had been free of the braid?

Her hand falling to her side, Sloane sat down on the edge of the bed. "I needed to talk to you as you are the only person I can trust with this information."

"Wait, before…" Torrie's eyes closed for the longest moment. With a heavy breath, her eyelids cracked open, her look grave. "I'm sorry I asked you."

Sloane's breath caught in her throat. She shook her head. "You don't need to apologize, Tor. I ken the pain you were in."

"It was unfair." Torrie drew a ragged breath into her lungs. "I'm a coward and I couldn't kill myself, but I never

should have asked you to do it. It would have been too
much to bear—for the rest of your life. I'm sorry I did that
to you. You were right to leave."

"You forgive me?"

"It never needed forgiving, Sloane. You were doing
what was right."

Her heart shattering just as violently as it had months
ago when Torrie had asked her to do it, Sloane had to lean
forward, searching for breath. She had failed Torrie—she
hadn't been strong enough to do as her cousin had begged.

But now, forgiveness. Who knew it would break her
just as easily?

Torrie's right arm moved, her hand splaying onto her
stomach. She inhaled a deep breath, her face cringing in a
flash of pain. "So tell me, what has happened?"

"I went after him—Lord Falsted. Except he doesn't
own the land. I saw the papers. The Duke of Wolfbridge is
the man. So I went after him."

"You did?" Torrie's beautiful big green eyes went wide.
"What happened?" She shifted, trying to sit up.

Sloane quickly grabbed several pillows, stacking them
behind Torrie so she could rest against them.

"I found him, Reiner—the duke. I went to his castle in
Lincolnshire and I went there to destroy him. Lord Falsted
helped arrange it. All I needed to do was steal a book from
him. A book that would ruin him were it to ever get out."

"What was the book?"

"It's a ledger of some sort with names. I have looked at
it, but I am not sure what it's for. Lord Falsted said with the
book, all of the duke's sins would be revealed—properties

would be revoked, his title removed, charges of treason against the crown. Ruined, fully and wholly."

"So it is done?" The smallest pained smile came to the corners of Torrie's lips. "He is ruined?"

"Not exactly."

"What happened?" Her cousin's forehead furrowed.

"I still have the book as there was a hiccup before I stole it."

Torrie's look narrowed at her. "What hiccup?"

"I slipped and fell when I was trying to gain entrance to the duke's castle. The fall knocked memories from my head, because I forgot everything of the last six months."

"Oh no." Torrie's eyes squinted in worry. "But you have remembered now?"

Sloane nodded. "I have, but not before I spent time with the duke. With his family." She drew a deep breath and exhaled it in a tortured sigh. "I like the man, Torrie. Had I known what had happened I could have easily hated him. But I didn't know and then I—I grew to like him. He is a good man…I think."

"What do you mean you like him?" Torrie's words hissed into the room.

Sloane shrugged, avoiding Torrie's glare by looking to the healthy fire adding heat to the already stifling hot room.

"Let me see your arm, Sloane."

Wary, her look shifted to her cousin. "Why?"

"Let me see it." Torrie wiggled her fingers at Sloane.

Her gaze fixed on Torrie's face, Sloane stripped off the long glove that constantly concealed her left arm.

Torrie grabbed her left wrist, her fingers wrapping along the twisted flesh. "Look at it, Sloane."

"Torrie—"

Torrie lifted Sloane's arm, shaking it in front of her eyes. "He did this to you, Sloane. That evil bastard did this. Did this to you."

Sloane closed her eyes against her own ragged flesh.

"You can't even look at your own damned mangled flesh, Sloane—much less mine."

"I—"

"No—no excuses. You haven't looked at my leg once since you stepped into this room. You're hiding from the truth. From the pain. It's easier for you not to look at it. Not to acknowledge it." She tossed Sloane's arm from her grip. "Look at your arm, Sloane. Look at it before you forget what it was like."

Sloane stared down at her wrecked arm. The twisted white threads of skin.

She hadn't stared at her own arm—hadn't truly looked at it save for quick glances as she washed her hands and then when her memories first came back—not since that night when she first discovered what had become of her arm and Reiner had come into her room to calm her.

She hadn't been able to bring herself to do it. To face what she was now.

"Now look at my damn leg."

Her breath quivering in her chest, it took every nerve in Sloane's body to lift her look to Torrie's leg.

Bile snaked up her throat.

Torrie's leg looked much like her own arm did months ago. Still healing. Still seeping pus. Red, angry flesh twisting together as it tried to close itself up from the air. Tried to heal itself in the most gruesome way possible.

"He did this. That demon did this to me. Did this to you." Torrie grabbed her left arm again, shaking it. "These are his sins and he needs to pay."

"It's not that simple, Torrie. It—"

"It is." A bitter sneer curled Torrie's lips. "You ken exactly what he took from us, Sloane. What he did to us. You need to make him suffer—suffer for all he's done."

The hatred palpitating off her cousin sent an icy shiver down Sloane's spine.

"Torrie, when—how—there is so much malice in your voice. It is not you. This was my idea to go after the man responsible—my want for vengeance. You—you tried to talk me out of it—you—"

"This pain has left only hatred in my heart, Sloane." The hard glint in Torrie's eyes didn't wane. "It is awful yet true. But hatred is all I have left."

"Tor, no." Sloane grabbed her hand, clutching it. Torrie was the kindest person she knew. She'd always held the softest heart out of all of them.

"I have not found a way to be otherwise. I cannot even cry on it anymore, Sloane. My tears are gone. The pain took too many and now I am left with none. Maybe someday, but I fear I have little hope for it. Every thought I have now is red—only anger."

"Torrie, you cannot mean that."

Torrie's eyes pierced her. "Even at you I am angry, Sloane."

Sloane's head snapped back. "Me? Why?"

"You pulled me out of there. You put the flames out. I should have died. I should have died with all of them."

Torrie's hand swept down to her leg. "Instead I am here, a grotesque mess of a being."

"No, don't say that—you're not grotesque, Tor—never. You just need to give it time. You're still healing."

"Am I?" A caustic chuckle left Torrie's lips. "From where I lay, I'm not healing. I'm turning into something that I don't recognize anymore." Her mouth closed, pulling back into a severe line as her look skewered Sloane. "So finish it or don't finish it with the duke, Sloane. I don't care. It's not going to help my anger. My anger isn't going away. Ever."

"Tor—"

Torrie's look swung to the fire, her arms clasping over her ribcage. "Just get out, Sloane. Get out, and don't come back."

"Torrie…" The name fell to silence on Sloane's tongue.

Domnall was right. Torrie had descended into a dark, dark place. And she wasn't sure if her cousin had hope of ever being whole again.

She scooted backward off the bed, her look staying on Torrie. Her cousin didn't so much as blink, much less look away from the fire as Sloane backed to the door.

Escaping out into the coolness of the corridor, Sloane paused to lean against the doorframe and drag a deep breath into her lungs.

What had become of her cousin? She had seen the signs before she had left months ago—but this was beyond anything Sloane could have imagined.

Torrie was drowning in so much hate that she couldn't move forward with life.

With her chest aching for the pain her cousin was in, one thing became clear.

She didn't want to become like Torrie.

Eaten to the bone with hatred.

Sloane had thought she needed justice. That she needed it to move forward.

But maybe it wasn't the key to moving forward.

Maybe she just needed to move forward.

{ CHAPTER 10 }

"Milly, did you discover if they will have a coach for us by early afternoon?"

The door clicked closed. Sloane didn't bother turning around to her maid as she finished folding her spare chemise and set it onto the bed next to her valise. She needed to finish packing if they were to leave the coaching inn today.

"Where in the bloody devil do you think you're going to next?"

Double—no triple hell.

He found her.

Sloane froze, her stare on the wall in front of her. Every nerve on her body spiked, prickling her skin from her scalp to her toes.

The air crackled around her, crackled like it did every time Reiner was within five feet of her.

But this was more. This was dangerous. The air not only crackled, it sparked—near to singeing her with the rage that accompanied the man behind her.

Hiding her motion, she picked up her chemise and slid it slowly into the valise in front of her on the bed. Her fingers dipped downward in the bag, searching. She found it. Blade. Handle.

Gripping her dagger tight in her hand, she whipped around, the blade pointed at Reiner before he could move across the room to her.

His chest lifted in a seething heave and he stepped toward her, directly at the blade aimed at his heart. "You remembered. Everything. And then you betrayed me." His words thundered into the room.

"What?" She jumped a step sideways.

He advanced, his words a growl. "You remembered what you were doing at Wolfbridge and you didn't come to me. Didn't tell me. You swore you would."

"I swore nothing." Her breath sped and she turned slightly to back up. Her shoulder blades hit the wall. She moved to her left, circling him with the blade still high.

He kept stalking her, his fury palpitating. Kept rounding about her, advancing on her until the tip of the blade was poking into his gut just below his ribcage.

His feet stopped, the deep lines on his face hardening into cold countenance until he was almost unrecognizable. He looked down at the blade, then dragged his vicious gaze up to her face. "You don't want to do that, Sloane." The words seethed through clenched teeth.

She twisted the dagger against his gut, the sharp tip tearing a hole in his waistcoat. "No? Do I have a choice?"

A blur in front of her eyes, he swung his arm through the air, his fingers gripping onto her wrist and twisting her blade-holding right hand away from his belly. Before she could blink, he snatched her other wrist and wrenched both of her arms above her head and shoved her backward.

The length of her backside slammed into the doorway. His clamps on her wrists tightened and he knocked her right hand against the door. The knife dropped from her fingers, clattering to the floor by her feet.

He leaned down over her, his fuming breath in her face. "You left me."

"I did." Her arms twisted under his fingers. Iron grips she wasn't about to escape. "You said I could leave at any time."

"And I never said I wouldn't follow." A savage growl vibrated his chest and he knocked her uplifted arms into the door again. His knuckles took the bruise of the blow more than her arms did. "You made Vicky cry—hysterically. And the look she gave me—she hates me—hates that I drove you away."

Sloane gasped. "But I—I left her a note—"

His lips covered hers, cutting her words.

Angry. Raw. Hard.

His mouth took hers in a kiss that demanded her silence. A kiss that she could feel him fight against, even as he took her very essence from her. A kiss that unleashed such harbored rage she was both lost and found as she drowned in it.

A snarl bubbled in his throat and he ripped his mouth from hers, then slammed her arms into the door above her head again. "And you stole from me."

"What?" Her eyes dazed, her gaze lifted, trying to focus on the split second change from him kissing her to his full fury showering down upon her. The rage in his eyes hadn't dissipated—if anything, it was more alive, more focused— pinpoints fixated on her.

"What?" She blinked hard.

"You stole from me, Sloane. No one steals from me."

"I stole from you?" Her own rage bubbled, exploding in hot droplets that seared up through her chest. "You dare

to say that to me? When you stole from me, you bastard—you stole everything—everything—from me."

His head snapped back. "I what?"

She twisted, trying to free her wrists of his grasp.

He yanked her arms upward, lifting her off her toes.

She stilled, glaring up at him.

"What are you talking about, Sloane?" The slightest measure of restraint appeared in his voice as he leaned in, his breath mingling with hers.

"You stole my brother from me, you bloody ogre—you killed my brother, you killed my cousin's family." The words spit from her mouth. "You're the one that set us aflame—my arm, Torrie's leg—you left our bodies in ravaged, scarred shells. You did this, not by your hand but by your order. You."

"I what?" He let her slide down the door until her feet touched the floor, but he kept her hands clamped above her head.

Smart bastard, for she was already eyeing her dagger on the floor.

"What in the hell are you saying, Sloane?"

"It was your land, Reiner. Your blasted land."

His head instantly flickered back and forth. "Whatever you're thinking, Sloane, you have it all wrong."

Her head shook between her upstretched arms. "I don't have anything wrong—don't try and deny you own that swathe of Swallowford land and that you ordered it cleared of tenants. I've seen the papers. You may not have been the one to light the torches, Reiner, but they were lit by your command. It was you. You killed them all—you killed an entire family. You killed my brother."

His eyebrows lifted. "I—what are you speaking of, Swallowford land?"

A hissing screech left her lips. "You don't even remember the terror you unleashed?"

His head dropped forward for a long second. A breath passed and his look snapped up to her, recognition reaching his eyes. "Swallowford? The land in Stirlingshire?"

"You bloody bastard—yes, that land." Her voice shrilled to a rage. "My brother's life and that's all it means to you—a tepid guess of some blasted land you may or may not remember?"

Reiner leaned in, his forehead almost touching hers as his voice dropped into a deep growl. "I never ordered anything—I just purchased it, Sloane. Or rather, my solicitor handled it so I don't know what the hell you're talking about."

"Don't lie to me—not now." She twisted her arms in his grasp, fury sending so much blood through her limbs she was sure she could break free. She couldn't. "It was the condition for your blasted purchase of the land—clear it of the tenants or you wouldn't buy it. You wanted the blood but you didn't want it on your hands, just another of the thousands of clearings haunting the land. Did you think no one would know? Clear it was the order—well, they bloody well cleared it, Reiner. Scorched it to the ground."

His forehead yanked away from hers and his chin dipped forward, his gaze on the space between them for several long breaths. Several long, heaving breaths.

Without warning, his fingers snapped away from her wrists, releasing her, and he took a step backward. His head tilted to the side, his eyes narrowing. "What exactly

happened there on the Swallowford lands, Sloane?" The rage palpitating in his voice had almost disappeared.

She wouldn't have it.

"If you don't ken already, then you don't care. You never cared." Her lip sneered. "And you'll not get the story. Not from me."

For long seconds his gaze skewered her and she braced herself for another attack.

Her look dropped to the floor. The blade was a foot away. By the time she bent to it, he'd have her in another iron hold.

With an exhale that fumed into the room, Reiner turned his head, looking about the chamber. Spying a silver platter on the table with a decanter of brandy, he walked over to it, his boots clomping on the floor.

"I'm not leaving this room until you tell me what happened, Sloane." He poured himself a dram of the amber liquid, quickly lifting it to his lips and tossing it into his throat. He poured another and took a sip as he turned to her. "Don't test me on this."

She stared at him for a long moment, her gaze skewering him with as much ferocity as his did to her. With a snarl of her lip, she opened her mouth. "Fine. The men you hired to clear the lands—"

"I hired no men, Sloane. You—"

She stormed across the room to him. "You're the one that bloody well wanted this story, Reiner, and I'm only going to tell it once. If you interrupt, I'm done. You'll get no more from me."

His jaw went slack for a long second, then he closed it and offered a single nod.

She grabbed the glass from his hand and swallowed what was left. The brandy burned a ball down her chest, but it was just what she needed to temper the fury that had swelled into a rock and wedged in her throat. Clunking the glass onto the table next to his hand, she looked up at him.

"I told you of my cousin, Torrie, how she is like a sister to me?"

Reiner nodded.

"She has lived with us at Vinehill since she was three. But her family lived on a small farm on Swallowford lands. They had been making the rent payments, but it wasn't enough. The clearing men were coming for them—coming to kick them off their land. The land that had been in their family for three generations. But the clearing men wanted Torrie's family gone—*you* wanted Torrie's family gone—so the land could be converted into grazing space for some bloody sheep."

She paused, staring at him, daring him to interrupt her. To claim innocence. He didn't.

She turned from him, walking over to the window on the side of the building and looking down onto the empty lane that ran beside the coaching inn. "So of course her family resisted. They had nowhere to go. They only knew how to farm. Torrie knew they would fight it and she was determined to go and stop her father—to save him and her mother and her brother." Sloane paused, swallowing hard. "And I was determined to go to save Torrie. And my brother, Jacob…he was determined to go to save me."

Her fingers lifted to the glass pane in front of her, tapping on it for several seconds. "When we got to the farm, the men were already there. Torrie's father had locked

him and his wife and his son into their cottage and was refusing to come out. The brutes had torches. Torches burning and crackling and ready to light everything up."

Her right fingers dropped from the glass, moving to the top hem of the glove above her left elbow. Slowly, she peeled it down, bringing the scars to the daylight. "Torrie begged the men to wait—that she could go into the cottage and convince them to come out. So she went in, but she couldn't make them move. Not quickly enough, at least. So the brutes ran around, setting every single one of the five buildings aflame. Though one of them stopped to let the animals out of the barn." A caustic chuckle left her lips. "Imagine that—they let the animals out—they were more important than the people."

She paused, her voice hiccupping, and she had to let a deep breath sink into her lungs. "And when they went for the cottage, Jacob tried to stop them—he killed two of them, but he was too late. One of the torches was tossed onto the roof of the cottage with Torrie and her family still inside. It burst into flames—hot—almost instantly. Like magic. Like the breath of a dragon."

She dropped the glove on the floor.

She shook her head and it fell forward, her gaze landing on the twisted flesh of her arm. "I managed to kick the door open while Jacob was fighting them. And I went in after Torrie. Jacob came in after me." She drew a quivering breath. "Part of the roof fell in right away and it set Torrie's skirts aflame. She was going to stay in there with them, with her family. But I caught her and started dragging her out and then Jacob lifted me, pulling the both of us out of the cottage."

Her right fingers lifted to her left arm and she traced the knotted flesh. "My arm was burnt when I was putting out the flames engulfing Torrie's skirts. Jacob ran back into the cottage to save Torrie's brother and parents. But the roof collapsed. Collapsed with all four of them inside."

She glanced over her shoulder at her blade lying on the floor by the door. "Then I tried to kill one of the brutes—the rage, the pain—it took me over and turned me into a demon. I attacked one of them with my blade, but I was nothing against him. If it hadn't been for Lachlan arriving and stopping him—killing him, the blackguard would have killed me as well."

Long seconds passed before she lifted her head, her gaze finding Reiner's face. "You sit in your fancy fortress, life-times away, Reiner. Oblivious. But the things you do have consequences. Whether you see them or not."

Silence.

He stared at her, his face set in stone. "You are done?"

She turned fully around to him and nodded. "That is all of it."

He exhaled, his look piercing her. "Then you have it all wrong, Sloane. Every last bit of it."

{ CHAPTER 11 }

"You cannot take away the fire, Reiner—take away the deaths that are on your hands."

Reiner stared at her, stared at the rogue droplet of amber in her blue eyes that marked her unique above all others. For all of the anger rushing through him, halfway through her story all he wanted to do was drag her into his arms.

Calm her.

Erase the past.

Those minutes in time that had damaged her so. Those minutes that upended her world and put such malice into her blue eyes.

"I don't mean the fire, Sloane. That happened and there isn't a thing I can do about that. And it was horrendous and I am in a rage thinking on the pain you must have suffered. But you're wrong about what happened before the fire."

"Before the fire?"

"You say I was the one that demanded the lands be cleared. Who told you I ordered it?"

Her brow crinkled. "Why does it matter? What matters is that I ken it was you."

He bit back a blasphemy. "Who told you it was me, Sloane?"

She sighed. "It was Lord Falsted."

A caustic chuckle left his throat. "Falsted. Of course the lying bastard would have sent you."

"Sent me?"

He shook his head. "I didn't order anything cleared, Sloane. There were no conditions to buying the land."

"But you said your solicitor handled the transaction, maybe he ordered it on your behalf."

"The man doesn't do anything I'm not aware of." His look bored into her. "Falsted used you, Sloane. He used you to come after me."

Her fingers clasped together in front of her. "That's not true. I saw the papers—I saw the agreement—signed by your own hand."

"You know my signature?"

Her head snapped back. "You expect me to just believe you? Believe you because you walk in here and tell me I was lied to?"

He inclined his head toward her, his look skewering her. "Yes."

"Yes?" she scoffed. "It's not enough, Reiner. What makes your word any more trustworthy than Lord Falsted's?"

The side of his mouth lifted in disgust. "If you even have to ask that question, Sloane, then we are done here." Reiner spun from her and stalked toward the door.

Without a glance back to her, he let himself into the hallway.

~ ~ ~

Sloane stared at the closed door to her room, waiting for it to open.

Willing it to open.

It didn't.

Reiner was gone.

Done with her.

Good riddance. She didn't believe a word he said. Didn't believe he had nothing to do with the fire. She had seen the documents—seen the caveat to the purchase that the lands had to be free and clear of all tenants.

Except…

Except he had looked truly dumbfounded when she had mentioned the Swallowford lands. Like they meant no more to him than a blade of grass at Wolfbridge. Strike that—a blade of grass at Wolfbridge probably did mean more to him than the name Swallowford.

The air prickled the skin on her left arm so she picked up her glove from the floor and tugged it onto her left hand and along her arm. Air usually did that to her skin after a few minutes. Dried it. Stretched it. Made her want to itch the scars so viciously she would draw blood. She'd done it before, too many times.

It wasn't until she'd had the long kidskin glove securely in place, the hem snug on her upper arm, that the thought hit her just as hard as her fall from the vines at Wolfbridge.

Reiner hadn't even mentioned the book.

He'd said she'd stolen from him, yes. But beyond that, he hadn't mentioned the book. Hadn't demanded it back.

She ran to her valise, ripping garments from the bag until she found the false bottom tucked into the dark shadows of fabric. Her fingernails went into the side of the flap, wedging it upward.

The book—the red leather-bound ledger—still sat in the bottom, securely hidden away.

She folded the false bottom down on top of it, tossing her half-folded clothes back into the bag with no care other than to hide the bottom.

Reiner hadn't demanded she return it.

So it was either not as valuable—as damaging to Reiner—as Lord Falsted had told her.

Or it was that Reiner trusted her with it.

Trusted her not to ruin him.

Blast it.

All she had done was spew hate onto him. Hate, just like Torrie's. Hate that demanded vengeance.

Vengeance she no longer wanted.

She realized that after walking out of Torrie's room. She didn't want vengeance if it meant Reiner was hurt by it. She didn't want it if it meant that he walked away from her and never looked back.

Damn the man.

Damn her own idiocy.

Several minutes had passed since he left the room, and she ran to the window facing the main road through the village and searched the thoroughfare in front of the coaching inn.

No Reiner.

She spun, racing to the door and out into the hallway. Down two and a half flights of stairs, her speed out of control, she ran into the broad back of Reiner.

He stumbled, slipping down two steps before using the wall to catch both himself and her from breaking their necks.

His arm tight around her waist, he held her upright. She wiggled to wedge her face from his chest and looked up at him.

"Reiner…"

Her voice trailed off, her tongue useless as she stared at him. For all she wanted to stop him from leaving, she had no words. No words when she could very well be locked in the arms of the man that killed her brother.

But it didn't matter. She wanted him.

Awkward silence hung heavy in the breath of air between them.

She cleared her throat, walking her fingers up along the lapels of his coat as she attempted to untangle her limbs from his body. "I thought you would be farther away."

He looked down at her, his golden brown eyes searching her face, searching for the reason she had just tackled him. Then a slow smile, almost carnal, curved the side of his mouth. "I walked slow."

One breath. Two. Three.

He descended, capturing her in a fire-fueled kiss. Consuming her, head to toe.

His mouth hard against hers, desperate as though he was drowning and she was the air he needed to breathe. Shifting, his arm around her back tightened, dragging the full length of her against his body.

The pool of need in her core swelled almost instantly—the last time he had touched her quick to her mind. He turned, lifting her slightly, and he walked up the stairs. Two more levels and his lips never broke with hers.

He set her down in the hallway outside her room and he lifted his head from hers. "Tell me this isn't my imagination, Sloane."

"It isn't." The words croaked out, forced through her breathless throat.

With a growl he leaned forward, catching her lips under his, his tongue breaching her mouth, hungry for the taste of her.

Her hands went up, wrapping around his neck, her fingers diving into his hair.

He broke the kiss, his lips trailing down along her neck as he started walking forward. She shuffled backward until they reached her door and they stumbled into the room.

The door slammed shut behind them and Reiner spun her, setting her back against the wall next to the doorway.

His fingers slid up along her sides, moving inward along her ribcage to cup the bottom swell of her breasts. She gasped at the touch, her back arching toward him, offering herself as her fingers clenched his hair. Just as before, her body reacted to his touch, out of control, thoughts of sanity and decorum instantly disappearing from her mind.

A knock rapped through the door next to her ear.

Reiner froze, his lips on the smooth line of her clavicle.

"My lady?" Though muffled, Milly's high-pitched voice rang into the room. "The carriage will be ready in two hours. Do ye need help packing?"

Sloane coughed, clearing her throat as she clasped her right hand over Reiner's mouth. "N-no, Milly."

With imp in his eyes, Reiner nipped at her pinky finger.

She gave him a death glare as she shook her head. Her eyes averting to the crown moldings that lined the ceiling of the room, she tightened her hold over Reiner's mouth and cleared her throat again. "Can you please go below and order us an early dinner to be served in a few hours? I prefer to be alone for another hour, maybe two."

Reiner nipped at her finger again.

Shaking her head, her look pinned him. "Actually, Milly, will you tell the driver of the carriage we're to be delayed for a day? I will pay him for his patience. I'll knock on your door when I'm ready to eat."

"Are ye well, miss?" The door jiggled. "Should I—"

Her gaze swung to the door. "No, Milly. I am fine. I would just prefer to be alone for a spell."

"As ye wish, my lady." Footsteps echoed down the hallway.

Sloane waited, frozen in Reiner's arms with her hand across his mouth until the footsteps disappeared and a full minute passed.

When she finally turned her gaze to him, his eyebrows cocked.

"What?"

He glanced down pointedly at her hand still covering his mouth.

She dropped her fingers from his lips.

"I have you alone—truly alone—since you fell into my life, and you're only giving me an hour? Maybe two?"

She chuckled. "How much time do you want?"

His hand lifted, his thumb dragging along her bottom lip. "Your lips, your body, and I could get lost for a lifetime." His face lost all levity, his gaze burning her with

the intensity of a blacksmith's forge. "Do you truly want this, Sloane? For there is no going back. Tell me to leave and I will."

It wasn't even a decision.

Her course had been set the second she stepped out into the hallway and chased after him.

She met his gaze, his golden brown eyes intense on her. "I don't want to go back—I cannot. Only forward."

His thumb dropped from her lips to make way for his mouth capturing hers. Searing her with all the wanton need that surged through his blood the same as it surged through hers.

He stepped in closer, locking her into place against the wall as his fingers tugged down the bodice of her black dress. His fingers weren't satisfied until her stays, her chemise dropped as well, baring her nipples to the air.

His look dipped and a rumble echoed from deep in his chest. "Bloody exquisite." His mouth dropped and took her left breast in between his lips, his teeth raking the sensitive nub.

The ache deep in her core started to throb, started to demand more and more with each swipe of his tongue on her nipple. The world closing in on her, nothing but pleasure from Reiner and all he was doing to her seeped through her body.

His tongue trailed a line to her other breast and lavished it with attention until it was hard, straining into his mouth.

"Do what you did, before."

He chuckled into her skin. "I thought you would never ask."

His hands went down and he bunched her skirts, lifting them. Air hit her bare thighs, sending her skin to prickle and a burning pang through her core.

His mouth still on her nipple, his right fingers went to the inside of her left thigh, brushing the skin with the lightest caress that shouldn't have existed from his large hands.

Upward. Upward.

His fingers reached her folds and slid into the wetness.

The touch shocked her body into full attention, no longer reveling in the ministrations of his lips on her breasts.

Her body wanted more. Demanded more.

Her fingers tight in his hair, her head fell back, clunking onto the wall.

The circles he swiped along her nubbin sent her body into a frenzy. Something she couldn't control. Hell—she could never control this—never control how her body reacted to his.

The build was fast this time. Faster than the last time, as though her body knew exactly what was in store for her and was in a rush to get there. But she needed more.

For a second, rational thought flashed through her brain. Every scold, every word, every reminder she'd heard throughout her life about giving up her body to a man. Rational thought that couldn't find roots. For this wasn't any man. This was Reiner. There was no stopping this—not now. Whatever blasted thing this was between them needed to happen.

"Don't stop—I want more." Her words came out heated, unrecognizable as her own. "I want you in me."

"You are positive?"

"You—you into me—take me there, Reiner."

A raw rumble slipped from his lips and he freed the front fall of his trousers and set his hand under her backside. He lifted her, propping her against the wall, and he set the smooth tip of his member at her entrance. The thought of the size of it entering her body should have given her pause, but she couldn't think on it, for he swiped her folds with his thumb and all words, all thoughts left her.

She was lost. Lost again in a dark world with a thousand points of lights flashing through her brain. Her body twisting, releasing all the sweet agony flowing through her into her core.

His shaft broke upward, breaking through her barrier, and he froze. "Hell, Sloane, I didn't think you were—"

She fought her way through the fog to him. "I—I am—was." Her fingers clawed at his back, her words jumbled. Even with the pain she wasn't ready for it to be done. "More. Don't stop." Her words desperate, her hips swiveled on their own accord, urging him onward. "Don't stop, Reiner."

An incoherent blasphemy exhaled from his lips and he eased out of her.

"More. I think I need you deep inside."

The blasphemy turned into a growl and he drove up into her. The sheer determination of attempting to not wreck her body sent the cords of muscles along his neck straining. He eased out and in again. "I don't know how long I can take this care."

"Then don't." She grabbed the back of his head, pulling his face to hers. "It doesn't hurt, not now." Her lips met his in a brutal kiss that told him just how much she needed him to be driving into her.

He withdrew, thrusting into her again and again until he swelled deep within her. A guttural roar shook his chest as he pulled from her lips and buried his head along her neck. The pulsating shudders of his body blanketed her as he reached the same pinnacle she was immersed in.

There was no going back.

Not for either of them.

{ CHAPTER 12 }

It was the exact proof he needed. Even as he lifted
Sloane's skirts, he wasn't sure what he was going to find. A
masterful courtesan. Possibly a lady who had tumbled in
the hay a number of times but not experienced. A woman
somewhere along the gamut between the two.

A virgin was not one of them.

But to him, it was proof. Proof that she wasn't another
actress sent by Falsted. She wasn't a whore sent to ruin him
with some elaborate ruse.

Sloane wanted revenge, yes—was dead set on it. That
single-mindedness had set her up to be used by Falsted. And
now she was an innocent being tossed about as a pawn.

Which was worse.

Much worse.

For now he was going to have to make Falsted pay for
his part in using Sloane.

Still embedded deep in her, he opened his eyes. A sheen
glistened across her brow and her breath came in short
pants that didn't fully reach into her lungs.

Her body wedged tight between him and the wall with
her legs wrapped around his waist, he lifted his left hand
from her backside to clasp her head, his fingers threading
into her hair. He swallowed hard against his own labored
breathing. "Damn, Sloane, you should have told me you
were a virgin."

She laughed, expelling what little air she had managed into her chest. She had to gasp a breath before she could talk. "You assumed I was a loose woman?"

"I didn't know what you were—for how you came to Wolfbridge was so suspect. And then it is how your body reacts to mine—just like it did in the library at Wolfbridge. The way you twist under my hands. It is…practiced."

Her eyes snapped open to him, a flush filling her cheeks. "It is wrong—what I do? I didn't—"

His mouth covered hers, cutting off her words. He kissed her, long and lazy, his tongue exploring the taste of her just for the sake of discovery.

He broke away, his forehead tilting forward to touch hers. "What you do is exactly right. Everything. From that little scream that gets caught in your throat when my lips are on your nipples, to the way you gasp and tighten around me when you come. Right. Perfect. All of it."

Relief filled her blue eyes, the dash of amber in her left iris sparking to life. "Good. I cannot control it. Not with you. I've never had that problem with other suitors—controlling myself—but with you, Reiner…"

"With me, what?"

She sighed. "With you my body does things my mind would normally refuse."

"We'll marry as soon as we can—we're in Scotland so it will only require a willing man to do so."

Her eyes flew wide. "Married? I—no."

"No?" He shook his head, not quite believing he had just heard the word. "What did you think this was, Sloane? I said there would be no going back."

"You didn't say anything about marriage." Her eyes closed for a long moment. When her lashes fluttered open, her look went upward toward the ceiling. "I assumed…ever since the fire…"

"What did you assume?"

Her blue eyes dropped to meet his gaze. "I assumed I would never marry."

His brow furrowed. "Never marry—why not?"

The words unable to breach her lips, she lifted her left arm, still covered from fingertips to her upper arm in that blasted glove.

"Your arm? The scars?"

She nodded, her voice catching. "I am damaged. Unmarriageable. That is what my grandfather said."

"Your grandfather—"

"Only spoke a truth most are too polite to say out loud. But it is a truth nonetheless."

"Truth only bears weight if it is believed. Me—I believe a different truth. That you are marriageable. What else would this be? What else could this be?" His fingertips curled against her scalp and his throat tightened. "Tell me this was not a mistake."

"That is just it. I don't ken what this is." Her hands moved from the death grip they had on his shoulders to wrap around his neck. "My body reacts, and my mind goes right along for the journey. I don't ken why it is that I seem to lose all sense around you, Reiner."

He exhaled a long breath. "And that is why I wasn't sure what I would meet here—as all common sense appears to elude me as well when it comes to you."

"So it is that we do not trust each other?" she asked.

As much as he didn't want to, he unthreaded his fingers from her hair and lifted her body off of his. He took a step backward and her skirts fell down between them. Turning to the side, he watched her out of the corner of his eye as he pulled his trousers into place and buttoned them. "You have to understand, Sloane, there was one before you—six months ago."

"One what?"

"One sent to ruin me." He sighed and walked away from her, stopping at the table to refill a tumbler of brandy. He took a long sip, letting it roll slowly on his tongue before looking to her. "There was a woman before you. She was sent by Falsted to ruin me. A mistress that plied her trade very well—had me fooled until the day I caught her searching my room."

"Lord Falsted sent her? She was there for the book?"

His eyebrow cocked at her. He hadn't mentioned the book. Not yet. "She was. It didn't take much cajoling to get her to admit to her true purpose for being at Wolfbridge. She was an actress and a whore. Nothing more." He shook his head, then swallowed the rest of the dram. "I am still coming to acceptance of the fact that you were not just another harlot sent to steal from me."

Her back still splayed against the wall of the room, her head snapped back and thunked against the plaster. "You think this is a farce—what we just did? What I let you do?"

A flush filled her cheeks to flaming. Fury or indignation or guilt—he wasn't sure.

Best to tread lightly. "Truthfully, yes, it is still in my mind. The possibility that you are trying to bamboozle me and you will stop at nothing to see me ruined."

Her palm flat on her belly, her lips pulled inward for a long moment. She shook her head, her look going to the ceiling. With a deep exhale, she looked at him. "An honest answer. One I do not think I can begrudge you. Not if there was another similar to me. But I…"

He waited in silence, waited for her to continue.

"I would never trade my body for vengeance, Reiner. Never. There are levels I would stoop to—but that—that is unthinkable."

"Is it?"

"Yes."

"I understand what you lost, but revenge is a slippery slope, Sloane. You compromise on one moral. Then another. Then another. Pieces of you are lost bit by bit until you lose all perspective and are praying you are still on the side of right."

"What do you ken of it?"

"Enough."

She pushed herself from the wall and smoothed the front of her skirts as she walked over to him. He poured a fresh dram in the tumbler and set it in front of her on the table.

She didn't take it, her blue eyes intent on him. "What is the book for? Why is it so important?"

"So you do have it?"

She shrugged. "Maybe."

"But you still don't trust me."

"I am trying, Reiner. I am trying to place all of this. Not but an hour ago I still thought you were the man that killed my brother. I was still trying to reconcile the reality

of how I feel about you with the reality of how I should feel about you."

His eyebrow quirked. "How should you feel about me?"

"I should hate you, through and through. Stop at nothing to destroy you."

"But what is it you truly feel?"

"The opposite of that. And then you appear out of nowhere and tell me you're not the abhorrent man I thought you were. That maybe what I was truly feeling wasn't tainted. That it was right—that it could be right. So much so that I needed your body in mine." She sighed, resigned, then grabbed the glass and took a sip of the brandy. "And I don't yet ken what to think about any of it."

For how easy it had been to find her—to follow her from Wolfbridge, as she hadn't been careful at all—she wanted him to find her. Wanted it from the moment she left, whether she would admit to it or not.

He would have to chance it—the truth.

"The book…there is treason in it. Evidence of a smuggling scheme like this country has never seen. Who the sellers are. Who the buyers are. Where things are moved to and from. Persons smuggled in and out of France during the war. The gangs involved. What is stolen. Coining. It involves people from the lowest dockhands to the most high-bred peers. From London to the Highlands, this operation is insidious and has brutal tentacles that reach across the land."

Her jaw dropped. "You're a smuggler?"

"No. Make no mistake about that. After I discovered the scheme's existence, I was encouraged by the crown to

infiltrate it. I have the resources. The connections. I have
been in the perfect position to gather evidence—to gather
the names that need to be gathered. I am incredibly close
to discovering the last peer that is involved—that man that
directs the whole operation." His voice hardened. "And once
I have him, all of them will pay for their crimes."

Her head snapped back. "You're angry—viciously
angry. What is it you're not telling me?"

Of course she would drag this out of him. She was too
observant not to.

He inhaled a seething breath. "You remember my
sister's midwife did not make it to Wolfbridge in time to
save my sister?"

Sloane nodded.

"She was on the journey north when she was killed."

Her hand flew to her throat. "Killed?"

"It was one of the smuggling gangs. The midwife
had taken a mail coach to get to Wolfbridge in the
quickest possible way, but the coach was stopped in
Huntingdonshire. The smugglers were after counterfeit
silver coins on board and apparently there was struggle.
They killed everyone in the coach."

He had to unclench his fists before he continued. "So
I went after the bastards, and what I discovered when I
did was one guilty man after the next. Each one leads to
another. The number of deaths by their hands are untold—
and each death they need to pay for. On top of that list, I
put Corentine."

Sloane sank onto the chair by her legs, her eyes glossed
over. For a long breath, she didn't move, didn't speak. She

shook her head and then looked up at him. "You're saying all of this to get the book back."

A flash of boiling indignation swept through his veins, heating his skin. "I'm not here for the damn book, Sloane. I'm here for you. Keep the blasted book, and if I'm a smuggler, I'll be brought down eventually. With or without the book."

"I've just been told something so very different about the book, Reiner. And you've told me none of this—none of this until now." Her fingers went to her forehead, rubbing. "How can I trust what you're saying?"

His look sliced into her. "I walk out of here."

"You what?"

"I walk out of here. And this time, I walk fast. I leave the book with you so you can do what you will with it. Can you say that about Lord Falsted? Do you even know he's in the book? That he's an integral part of the scheme? What would he do in this situation—snatch the book from you the moment it was within his reach? Then what? What would he do with you? Discard you—kill you now that your purpose was served? You're being used, Sloane, why can't you see that?"

"I—" She shook her head, cutting off her own words. Her hands flustered, she stood. "I think my body may be playing tricks upon my mind and I don't ken what I believe anymore, Reiner."

He stepped in, closing the distance between them. "I have every reason not to, Sloane, but I believe what's in front of me. Whatever blasted thing this is that has happened between us. I believe in that over what you thought to do to me."

He leaned in, his lips landing on her neck, his tongue caressing circles against the fine cords of muscle. "I believe in our bodies colliding. I believe the moments when we are pressed into each other possess the rightest thing I've ever felt in my life." He pulled up slightly, his look searching her eyes. "I believe for all the suspicion still laced in your canny blue eyes, you want to believe me. And are trying desperately to do so."

She held his look for an extended, quavering breath.

But then she jerked a step backward, empty air filling the space between them. "I don't ken, Reiner. I want, I want to believe you—I just"—she spun from him and moved to the door—"I just need a moment of fresh air. I need to think."

Before he could say a word, she was out the door, her footsteps racing down the hall and stairwell.

Reiner stood in her room. Stood and stared at the door for thirty seconds. He turned to the front window and searched the main road. In a flash, her dark skirts appeared against the grey gravel of the road and she moved down the lane toward the edge of the village.

He was going to follow her, whether she liked it or not.

But he'd give her a modicum of space. After another thirty seconds of watching her walk down the road, he turned to the door, but then spied her open valise on the bed.

He paused and went over to it, rifling through the contents. Chemise, cloak, dress, stays, and stockings. Nothing else. Just as he was about to put the contents back into the bag, his forefinger slipped along the inside bottom seam of the bag. It shifted.

He picked at the edge of the fabric a moment, and it lifted. A false bottom.

Breath held, he tugged it open.

His red ledger.

He flipped open the leather cover. Written in his own hand, the start of transactions unveiling the web of trickery and smuggling and murder.

With a long exhale, he looked to the window. He couldn't see Sloane from his angle. But her presence was still with him. In his bones.

As brutal as it was to admit, he doubted he would ever be able to shake the feel of her from his mind or his body.

He closed the book, setting it back in place in the false bottom and restacking her belongings on top of it.

With a sigh at his own stupidity, he spun to the door.

He had a Scottish lass to catch.

{ CHAPTER 13 }

The clanging metal ringing in her ears, Sloane walked past the last building on the road that cut through the village—a blacksmith's shop that stood in front of a livery stable.

She stopped at the split in the road at the end of the town. To the left, the lane rolled through hills and crags. To the right the road weaved a line through the vast misty moors that sat south of town. Barren, both directions. Neither path held much interest to her.

Not when the only thing she could see was Reiner's face in front of her. Raging. Gentle. Consumed with passion. Hungry—ravenous for her—for everything she was.

She just didn't know if she could give him what he wanted. Her. All of her.

Not when there were still too many unanswered questions. Not when he was asking her to trust that he wasn't the man that killed her brother. For if he was…

If he was, then there would be no escaping the ultimate betrayal. Grandfather would never forgive her. Her brother would never forgive her.

She would never forgive herself.

Yet, despite that real possibility, she wanted to believe him. Believe everything he was telling her—be she a fool or not.

Her feet veered to the right, passing by the clanging from the smithy and the horses standing outside the stables, their snouts in a trough.

Just as she moved beyond the stables, she heard a wagon behind her and moved to the right side of the road to let it pass.

The man at the reins on the driver's bench tilted his head to her, his hand to his cap. Hay fluttered out past the open end of the wagon as it passed.

She didn't see the other man behind her.

But she felt him as he barreled into her from behind, knocking the air from her lungs. He half carried, half threw her onto the back of the wagon, his body landing on top of hers and smothering her face first into the hay.

Screams tore from her throat. Screams muffled by the brute atop of her and the thick bed of hay below. Screams she wished she would have saved, for no one would hear her over the constant clanking of the blacksmith.

The brute atop her wedged a hand under her face and clamped his putrid palm across her mouth.

She twisted, clawing through the hay for something to grasp, something for leverage so she could squirm out from under him and escape. But she couldn't see anything. Nothing but the hay beneath her. Nothing but straw poking into her skin.

Don't waste energy. That's what Lachlan would say. And he was the soldier. He knew. Save energy for when she could truly escape.

Sloane stilled.

And started counting. One minute passed. Two. Four. Six. Ten. The nag kept at its fast trot hauling the wagon down the road. They would be a distance away from the village now. Too far to scream. Too far to outrun.

The man above her shifted, lifting himself to his knees.

She stayed splayed on her belly, frozen in place.

He removed his hand from her mouth and he grabbed her arm, yanking her to flip her over flat onto her back.

"Where did ye put the book, wench?" His cockney accent gave him away instantly. He wasn't local. Not from Scottish lands. Hell. Falsted must have had these men following her.

She shook her head. "What book?"

His meaty paw clamped around her jaw, his fingers digging into the soft flesh of her cheeks. "Don't play dumb with me, bitch. We looked in yer room and it's not to be found."

Her blood crystallized in her veins. She'd been followed. Followed all this time.

Damn, Reiner was right.

Lord Falsted would just dispose of her once his greedy hands got a hold of that blasted book.

She shook her head, trying to wedge it backward into the hay and out of his grip. "You don't need to do this."

"Then ye best be telling Joe where to point the wagon to retrieve it, or it's yer neck, wench."

"I don't have it."

His fingers tightened on her face, making her teeth cut into her cheeks. "We saw ye looking at it in that drawing room at the inn back in Carlisle, so ye cin stop yer lyin' now."

"Fine. Fine." She nodded the best she could with the clamp of his fingers tearing at her skin.

He loosened his hold on her cheeks.

Perfect.

Anything to draw these two brutes away from Reiner and Milly.

"I left it with a friend in Stirling."

"Ye care to share that name with us?"

"I'll not put him in danger."

His hand flashed through the air, the slap striking her cheek. "Then ye'll be coming with us to retrieve the book."

She nodded, hoping she cowed adequately for him. The pain of the slap alone helped with that. She had no intention of letting these two drag her to Stirling, but the more docile and afraid they thought she was, the better.

The brute rocked back onto his heels and flipped to sit on his backside. His back propped against the side rails and he stretched his legs out long across the back of the wagon.

Sloane used the moment to scoot herself as far away from him as she could, shifting upright to see her surroundings. She could no longer see the village and there wasn't another soul on the road. Alone with nothing but the misty moors surrounding them on both sides.

Her head snapped up.

Empty moors. Empty moors that shifted into bog-land.

She searched the bogs that lined the road. Peat bogs as far as she could tell. Her head tilted down, she snuck a long assessing glance at the brute stretched out behind her. Everything about him indicated he was a city dweller. Soot-stained clothes. His accent. His smell. She shifted her gaze to the driver of the wagon. She couldn't see the front of him, but his ill-fitting clothes were the same.

What did a city dweller know about bogs?

With any luck, nothing.

Her mouth closed tight and she inhaled a long breath
to fill her lungs, then coiled.

She waited for the brute in the back to look behind
them and she jumped, leaping over the side of the wagon.

Straight down the embankment toward the bog.

It was a risk. But this was land she knew. Land she
could identify. Land they could not. And they wouldn't be
so stupid as to follow her into a bog.

She spied her first chunk of solid ground to leap
onto. One leap. Two. Her foot slipped, the toe of her boot
splashing into water. Arms swinging, she caught herself.
Three. Four leaps.

Ignoring the shouts behind her, she hopped and
jumped from one clump of solid ground to another,
avoiding the mushy wet mosses in between that would for
sure sink her to her death.

Bogs were like that. Hungry for humans.

But she didn't intend to be eaten.

Her eyes scanning the grasses, searching for solid
lumps, her concentration stayed fully on the ground before
her. She was forty steps into the bog before she realized
the brutes were following her, their bitter swearing getting
louder and louder.

She glanced over her shoulder. The thin driver was
faster, more nimble as he slipped and scampered across the
squishy spots of the bog.

He didn't even see it as his fellow brute dropped behind
him. One loose foothold, and the blackguard slipped,
sinking into the muck of the bog.

His arms flailing, he struggled to stop the sinking,
grasping at grasses, screaming.

Sloane wanted to shout out for him to still. To calm.

But it was too late. Panic and his massive form were exactly what the bog wanted. What the bog feasted upon.

The brute's head slipped below the moss and his hand went motionless, still clutching a fistful of grass.

Swallowed.

She shouldn't have stopped. Shouldn't have looked back. For in the next breath the driver was almost upon her.

"Stop right there, ye fuckin' bitch." He stretched out with his long limbs, his fingers snagging her left wrist.

Sloane yanked her arm and leapt onto the next mound closest to her—or what she hoped was a mound. His fingers slipped off her arm in midair, and the sudden absence of resistance sent her flying too far. She slid off the mucky grasses, her right knee and arm sinking into the bog.

The solid ground not nearly solid enough.

Behind her, a splash, and then silent thrashing. The driver had fallen face first into the bog, crashing through the top layer of moss. What little there was of his backside stuck high in the air went still, then slowly started to slip below the moss.

Swallowed.

Sloane couldn't spare even a thought for the brute, as her right arm and right leg were quickly being sucked into the thick muck of the bog.

She froze in place, attempting to fight the panic threatening to take over her muscles. Her eyes squeezed closed and she tried to conjure everything Jacob had ever told her about bogs.

Do not struggle. Do not fight against a bog. You have to fool it. Move slowly. So slowly you are tricking the bog into

*thinking you are still. It is the only way to dupe it. The only
way to escape it.*

Her left leg was still partially on a solid clump of
ground next to her left hand, her thigh shaking with the
ferocity of gripping to the last thing keeping her from
drowning.

"Sloane." A thunderous yell flew across the bog.

She popped one eye open, then the other.

Reiner on his horse at the road, just behind the empty
wagon.

She carefully drew air into her lungs, trying to cause no
movement.

"Reiner." The word exhaled softly from her throat.

"Sloane." Panic laced the word and he jumped from his
horse, charging into the bog.

"Stop." Her screech echoed over the bog and it cost her.
She sank. Another inch toward her death. The whole right
side of her body had descended into the cold tentacles of
the muck.

But she could still crane her neck upward. Still see
Reiner moving into the bog.

"Stop. You'll sink." Another inch down.

He stopped, thank the heavens.

His fingers flickered, flipping in and out of fists out of
sheer frustration. "I have to come after you, Sloane."

The determined glint in his eye told her he was
coming, death or not.

She nodded slightly, not that he could see it. She drew
a shallow breath, trying to talk without her chest moving.
"Wood. A piece of wood to throw out to me. There's no
solid ground here."

His look went frantic around. And then he ran toward the wagon as he stripped off his coat. He tossed it onto the hay in the rear and then brought his leg high and kicked at the long planks running the length of the wagon. Five sharp blows of his heel, and one plank splintered. He grabbed the edge of it, twisting it from the frame of the wagon. It was half as tall as him and it would have to do.

He ran back to the edge of the bog, his look frenzied on the mounds of grasses and moss. His first step out, he missed the solid ground and sank up to his shin.

"Bloody hell."

"Slow. Pull it out slow." She waited, breath held until he freed his foot.

Once his balance was set again, Sloane watched him lift his foot and aim for another wrong area of grass.

"Stop."

His foot froze in midair.

"It's forward to your right."

His hovering foot moved in the air until it was directly above a solid clump she could recognize. "Yes." The cold muck crept upward to reach the base of her neck.

He dropped his foot and moved to the clump.

She exhaled. It held him.

"Next one, Sloane." He lifted his left foot in the air, waiting for direction.

"Straight ahead. A foot further than you can stretch. You need to jump."

He leapt forward without hesitation. No skidding. Impressive for his size and weight.

"Now to your right again."

"It's sending me farther from you."

"Trust me."

He lifted his right foot.

"Directly to your right. A long step." Damn. The muck was crawling up her neck and she could barely see above the grasses in front of her.

He moved.

"Now three right in a row directly in front of you. Normal stride. Do you see them?"

"Yes." Three quick steps and he looked to her.

"Now look forward to your left. Two short jumps."

He nodded, then jumped from one to another.

"Stop." Her chin dipped below the surface and she had to fight the instinct to start gasping for air before she went under.

He looked at her. He was close enough now that she could see the terror in his eyes. He wasn't used to this. He was huge and strong and fearless. Nothing could stop him.

Nothing but a death-sucking bog.

His eyes flickered down to the right. The last lump of the driver's backside still hovered in the air. "He…" He looked to her.

"The bog has him now. It's not safe past where you are. The board." She twisted her neck up as high as she could so the thick water didn't get into her mouth.

For a moment he looked dumbstruck, his stare was so intent on her, but then he looked down, finding the board he forgot he carried in his arm.

"Just slowly onto your knees. Get a solid spot and don't lose it."

He dropped to his knees, digging his toes into the fleshy mound. "Hell, Sloane."

"I hope not today." She smiled at him.

His look seared her in place, then he stretched the board out toward her gloved left hand sitting precariously still next to her left thigh clutching the mushy mound.

He nudged the tip of it under her fingers and she clutched the edge of it.

The mud had splattered onto her glove, making the leather slippery and she swore to herself. Of all times she wished she weren't wearing the blasted thing. She conjured a smile and looked to Reiner. "I ken you want to pull me over to you fast, but that's not going to work." She stopped, spitting out the mud that had just slipped into her mouth past her bottom lip. "If I lose grip, I can sink fast. So slow. Slow."

He nodded, then started to tug. Her leg shifted off the one solid piece of ground she was clinging to and sank.

He pulled her, inch by inch to him until her fingers slipped. "Too fast."

He stopped, jabbing the board into her palm so she could re-grip the edge of the wood before she sank further.

"Just keep your head above the water, no matter what." The growl in his voice shook the air around her.

"I don't intend to die today, Reiner."

"Good." His arms straining against the force of the sucking bog on her body, he got her close enough to reach her wrist.

Done with the torture of moving slow, he flung a hand out, grabbing her wrist as he dropped the board. His strength against the bog, and he didn't bother to slow, merely dragged her with all his might—the bog battling him with every inch gained—until she was on the edge of his mound of solid ground.

Shifting backward onto his calves, he yanked her fully from the suck of the bog, clutching the muddy, sopping mess of her to his chest.

"Dammit, Sloane," he growled into the top of her head.

"Don't yell at me—we're not on solid ground yet."

"Strip off your dress."

Her head jerked away from his chest. "What?"

"It has doubled your weight—you cannot jump with that thing swinging and weighing you down. I'll not chance you losing your balance."

Her look veered across the vast open bog. "But we are in the open. And it is one of the only two dresses I have with me."

His eyebrows cocked as his gaze swept downward. "You think it is salvageable?"

She glanced down at the putrid muck now sunk into every fiber. "No."

He nodded and stretched his arms around her, his fingers working the buttons down her spine.

After tugging the fabric wide, he helped her strip down the soaking cloth from her arms and torso. She stomped her way free of her skirts that clung to her legs.

He studied her from head to toe. "Your legs are steady? You can make it back? I'll carry you."

"No. I'll not chance you losing your balance and both of us sinking into the bog." She lifted herself on her bare toes—the bog had sucked off her short boots as Reiner had dragged her through the mud. Her feet worked, her legs solid enough. "Follow me back, exactly."

"I don't intend to step anywhere but in your footprints."

She nodded, then shuffled around him on the tiny mound they stood on. With the heat of Reiner long against her backside, she studied the undulating shifts in the grasses and mosses that covered the bog. She traced a trail along the clumps back to the roadway, then started to move.

Hop to the right, long stretch, three steps, a leap, and she kept moving quickly, hearing Reiner's thudding feet squishing into the soft mounds in her wake.

It wasn't until she jumped to the edge of the roadway, falling to her knees as she scrambled up the embankment—with full, beautiful solid dirt under her body—that she allowed herself a full breath.

She reached the road and stood, spinning around just as Reiner stepped onto the roadway.

He didn't give her a chance to take another breath before he wrapped his arms around her, crushing her to his chest.

"What in the blasted hell was that, Sloane?"

"Two men." She wiggled her head backward to look up at him. "I was at the edge of town and one of them grabbed me and tossed me into the back of the wagon."

"Tell me the bastards didn't hurt you." His arms tightened to iron clamps around her.

"No. Suffocated me at best. I saw the bog and hoped it would be my best opportunity to escape. Neither looked able to navigate bog-land. So I chanced it."

He nodded, an odd mixture of fury and curiosity in his golden brown eyes as he studied her face. "They both sank in there? I only saw the one."

She looked out across the bog. Grasses swayed in the slight wind, calm, as though the ground had not just eaten two men. "The other sank fairly close to the road." Her gaze shifted back to his face. "They wanted the book, Reiner. That's why they took me."

The slight relaxation of his arms disappeared, and he tightened his hold on her until she squeaked. He abruptly released her, taking three fast steps away as a growl thundered from his chest. He spun back to her. "You should have never been involved in this, Sloane—never. When I get a hold of Falsted I'm going to crush him—taking advantage of you, an innocent, like this." His knuckles slammed into the wooden side of the wagon.

She let him seethe for only one moment before stepping to him, her hand landing softly on his shoulder. "I'm not an innocent, Reiner. Far from it. I went after Lord Falsted first. I did that. We thought he was the one that ordered the clearing. And then he turned my hate for him onto you—he used me to come after you. He lied to me, yes. But I volunteered. I came to Wolfbridge on my own. I came with nothing but vengeance and hate boiling in my chest. I wanted to see you ruined. To see you suffer. Suffer like I did. Like Torrie did. I had that malice in my soul." Her head shook. "So no, I wasn't an innocent."

He looked back at her over his shoulder, his golden brown eyes piercing her. "And now?"

"And now I thank the heavens that I fell outside your window. That I knocked my head. That I forgot exactly what I was doing at Wolfbridge. It was the only way that I would have ever seen the truth."

"Which is?"

"You're not my enemy, Reiner. You never were." She drew a shaky breath. "I think you may just be the true opposite of my enemy."

He turned fully to her. "So then marry me, Sloane."

"You are still to insist upon it?"

"Insist, ask, whatever you need to hear. I want to marry you." The side of his mouth drew back in a slight cringe. "But I don't want to tell anyone about it."

She blinked hard, her head tilting to the side as her bottom lip jutted upward. "That's not exactly a proposal."

His hands wrapped around her wet upper arms. "This—you—your body, your mind. I want us married, Sloane. I want your skin under mine without having to feel as though I've lost all sense of honor. I want us united not only for that, but also for how I don't want to ever have to suffer through a week like I just did when I thought you were lost to me forever."

Her lower lip relaxed a modicum. "Your proposal is getting better."

"You left me, Sloane, and I'll not have that again. I cannot bear it. And then when you were just sinking into the bog…" His words stopped as he looked out at the landscape for a long moment. His gaze returned to her, pinning her, his words a low rumble. "My world stopped and I couldn't fathom moving into the next day without you on this earth."

Her breath caught in her throat.

He stepped in, his chest brushing the hard nubbins of her breasts through her sopping shift. He looked down. "You realize I can see everything of you through your shift and it is driving me quite mad."

She had to fight to not touch him, to not splay her hands across his chest. "Don't change the topic."

He sighed. "The not telling people—it is just for now. Just until we can marry properly in England."

"A Scottish marriage isn't proper?" Her nose wrinkled, miffed.

"It's proper enough to call you my wife. To have you in my bed without tempting the gates of hell." His hands moved from her arms and wrapped around her waist. "No, I want to use our proper English wedding to flesh out the very people that have used you to come after me. Those that decided kidnapping you in broad daylight was something I would allow. Falsted is one of them, yes, but there are a number of known entities in the smuggling enterprise arriving at Wolfbridge in a week's time. A summit, if you will, cloaked in a house party, and I am a breath away from pinning the last leader—one man in particular. Falsted has been my entry to this world, but he's also long had his suspicions about me—it's why he sent you after me. Why he sent the one before you. But he's never had proof of what I've been doing—whose names I know, the evidence I've collected."

"Why he's needed the book."

"Exactly. I've invested in enough of his plots that I'm too valuable to cut out of the scheme without direct proof. Falsted sent you, which means he's getting desperate. And desperate men break. If we can set him so far off-kilter, I am positive he'll break and tell me who the mastermind of the whole smuggling scheme is—one way or another."

She couldn't help the smile that curved her lips. "Now this is interesting. Your proposal almost sounds enticing—flipping this back upon Falsted and his brethren."

A smile turned up the corners of his lips. "I hope it sounds more than interesting—at least the marriage part."

She couldn't resist any longer and her palms went flat against his wet lawn shirt. "You do realize my grandfather had very different plans for marrying me off? Though only the heavens know what he has been concocting since he finds me unmarriageable now. But I was originally only to marry a man that will prove to be advantageous to the Vinehill estate."

"Done." He pulled her tighter into him, her body long against his hard muscles. "If you'll recall, I just happen to own some of the Swallowford lands—I have no business with them—I merely bought them to gain Falsted's trust. So I'll happily sign them over to your grandfather or your brother. They can do with them whatever they want—sheep, tenants—whatever is best for your people."

"You didn't even ask of my dowry." Her eyebrows drew together. "You would do that? Marry me with no gain for yourself? A loss, if anything?"

"I gain you, don't I?" He said the words so matter of fact, as though marriage was that simple. There was always a gain, always an alliance to be had. What he proposed was not marriage. What he proposed was...

Love.

The realization hit her and stole all the breath from her lungs.

One did not get married for love. Sometimes for lust. But never for love.

And never to a man that one had only a month ago vowed to destroy.

Her look dipped down and she stared at the cut of his white lawn shirt, now splattered with fat splotches of mud.

This was the moment.

The moment she would be trading away all thoughts, all ambitions of vengeance if it truly had been Reiner that had ordered the Swallowford lands cleared.

He could be the entire reason her arm was scarred. Torrie was scarred. Her brother dead. Torrie's family dead.

It was still possible he was the reason.

But Reiner wouldn't trade his honor to save his own hide. If she knew anything, she knew that. He could have disposed of her in a thousand ways when she was at Wolfbridge if that was his game.

But he didn't.

Or in the inn after he knew she stole the book. He could have used her own dagger on her and left her in a pool of blood.

But he didn't.

He could have walked away from her in the bog.

But he didn't.

He didn't because he wanted her.

Wanted her, consequences be damned.

Even if he had ordered the lands cleared—even if he was lying to her now—she didn't know if it even mattered anymore.

For if she couldn't let go of her vengeance—of that hate being her sole purpose—then she wouldn't be moving forward. Ever.

She would be Torrie, wishing for death every second of the day. Wishing for her soul to wither away and die. Wishing for everyone around her to feel her pain.

She didn't want that.

She wanted a future.

A future with Reiner in it.

Her look snapped up to him and she caught his face in between her muddy palms. Her eyes locked onto his. "You walked across a bog for me."

The side of his mouth lifted. "How far do you need me to walk?"

An uncontrollable smile carved into her face and she lost herself in his golden brown eyes. "No farther. Aye. I will marry you, Reiner."

{ CHAPTER 14 }

The thick scent of baking bread wafted into his nostrils and Reiner halted his stride. "This is it."

Sloane stopped, leaning forward to look past Reiner into one of the shops that lined the main road through the village. She looked up at him. "It is?"

"Yes. The baker will do it."

"You ken that?"

"I do. I asked when I arrived in the village who the best person to marry a fool was, and this was the answer." Reiner pointed in the open door. "He's the man."

She laughed. "Should I be more miffed that you planned this without me or that you consider yourself a fool?"

"You should take both of those things as the highest compliment. Both of them are testament to your undeniable charm."

"Charm?" She chuckled. "I didn't ken you considered attacking you with a dagger charming. I will have to keep that in mind for the future."

Her fingers flexed forward and she glanced down at her mud-caked right hand that poked out of the sleeve of his tailcoat. He'd watched her try to slough off the mud caked onto her skin while she sat in front of him on his horse on the ride back into Buchlyvie, but she'd only managed to flake off half of the dried muck.

Her bottom lip drew under her teeth. "I'm not at all proper."

"We are to be married by a baker." Reiner set his hand onto her lower back and steered her toward the shop's entrance. "I would venture to say not much of this leans on the side of propriety."

"But I'm a disaster and not in proper clothes." Her left hand shifted, hidden in the folds of his dark coat as she clutched it tightly closed in front of her. Her right hand dipped to tug the bottom hem of the coat lower on her thighs. "Maybe I could wash first? He'll be able to see through my shift to my legs and think I'm a trollop—or worse."

"Or possibly your shift will silently explain the necessity of a quick wedding." A lascivious grin that he couldn't quite control took over his mouth. "Besides, I have grand plans of helping to scrub your body clean and I think it only proper if we're married first."

An enchanting blush tinged her cheeks pink. The streaks of mud across her face made it all the more captivating.

He nudged her in through the doorway of the baker's cottage. "Come—you've already managed to ignore the stares of all the passersby on the road with your head held high. Only ten more minutes and we'll be sequestered in your room."

With a sigh and a smile, Sloane nodded.

Just as they stepped into the empty shop, a woman—Sloane's maid by the sound of her—called out from down the lane.

"Lady Sloane, oh my—blazes be the bull. You're a dreadful mess. What happened?"

"Milly." Sloane stepped away from Reiner and back into the road. "I took a turn in the peat bog outside of the village."

"All saints—not the death moors?"

Sloane nodded.

Milly looked Sloane up and down. "And it took yer dress?"

"And my boots."

Milly's skewering gaze swung to Reiner. "And who be this? A fine gentleman that saved ye?"

Sloane glanced up at Reiner, a mischievous grin on her face. "Yes. And he is also the Duke of Wolfbridge."

"What?" Milly made the sign of the cross, backing away from Reiner. "Devil take it, my lady, why are ye letting him touch ye?"

"Because I plan to marry him."

"No." Milly gasped, stepping backward, her hand flat on her chest. "Yer not in yer right mind, miss. He's bewitched ye. Bewitched ye like the devil he is."

"One could say that." Sloane's head tilted to the side. "Or one could also say that he has been unjustly vilified. Either way I plan to marry him in this very moment and if you could see your way back to the inn to request a bath"— she looked to the muddy mess Reiner also stood in—"or two, be brought up to my room, I would appreciate it."

"Tell them I'll pay triple for it if it's done by the time we arrive back there," Reiner said. "For you as well."

"I don't take the devil's coin." Milly's head flew back and forth and she crossed her fingers at Reiner, lifting them high in the air.

"Then do it for me, please, Milly." Sloane reached out and grabbed Milly's fingers, pushing them downward. "I will explain everything to you. Just trust that I ken what I'm doing."

"Don't rightly know if I can trust yer judgment, my lady, not with him at yer side." Milly shifted her look to Sloane. "But I will have the bath brought up for ye, miss. For ye'll need it before we travel onward."

"Thank you."

Milly turned away and walked toward the coaching inn.

Sloane looked to Reiner. "I apologize for her behavior."

"You shouldn't apologize for other people, Sloane. You were not the one ready to spit upon me."

"No, but I was the one to put the thought in her head that you were the devil, so it only seems fitting that it has come back about to bite me."

She turned fully to him, her right hand going to his chest and resting along the cut of his waistcoat. "In recompense, if she only manages one tub, you can go first. I'm far muddier as it is."

"And I was thinking that's exactly why you should go first."

She blinked at him, silent for a moment and then she gave a slight nod. Her right cheek lifted in a half smile. "I wasn't ready to go in before, but I am now."

And so, as she stood next to him in a damp chemise, wrapped in his tailcoat, barefoot, her hair a muddy mess, he made Sloane his wife.

And she'd never looked more beautiful.

Never as when she'd smiled at him and the words "I will" slipped from her lips, breathless as though she couldn't quite believe what she was doing. But she was doing it anyway. Charging forth, not letting doubts or sanity get in her way.

Exactly as he wanted her.

Ten minutes later, Reiner opened the door to her room and ushered her in.

There were two tubs.

Side by side, two large tin tubs swallowed the modest space. Steam lifted off the water as the draft of air from opening the door rushed into the room.

"Wonder upon wonder," Sloane said as she walked in.

"Maybe Milly reconsidered the beast you just married?" Reiner closed the door and locked it, then moved across the room to set the loaf of bread and wrapped slices of cake the baker's wife had insisted they leave with onto the table.

"Or maybe she's afraid of the devil?" Sloane stepped to a tub and swished a finger in the water. Her head lifted and she caught sight of herself in the cheval mirror in the far corner of the room. With a squawk she ran over to it. "You married me like this?"

He spun to her. "Like what?"

She grabbed a muddy clump of her dark blond hair, lifting it to him. "This. Everywhere on me. I knew I was a mess, but this...this..." She turned back to the mirror, her shoulders drooping as she took in her reflection. "No wonder the baker's wife kept wrinkling her nose."

Reiner went across the room to her, stopping behind her and looking at her reflection in the mirror. "You were a beautiful bride—the mud can't hide you." He lifted the back of her hair, thinking to find a spot on her neck where

the mud hadn't caked. There wasn't one. He set his lips to her skin anyway.

It drew a slight giggle from her and she spun around, then pointed past him to the tub. "One for you and one for me?"

His eyebrow lifted. "Or one for the first dip and the second to clean off what was left from the first?"

She sighed, her eyes on the steaming water. "Then do go quickly. Maybe the water will still be warm when I get in."

He grabbed her hand and tugged her to the tub. "What if we both went first?"

Her eyes went wide and she looked down at the tub closest to them. "We can share? Well, that sounds… delightful." She looked up at him. "But I don't think we'll fit."

"We can—we'll make the room." His fingers went down, pushing his jacket back off her shoulders. It dropped to the floor. The air, not as suffocating as it had been in the few coaching inns he'd stayed in on the journey north, was cooler, crisper here in Scotland.

Before he could thread his thumbs under the straps of her chemise, her hands went to unbutton his waistcoat and then onto his shirt. She pushed it up, slowly, dragging the fabric along his body, torturing him with every fold brushing against his skin. Her fingers trailed against his rib cage, his chest. She tugged the shirt over his head, then stepped back, her gaze on his chest, studying him.

Her eyes greedy, the heat in them was unmistakable and she took a step forward, setting her lips—still cool from her dunk in the bog—to his chest. The cold juxtaposed with the heat of her tongue as she tasted him. It nearly set him into action, ready to throw her on the bed—mud be damned—and slam into her.

But he held steady, his arms clenched to his sides as he suffered the torture of her lips on his chest.

Her fingers walked down, flicking free the buttons on the front flap of his trousers, then slid between the fabric and his skin, sliding over his backside as she pushed them down.

Hands of an angel by way of the devil. He had to bite back a blasphemy.

She went to one boot, pulling it free, then the other, not satisfied until he was free of every stitch of clothing and naked to the world.

Her stare hungry on every spot she touched, she stood slowly, her fingers running along his calves, his thighs, backward to run along his butt, then upward to his abdomen, his chest. Tracing the contours of his body like she was sculpting a masterpiece. Her touch exquisite against his skin, his only complaint aside from the muddy glove that was still on her left hand, was that she didn't dare to touch his cock stretched large and high. But there would be plenty of time for that.

Her look lifted to his face. "Your body is stunning, Reiner."

"You thought me fleshy?"

"No. I knew you were strong. I recall flashes of your bare chest when you came into my room after I discovered what happened to my arm. But my mind was in a different place then—not able to recognize what was in front of me." She shook her head slightly. "I've seen plenty of strong men in Scotland with their shirts removed. I just didn't realize

you would rival any of them." Her smile turned wicked. "And I've never dared to touch any of them."

"I wouldn't want to hear about it if you did." A growl he couldn't quite control at the thought of her fingers running along any man but him echoed in his words.

His thumbs slipped under the straps of her chemise and he pulled it down slowly, letting the wet fabric slide down her body until gravity took hold and she was naked before him. Naked except for the blasted glove covering her left arm.

He stepped closer, his breath mingling with hers as his fingertips went to the top hem of the long glove covering her arm. Her right hand snapped up between them, grabbing his wrist.

"The glove has to go as well." His eyes met hers, challenging.

He wanted all of her. He wasn't about to accept less. And all of her meant removing that bloody glove of hers. A glove he'd grown to hate. He'd seen why she wanted to hide her arm from the world. But that didn't mean he wanted her arm hidden from him.

"It—it is just—I don't like to look at my arm myself. So I don't want to subject you—"

"Your arm, scarred or not, is part of you, Sloane. I didn't marry only the unmarred parts of you."

Her look dropped to his chest. "There is more of me marred than you think, Reiner."

"You mean your stubbornness? How angry you can get at me? How you like to swing a knife in my general direction far too often? How you still look at me with eyes laced with suspicion?" He stepped in closer, only the thinnest slice of air between his naked skin and hers. "I see all of it, Sloane, and I married all of it. Your arm—the scars on it—are all part of what led you to me."

Before she could protest, he slipped his forefinger beneath the edge of the kidskin and tugged the glove down her arm. She didn't resist. And with every inch he pulled it down, baring her scars to the light, his cock grew harder. Harder because she was letting him in.

Finally.

Letting him past the deep and deadly moors she had surrounded her heart and head with.

"So I take all those parts." The glove went down past her wrist and he dragged it free of her fingers. Gently, he took her left hand and lifted it to his lips, the puckered skin oddly soft under his touch. "I celebrate them, for your body is amazing."

Her eyes lifted to him, narrowed with suspicion. "Amazing?"

"That this could happen—your arm could go into flames, burn you, and your body managed to rebuild itself out of nothing. Out of charred flesh." He lifted her hand in front of him, studying the tight, white stretches of skin. "It is a wondrous thing. True, I don't imagine it looks like it once did. But it is whole, sealed again from the world. Tougher because of the trauma. It is amazing."

The suspicion in her look drifted away, leaving only her blue eyes sparkling, glossy with tears in the light streaming in through the window. Accepting what he said, even though she fought it with every breath. "You are exasperating."

He grinned. "And I would also like to bed my new wife." His eyes flicked to the tub. "Or bathe her." He looked back to her. "Actually, both."

She lifted herself on her toes, her hands going about his neck as she kissed him. Her lips parted instantly, and he tasted her, savoring the sweetness of her mouth. Hell, he was hungry for her.

But he needed to slow this.

The first time was too fast. There had been no savoring of his body in hers. Of her folds stretching around him, taking him in so leisurely it was torture to move slower and torture to move faster.

He wanted all of that. Time to revel in every inch of her body.

And it needed to start in the tub before they lost all of the warm water.

He broke the kiss and stepped into the tub, grabbing the washcloth and the bar of soap on the floor as he did. He settled into the tub, leaning back against the slope of the metal. It had more space than it appeared and he spread his legs, even though he had no intention of having Sloane sit between his legs. She was going to sit on top of him or he was likely to come on her backside.

He reached out and grabbed her hand, tugging her toward him and only releasing her when she had to grab onto the side of the tub for balance.

She stepped into the tub, her feet between his legs, and for a breath, she looked unsure of what to do. He would have dragged her down onto him immediately, but he caught sight of the smooth creamy skin on her backside and couldn't resist running his palms over the rounded swells.

He tortured himself until the need to have her tucked tight to his body overrode all his thoughts.

With a groan stuck in his chest, he pulled her downward into the water, setting her on his lap just in front of his shaft. Damn. Not enough space. Not for how he wanted her body spread out and writhing.

Soap first. With discipline he never knew he possessed, he scratched the soap against the washcloth and set to scrubbing her back. Her head moved back and forth, soft moans coming from her throat.

"Dunk your head so I can get your hair."

She moved slightly forward and leaned back the best she could in the tight space, sinking her head below the surface of the water. Mud seeped from her hair, spreading into the tub. He set the soap quickly into the strands, scrubbing the dirt free the best he could, and then tugged her upright in front of him.

He scuffed the soap onto the washcloth and dragged it up and down her arms, then purely for his own pleasure, dragged the cloth, and his fingers across her breasts far more times than necessary to clean her skin.

She leaned back against him as the washcloth took to every nook and cranny he could reach. He had taken to the task of cleaning her body with his control intact. But as his hand holding the washcloth slid between her legs, she wiggled on top of him and her right hand reached up to wrap around his neck. The movement unhinged him. Agony set into his member as her backside writhed against him.

The pain swelled so intense it forced him to jerk his hand from between her legs. "You're clean."

She craned her neck to look up at him. "I am?"

"Yes."

"Oh." Her head dropped, her look forward as she wiggled her backside against him. On purpose or inadvertently, the cruelty of it sent him near the edge of sanity. "I did think there would be more to bathing together."

"More?" The word strangled from his throat, his control almost gone.

She shrugged her shoulders and then she stilled.

To hell with the blasted lack of space.

He lifted her and slid her onto his member. Slick, wet. The tightness of her encased him, ripping him to shreds with nothing more than the sleek warmth of her body.

He moved her upward and then dragged her down onto him—three strokes and his body was shaking beyond control. Too soon. He set her tight on his cock and slid his hand forward, finding the nubbin, his movements fast and quickly drawing her to a screaming edge.

But this one was his. All his. He lifted her off his cock once more, slamming her body down onto him. It was enough. Water sloshed out of the tub as she came, her body doubling over, the tightness ravaging his cock, drawing him into his own brutal release that shredded every muscle in his body, threatening to never let him free.

Shattering everything he knew of how his body could react to a woman's. Shattering everything he knew of how he wanted to live life.

It left him with one thought alone.

She was everything.

And he had better become accustomed to that fact.

{ CHAPTER 15 }

Sloane shifted on his chest, a soft sigh coming from her throat. "The water is getting cold."

"Then we better move to the next bath before it's freezing."

He lifted her, slipping her into the adjacent tub, then slid over himself. The water was tepid, not exactly cold, but no longer steaming.

Sloane reached back into the first tub and dug out the washcloth and soap, then snuggled herself onto his lap again, leaning back against him. She grabbed his arm and started scrubbing the mud that had caked through his shirt onto his arm.

Reiner leaned his head back on the rolled edge of the tub. He liked it, liked her hands on his body doing the most mundane actions. Her delicate fingertips pressing into his skin. Her bare lap on his thighs. Heaven help him, he was already getting hard again.

She cleared her throat. Suspicious.

His head lifted from the edge of the tub. "What?"

She glanced over her shoulder at him, then her attention went back to his arm, her strokes against his skin faster. "You need to ken—Milly isn't the only one. She had two tubs brought up, but she did that because it's her job and the extra coin was too hard to pass up, even though she wouldn't admit to it."

He stared at the back of her blond hair, the streaks of red deepened into russet with the wetness. "She's not the only one that what?"

"That despises you." Her face went into a cringe as her eyes flickered back to him. "Everyone in these lands thinks you killed Jacob. That it was you that ordered those men to kill Torrie's family. Though they blame Falsted just as much. He has been a scourge upon this land for far too many years."

He sighed. "So everyone in these lands hates me?"

"Those that ken of you, aye." She stopped scrubbing his arm and shifted on his lap to turn and look at his face. "Once I learned of it from Falsted and then told my brother, it was only a matter of time before word spread from Lachlan's mouth. Torrie's family had lived in the area for generations and were well-respected. It was why she was the cousin chosen to be my companion when we were three—their unfailing loyalty to my grandfather. It's why she's as a sister to me."

"So everyone in this land hates me and I just married a daughter of their lands?"

The cringe around her eyes deepened and she nodded. "Aye. You did. So you can see why you won't be exactly welcomed in the area. I just want you to be aware, in case Milly's reaction is repeated by others." She set her wet hand on his chest, her fingers curling into the divot centered along his breastbone. "It will just take explaining to people, that is all. The only trick is to get them to listen when they've already made up their minds about you."

"A disadvantage, absolutely." His bottom lip jutted up. "I assume your grandfather and brother are the sorts not to be swayed easily?"

"You guess correctly." Her right cheek lifted in a half smile. "But you managed to change my mind about you and you yourself noted how stubborn I am."

"You didn't have a chance to hate me before you liked me. That was my only saving grace."

Her lips pulled to the side. "Maybe we give it a few weeks before you meet them. Or months. Or years."

"I'll not be skulking about in shadows with you, Sloane. After we marry again at Wolfbridge, I have full intentions of traveling to Vinehill to properly meet with your grandfather and brother."

She inhaled a long breath, then expelled it in a sigh. "Or we could delay it."

His eyebrow cocked. "Or we could do it now while we are still near Vinehill."

A bright smile—straining with fake force—locked onto her face. "After Wolfbridge, then. I think that's best."

She spun around and picked up his other arm, scrubbing with vigor.

Reiner shook his head.

His wife would certainly keep him hopping. Best he limber up.

~ ~ ~

"I have been churning it over in my mind. And I may be wrong."

Sloane peeled her naked skin off of Reiner's and shifted to sit up next to him on the bed. His fingers dropped from the tangle of her hair, his chest still quickly rising and lowering from the all-too-enjoyable early morning rout with their bodies.

Her hip jutting into his, she folded her legs under her and pinned him with an incredulous look. "You, wrong? Do I even want to ask?"

He grinned. "It rarely happens." His hand dropped onto the top of her bare thigh, his countenance growing serious. "But I need to tell you this because I don't want it to ever appear I tried to lie about it or hide it. And if I find out that I'm wrong about this particular topic, you will hate me for it."

Her eyebrows slanted inward. "What is it you're bandying about and refusing to say, Reiner?"

He drew a long sigh. "It is possible that my solicitor put conditions on buying the Swallowford land unbeknownst to me. I recall signing the document, but I don't recall reading it other than a cursory glance."

"You what?" Her words filled the room in a shriek.

"I didn't want to tell you—I truly just imagined it as a possibility this morning after what you told me yesterday. But I need you to know in case it is true. If I had to guess, the contract Falsted showed you was a forgery of my name. But…"

"But what?"

"With my holdings, I sign a number of documents from my solicitor every day. The possibility is slight that he put something atrocious in there about clearing the land—or the document came that way from Falsted—but regardless, it was not by my request. You need to know I would never order something like that done, Sloane."

She moved away from his heat, sliding to the edge of the bed. "And you're just telling me this now?" The ice in her words sliced through the cool air.

He reached for her arm. "Sloane."

She snapped it away, standing from the bed and pulling her chemise on, the chill in her voice quickly spinning into hot rage. "You got what you wanted—me in your bed— then you turned me into your wife so I would have no power to ever ruin you. And *now* it's okay to tell me this?"

He sat up. "I didn't time this, Sloane, I swear it. I've been thinking on it—thinking on everything you told me." He shrugged. "Yesterday I would never have even considered it a possibility that I signed papers I shouldn't have—my solicitor is above reproach. But yesterday I also believed that once I caught up to you, I would throttle you and that would be it. I could wash you out of my bones."

He shifted on the bed toward her. "But then I saw you and the exact opposite happened. I wanted you more than ever. Needed you more than ever. I never would have considered that a possibility. Never."

"Don't twist this to make your half-truths seem negligible."

"I'm not twisting anything, Sloane." He stood from the bed, reaching for his drying trousers hanging over a chair by the fireplace. "What I'm trying to explain is that something I thought was fact wasn't. My reasons for coming after you were all lies I told myself. And this is the same thing—why was I so confident in my man?" He yanked his trousers into place. "There are no guarantees. My solicitor has a number

of men working under him drafting documents and I cannot ensure that he reads everything as well, even though it is expected of him. So it's possible something slipped past me that shouldn't have, even though I never would have intended it."

"But you signed the document, Reiner—you. You bound your name to it. You're responsible. You did that— you did this." She flung her scarred arm up in the air to him.

He visibly blanched.

Good.

She spun from him, stomping over to her valise. She didn't want to see it—see the tormented look in his brown eyes.

The damn man had made her believe he had nothing to do with the fire, and now this. A possibility.

A possibility she didn't want to acknowledge—that she'd just married the man that had ruined her life—that had killed her brother.

Her tongue flew to the roof of her mouth, gagging on the thought.

She'd ignored her instincts. Her common sense. Let a moment of raw desire overtake every sane thought she owned.

She should have stuck to vengeance. It was easier.

"Sloane." Reiner moved behind her, so close she could feel his heat along her bare shoulders. "I know this is messy and wrong and I wish I knew the truth of the matter myself right now. I won't know until I'm back at Wolfbridge and can look into the papers. But I needed you to know so if I am wrong about it, you won't be caught unaware later."

"Caught unaware?" She spun to him. "Caught unaware? That is exactly what this is, Reiner. You swore to me you had nothing to do with it—and now—now what? A day later and maybe you did do it? What am I supposed to do with this information? My brother died. *Died*."

She whipped back to her valise, yanking it open and reaching in. Her stays, crumpled in the corner. The only dress she had now stuffed haphazardly into the bag.

This wasn't how she'd packed it. Her clothes had been half-folded when she had tossed them back into the bag yesterday. Careless, yes, but not stuffed with all disregard to wrinkles.

Her mouth went dry as she started yanking garments from her bag. "Tell me you didn't go through my bag, Reiner."

He didn't say a word.

She ripped her dress free from the bag, digging, tossing stockings and gloves to the floor by her feet. "Did you go through my blasted bag, Reiner?"

"I did." The words came out in a sigh.

Hell. He wouldn't have.

She reached the bottom of the valise, her fingers shaking as she worked her nails into the lining to flip the false bottom upward.

Her nails setting hold, she tugged up the bottom flap.

The red leather book sat in its place, just as she'd left it.

Her breath held, she flipped open the cover and thumbed the pages to the air. The rows and columns of names and items and numbers, just as before.

The air in her chest stuck, unable to move outward or inward.

Her brow furrowed and she looked over her shoulder at him.

"What?" Fear struck through his brown eyes. "The book?" He ripped the bag from her hands and looked in the bottom. He exhaled relief.

She stared at his profile, her words breathless as she still could not find the air in her lungs. "You knew where the book was?"

His mouth pulled back in a terse line as he set the valise on the table and glanced at her out of the corner of his eye. "Yes, I did. I found it after you left the room yesterday before I went after you."

"You found it, yet you left it in there?"

He looked to the book and his lips pulled inward for a long moment as he shook his head. A man on his way to the gallows. "I did, but I didn't want you to know I pawed through your belongings."

"But why? Why not take the book? It's what you came here for."

His look whipped to her, his eyes narrowing as his voice dipped into a barely controlled roar. "I came here for you, Sloane. You. How many times do I have to tell you that?" His body turned to her, his bare chest grazing her breasts. "The book—yes—it's what I told myself I was after—what I was here for. But when I found it…"

"What?"

"When I found it I realized it was just an excuse. I'm irate you took it, yes. Livid, actually. But when I saw it, I instantly wished I never had. It was just a bloody excuse." His hands went to the sides of her face, his palms cupping her jawline. "Because it was you. You are what I was here for. You. And that damn book—you can take it and do whatever the hell you want with it."

Her breath finally dislodged from her chest in a rushing exhale and her head went light. He could have taken the book yesterday and disappeared.

But he didn't.

He stayed.

Stayed for her.

Her hands went to his wrists next to her face, clasping them with all her might. Her look skewered him, attempting to read his every intention down to his soul, and then she pushed words up through her chest. "You stayed for me?"

"How many times do I bloody well have to say it, Sloane?"

Her eyes flickered to the bag, then to her husband.

Husband.

In that moment, it truly struck her—the first time she'd dared to truly consider him her husband. Dared to let blind faith in this man standing before her take over all her misgivings—overcome all her distrust.

Husband.

Her husband.

And that meant a lifetime with this man.

No matter what he'd done. No matter what errors in judgement he'd made in the past.

Which meant she had better start letting trust win the constant battles in her mind.

Her eyes locked onto his. "No more times. I think…I think now I heard you. Believe you."

{ CHAPTER 16 }

"Is it much farther from the main road?" Adjusting on his saddle, Reiner looked past Sloane on her horse to the rocky outcroppings that butted into the rolling fields along the road.

Sloane had insisted she needed to take a detour from the main road south. When he'd believed it was to be just a quick side trip to a friend of Sloane's, he'd thought to indulge her. But now they were far from the main road and they needed to be on their way if they were to make it to the next coaching inn by nightfall.

His gaze landed back on his wife. Wife. The word swirled around in his mind with an odd mixture of disbelief, relief and—if he was honest with himself—joy. His body needed hers like no other, and he was quickly finding out just how much his mind and soul needed her as well.

A gust lifted a wavy strand of blond hair across her high cheekbones that had turned rosy in the brisk wind. He took in her profile—for as delicate as her features were, they hid a fiery soul of iron. She didn't shrink to anything—including him. The exact opposite of what he'd imagined wanting in a wife. But also the exact match he needed.

He shifted the reins in his hands. "What did you give to your maid before we left Buchlyvie? You are positive you can survive without her until we reach Wolfbridge?"

Her gaze shifted to him. "Your fingers work buttons just as well as hers do, Reiner. Unless you think it beneath you to help me dress?"

"I will happily button up anything in the morning I get to unbutton at night."

A wanton smile crossed her face and she laughed. "So then I will survive quite nicely until we get to Wolfbridge." She glanced over her shoulder at the craggy hills they had just passed and then looked back to him. "I wrote a letter this morning while you were arranging Milly's coach and our horses. Milly is to deliver it to my brother at Vinehill in five days' time. I told her it shouldn't be in Lachlan's hands until then, so I can only pray she has the patience."

"What did it say?"

"I was reporting upon our upcoming nuptials at Wolfbridge. I didn't want it delivered earlier, or there will be hell to pay with both Lachlan and my grandfather. Five days should give us enough advantage in time to travel back to Wolfbridge and for the marriage to take place. By then, it will be too late for Lachlan to attempt to stop the wedding, if he were to get the rogue thought to do so into his hard head."

Reiner nodded. "Your brother was a soldier, you said?"

"He was. He fought for years on the continent, and I do believe he was most at peace with himself when he was fighting. He had come back for a visit just days before the fire. And then he just stayed at Vinehill after Jacob died. He's heir to Vinehill now, so he's been making a poor attempt to adjust to the new role thrust upon him."

"Poor, how?"

She shrugged. "Everything makes him angry. Our grandfather. How things are managed. The numbers. The petty problems that come through his door. I think the anger is still his reaction to losing Jacob."

"You three were close?"

"The four of us, including Torrie—yes." A bright smile lit up her face. "We were a band of glorious mischief upon Vinehill. We probably were until the day of the fire. Our grandfather never much regarded us—except for Jacob, as he was heir. But we were happy—I was happy—we had our own little family that no one could break."

A pang cut across Reiner's chest. "I could describe my sister and myself in just the same way."

Her eyes went wide. "You? Mischief? I don't believe it."

"Well, maybe not blatant mischief. But Corentine and I were each other's unfailing rocks."

"You still deeply feel her death?"

He nodded. "So I can imagine how raw Jacob's death must be for you. For Lachlan. I understand why you came after me. Corentine's death is why I'm determined to take down the smuggling scheme and I've let nothing get in the way of it. But even at that, I fear it will not be enough."

"Not enough?" She stared at him for a long moment. "Because you blame yourself. You said that very thing. All that anger that I have, I turned it outward, toward Lord Falsted and then you. But you—you turned all that inward upon yourself, didn't you? That raw, raging pit in the bottom of your stomach that is determined someone should pay for the death." She blinked hard, an exhale leaving her mouth. She glanced about for a moment, then her gaze pierced him. "You hate yourself for it, don't you, Reiner?"

His breath unsteady, the horses continued for twelve more steps before he dared to meet her stare. "For those moments in time. For my stupidity in not calling for her midwife sooner. For not stopping the decrepit old midwife and the doctor from everything they did wrong to her body during the birth. Yes. Yes, I absolutely hate myself. If I had only listened to my sister when she'd first told me to send for her midwife, Corentine would be alive today. If I hadn't been too busy. Too absorbed in things that didn't matter, I could have saved her."

"You cannot ken that."

"Yet I cannot escape the possibility."

Silent and with a slight nod, she drew a deep inhale that lifted her chest, the cut of her lavender riding dress rustling against her skin. Silence he was grateful for.

She looked around her and her hands tugged on her reins, stopping her horse.

"This is it."

Reiner halted his steed and looked about. What looked like ruins of several cottages and barns sat just to the left of the road.

Before he could even think on it, Sloane slid off her saddle, dropping her reins, and started walking into the group of buildings.

He looked closer at the rubble. The overgrown summer grasses hid much of it, but he could just make out the blackened stones. The scorched earth.

All of the buildings had been burned to the ground, possibly in the not too distant past. Weeds snaked up the triangular wooden poles in an abandoned vegetable garden in the center of the buildings. Reiner studied the land from the height of his horse as Sloane walked past the garden. Four—no, five buildings had once stood in this spot. Two cottages, possibly. A couple barns.

Buildings that had been burnt to the ground, only the charred skeletons of stone foundations giving evidence of where they once stood.

His chest heavy with stones he could not shake, Reiner dismounted, following Sloane into the center of the destroyed buildings, his look riveted on her back.

This was it. This was the place.

She paused ten feet from the remains of one of the cottages, her gloved left forefinger pointing to the ground. She didn't turn back to him, her voice wooden. "This. This was where Jacob dropped us after dragging us from the burning cottage. Where Torrie rolled, screaming, writhing as the flames ate her legs. Where my arm was burned trying to help her."

She veered to her right, stepping over the low stones that had once marked the foundation of a cottage. As she walked through the rubble, her head remained down, her eyes searching. "This. This was where I searched the earth for Jacob. It was days later when the agony of my arm wasn't so overwhelming that I had finally ceased retching every hour with the pain. I came here and I stood, railing at myself for hours. What if I had stopped Torrie that day from ever leaving Vinehill? What if I hadn't agreed with her that it was a good idea to try and stop the clearing? What if I hadn't run into the cottage after her? What if I had grabbed Jacob's arm and not let him go back into the inferno in the cottage?"

Her voice drifted off and she spun in a slow circle, her gaze still locked onto the ground, searching. "Lachlan said they couldn't find any remains, that the fire burned too hot. But I didn't believe him. So I made him bring me here. And I searched, searched for hours in here and could find nothing. No evidence of any of them." Her fingers flipped upward into the air. "Like they were just gone. Never even existed. Jacob. Torrie's parents. Her brother. It was as though the world had refused to acknowledge that any of them ever even set foot on the earth. That they were ever anything—walking, talking, breathing, laughing—loved."

She drew in a sob, her voice catching. "That they meant something. They were just…gone."

She shook her head, her face tilting up to the sky as she blinked away tears that had swelled in her eyes. Streaks of wetness clinging to her cheeks glistened in the sunlight. "It wasn't until it was dark and I was heaving up bile that Lachlan dragged me away. He didn't ken what to do with me. Leave me or pull me away. And I didn't ken what to do with him. He wanted to find Jacob just as much as I did. Or maybe he lied to me to spare me of how he looked in the end—I don't ken."

Her lips drew inward for a long breath. "That month at Wolfbridge when I believed he was still alive—and then I remembered. It was like losing him all over again. All of it, all over again. All the pain…" A sob choked her words away.

For how brutal the need was to go to her, to gather her into his arms and hold her against all of the terror she'd suffered, Reiner remained rooted to the ground. She had brought him here for a reason, and he was terrified at what that reason was.

Her face still upturned, her eyes closed for agonizing minutes until the tears stopped streaming and her head dropped. She swiped the wetness from her cheeks and looked at him.

"I needed you to see this. To see what happened here."

His voice as even as he could make it, he took three steps toward her, his toes touching the barrier of fieldstone between them that had long since tumbled from the foundation. "Why are you showing me this, Sloane?"

Her gaze pinned him. "You ken why, Reiner."

"I didn't do this. I explained that…unless…unless it is that you don't believe me?"

She shook her head. "It doesn't matter whether I believe you or not. You took on this land as your responsibility—how many more lands are there that you don't ken what is happening upon? I needed you to see this so that you ken—I need you to be responsible for whatever you bring upon these lands. I want you to be a force for good. Not for…" Her left hand lifted, sweeping around her. "Not for this. Not for unleashing terror across the land—erasing innocent people from their homes. Not for destroying lives."

"If I could change anything of what happened, Sloane, I would do it in a heartbeat."

"That, I do believe." A smile, achingly sad, lifted the corners of her mouth and she stepped toward him, her feet stopping on the other side of the foundation. "We are both living in maelstroms of ifs, Reiner. And I have not been able to bring myself to ken what to do with all of them."

"But you do now?"

"No. I don't." She shrugged, looking over her shoulder at the carcass of the cottage. "Maybe I'll never ken how to deal with the ifs and they will always hold a cloud over my head, dark regrets that will weigh upon me until my death."

His heart splintered for her pain. For pain he wanted to take from her but didn't have a clue as to how to do so.

"I visited Torrie several days ago."

"You did? How is she healing?"

Her gaze swung back to him. "Terribly. She is so bitter—so very, very bitter—and I cannot blame her. She is in pain constantly. How could she not be bitter? How could she no longer want life? How could she not rail and hate everyone around her?"

His words dipped low. "She wants to die?"

Sloane nodded, fresh tears cresting on her lower eyelashes. "But she was such a beautiful soul before this. The best out of all of us."

"She was?"

Her lips drew inward for a long moment. "If one is lucky, it is the people around you that make you a better person—Torrie did that for me—for all of us. We were all better people because of her kind spirit. A spirit that has been extinguished and I fear will never return." Her hand swept around her, and she followed it, stopping with her back to him. "She could have died here, just the same, for how this has destroyed her."

Reiner stared at her back. She was pulling away from him. Removing herself. Not a full day married and his wife was already leaving him.

And he couldn't do a thing about it, for this could very well be his fault.

He could reach out and touch her, grab her, pull her to him. But that would be forcing her—capturing her. And the one thing he knew was that she needed her freedom. It had been the only way to her heart at Wolfbridge. He prayed it would be again.

The wind caught the loose length of her hair, lifting it and setting it about her shoulders. It made her shake her head, snapping her out of the past, and she turned fully toward him.

For a long breath, she stared at him with her blue eyes. Stared at him with the weight of the world in her gaze.

Then her right hand lifted, reaching out over the stones of the foundation to slide along his palm. Her fingers entwined with his, her voice shaking. "I don't want to be destroyed, Reiner. I have to move forward—push onward whether I wish to or not. Push forward and not make the same mistakes again. Learn from the past."

With a sweeping glance about her, she stepped over the stones to stand before him. Her head tilted up, her gaze intent on his face. "And you do too. I needed to see this place again. I needed *you* to see this place. Because what matters is the future, Reiner. Our future. And with that, everything you touch, everything you have control over. I need you to care. Care enough to never let something like this happen again."

His lips parted and the inhale of breath into his chest slammed into him, shaking him to his core. It took three heartbeats before he could form the realization of why she'd dragged him here into words. "You want me to be a better man."

She nodded. "I do." Her look dipped to his chest for a breath before lifting to his face. "And not only that, I want you to give up your own insatiable need for vengeance. I worshipped at that altar and almost lost you. My hatred not letting me see what was in front of me. And I don't want the hatred twisting you into something you cannot control."

He stared into her eyes. The cool blue he could lose himself in forever, the drop of amber a buoy in the depths. For as much as he knew what she was asking of him was what he needed to do, he could not bring himself to it. His voice came into the air rough, breaking. "I cannot. I'm not ready."

Her eyes closed for a long moment, her chest lifting in a heavy breath.

One, two, three seconds passed.

She opened her eyes to him. "Then I will walk beside you until you are."

{ CHAPTER 17 }

Sloane glanced over her shoulder at the rough grey stones lining the entrance to the empty circular staircase she'd just escaped up through. For how Wolfbridge Castle had been crawling with people the last three days—guests and servants alike—she could scarcely believe she'd managed to escape the throngs for a spell. The guests had given her very few moments alone with Vicky, much less Reiner.

At breakfast before he went out with the hunting party, Reiner had whispered to her that a solar at the top of the east tower should be empty, as it was one of the few rooms in the castle that hadn't been renovated.

But he hadn't had time to tell her how to get up to the room before they were interrupted by Lord Langton inquiring about the stretch of land they would be hunting on for the day.

So she'd had to search for it. After a solid half hour of wandering halls and dodging conversations, she'd only minutes ago stumbled upon an inconspicuous door in the passageway to the great hall that hid a circular stone staircase winding its way upward. For all of Wolfbridge's grandeur, its heart still held fast to the medieval bones of stone.

She stood in silence for a breath, shocked she could hear her own thoughts for a change. A short hallway sat before her, five steps deep at most, with two opposite closed doors. She chose the right door first. A simple black iron latch held the door closed, and she lifted it, pushing on the heavy oak planks. The hinges creaked, filling the hallway as she shoved the door open. If anyone needed to find her, all they would have to do was follow the echoing wail of metal scraping against metal.

She peeked her head into the room. Small and dark with only three arrowslits letting light into the room. Definitely not a solar.

A hand snaked around her waist and dragged her backward.

With a scream sputtering from her throat, her feet left the ground. Another hand clamped across her mouth, cutting her scream.

"It took you far too long to make it up here." Reiner's voice, low, whispered in her ear.

She twisted in his arm, a screech on her lips. "You're supposed to be hunting. You scared me half to Hades."

Still holding her in the air, he walked backward into the room across the hall. "And you have driven me as mad as the devil the past three days."

He set her on her feet, his lips quick to her neck, warm heat instantly prickling her skin. She couldn't keep the smile from her lips. "Mad, you say?"

"Utter bedlam." His lips worked down her neck to the bare of her shoulder next to her cap sleeve. "Having to sleep in another room than you. Every blasted second we are awake being commandeered by the insufferable masses below."

She laughed, her fingers squeezing his shoulders as she angled her neck to allow him better access to her skin. "You

were the one that wanted the appearance of the utmost
respectability—to obtain the special license. I am more than
happy to acknowledge that we've already been married in
a very proper Scottish wedding by a very proper Scottish
baker."

He chuckled into her skin, a low hearty rumble.
"But that gains us nothing as far as the smugglers are
concerned. I need Falsted to make his move. He's already
nervous as all hell, watching you, wondering what game it
is you're playing. I need him to break and give up the man
above him. And for that, he needs to think we are about
to marry and he will soon go down in flames. So no. No
acknowledging our very proper Scottish wedding or he will
think the game is already over. As of now, he still believes
he has a chance of continuing forth with his treacherous
activities without anything befalling him."

"Does he still think I am his puppet?"

"I believe so. I have painted myself to be a besotted fool
when it comes to you."

She twisted away from his lips. "You're not?"

He chuckled, jerking her body back into him, his
mouth ravenous on her skin. "It is not a hard role to play."

His head lifted from her skin and he met her gaze.
"Plus—beyond all of that—I want you to become my wife
with the utmost propriety. I don't want a single haughty
nose ever to be turned up when it comes to you. And there
are far too many supercilious wives here with their doors
cracked at night waiting to witness the slightest slip of
impropriety."

"So all here are not part of the smuggling ring?"

He shook his head. "Most aren't. Most are here for the free food and hunting and lodging." He leaned down, his lips capturing hers and kissing her thoroughly. He pulled slightly up. "But many of the smugglers like to mix amongst the upper crust of society, so my house parties bode well for them."

She looked at him blankly.

"What?"

"I've lost any and all thoughts of smuggler schemes and can now only think on raiding one thing." A wicked smile curved her lips as her hands dropped between them and she worked the buttons on the front flap of his riding breeches.

"Please tell me you mean my member."

"I do." She pushed him backward toward the settee sitting below a leaded glass window on the far side of the room as she shoved his britches down over the strong muscles of his backside.

The back of his calves hit the front of the faded, but once splendid blue silk upholstery. She nudged him downward and slipped onto his lap, straddling his legs.

"This is the best hunting I've had in years."

She caught his face between her hands. "You mean the best hunting ever."

"I do." He leaned forward, nipping her chin and then his lips dropped to the bare expanse of her chest above her bodice. "I stand corrected, again."

She didn't wait for his hands to bare her breasts, instead, dragging down the front of her muslin dress, stays and chemise, her thumbs gliding over her own nipples, readying herself for him.

She'd learned during the past days it drove him mad when she touched herself. Slow. Torturous.

A groan rumbled from his chest and he wrapped his hands around her backside, yanking her into him, his engorged cock grinding though her skirts.

"Luckily, I'm prey that wants to be caught." Her thumb circled her nipple. "And devoured."

His groan shifted into a visceral growl and his hands twisted through the fabric of her skirts, finding way to her bare thighs. His mouth dove forward, clamping onto her nipple, his tongue swirling over the sensitive nub.

Under her skirts, his right thumb slid inward, dipping into her folds, finding her nubbin. Slowly circling, just the same as she'd just tortured him. She swiveled her hips against his hand, speeding his strokes. It sent a rush of tingling heat outward though her limbs.

His left hand tightened on her backside, halting her motion. He looked up at her with a carnal gleam in his eyes, his lips not leaving her nipple. "I want you begging. The moans from deep in your chest."

She tried to move her hips against his hold on her body. Nothing.

"Damn you."

He smiled, his teeth nipping the tip of her nipple as he flicked his thumb deep into her folds, his forefinger sliding into her body.

Her head fell backward, arching her body to him. Her left breast. Her right. Her thighs parting wide above him. Giving herself over to him. Over to everything he needed to do to her body.

His hand, his mouth, plied her body, pulling her into throes she couldn't control. The intensity turning her inside out.

She broke.

A guttural moan bubbled from deep in her chest. Breathless. Demanding. "Please."

"Please what?"

"I want you inside me." She could barely form the words, her voice sinking into an uncontrollable mewl.

Her skirts bunched around her, and he lifted her. With one swift motion, he drove up into her.

She gasped, looking down at him. Heaven to hell. She didn't think she'd ever grow accustomed to the glorious size of him deep within when he first entered her, stretching her body in ways she craved with every speck of her being.

His tongue flickered over her nipple, but he didn't lift her hips.

She was done waiting. Done with slow.

Her knees digging into the settee, she lifted herself and descended, her hips swiveling along his shaft.

Yes. All of it, yes.

Up and down. The full slick length of him sliding along the core of her, pushing her body into writhing she couldn't control. Tormenting her ever higher with every thrust.

He'd had enough, his hands locking onto her hips and taking over all movement, slamming her body deep onto him.

"Harder…harder…harder…har…" she repeated, until the ability to form words left her.

He obliged. Again and again, until a brutal breath left his lips and he expanded, deep within her. A swell that filled her and sent her own body into brutal deliverance.

Surge after surge rushed up from him into her. Her core clamping around him in matching waves, taking his breath, his very soul from him.

His arms tightened around her, his lips burying into her neck. "Another day and I can take you properly in my bed."

Her breath still hadn't fully come back to her. "I don't mind the settee."

"I mind you not naked. All these bloody clothes." His head lifted and he kissed her lips. "It can't come fast enough. One more blasted dinner. One more blasted morning and then you'll be mine again and if I disappear with you for the next year straight not one can say a word about it."

She laughed. "I'd like that."

"Hell." His head cocked to the side and he fell silent. "Do you hear that?"

She listened, then nodded, her voice a whisper. "Footsteps up the stairs."

"Dammit. They're light. Women, probably three." He lifted her off his lap and set her down next to him, jumping to his feet as he tugged her skirts down her legs.

Her right cheek lifted in a cringe as she pulled up her stays and dress. "You still think to attempt propriety? For I am ready to forgo it."

"I waited an hour up here for you for that very thing. So for your reputation, yes." He kissed her forehead as he haphazardly yanked his breeches into place. "I'll go next door. Sit here and leave the door open—they'll come right in and I'll sneak out and down the staircase behind them."

A groan rumbled from her throat. "Maybe I can be the one sneaking away?"

He smirked. "Not plausible. I'm supposed to be out riding with the hunting party at the moment."

With a quick squeeze of her thigh, he moved out the doorway. At the room across the way, he lifted the heavy oak door as he opened it, minimizing the squeaking hinges to a low grind. He disappeared behind the door with the most mischievous grin she'd ever seen on his face.

He'd said he was never one for mischief, but her husband was certainly prone to it. Mischief she would much prefer to be basking in, fully naked, under his hands at the moment.

With a heavy sigh she plastered her most benign smile on her face and smoothed out her skirts as she looked out the leaded glass window.

She caught her breath just as the troop of giggling ladies cleared the top step of the staircase and tumbled into the hall. The smile on her face widened and she hoped the flush in her cheeks didn't speak volumes of where her mind truly was.

~ ~ ~

The dancing that evening was a mild affair, nothing compared to the previously planned harvest ball that was to take place the next evening after their wedding in the morning. Reiner had coordinated it months ago to coincide with the full moon—long before Sloane had ever stumbled into his life. But now the ball, along with announcing their impending wedding to guests as they arrived, made the perfect opportunity to spook Falsted. Spook him into doing something stupid—like search for the book himself or in a panic, bring Reiner straight to the last unknown man at the helm of the smuggling scheme.

Sloane rounded the corner in the last steps of the dance, and her look caught Lord Falsted just outside the billiards room, staring at her. The bastard.

His glare would unnerve her if she didn't know Reiner had been watching every step Falsted took since he'd arrived at Wolfbridge. At their last meeting, two months prior, Falsted had indicated there was one last man that Reiner should meet, and that the gentleman would be present at the ball. The last one Reiner needed to know before he dismantled the whole smuggling scheme.

It couldn't come soon enough.

Stepping off the dance floor as she caught her breath, Sloane wiggled her toes in her satin slippers. Reiner had said the evening would be mild. She shook her head to herself. Mild, if having enough people in the castle that she could have danced with only a quarter of the men before the night's end could be considered mild.

She'd perfected her steps under the tutelage of her governesses and could physically match the most ambitious of the dancers, but her toes were aching as the evening drew to a close and she had yet to dance with Reiner.

The first strains of a waltz filtered down to her ears from the string ensemble seated high in the minstrels' gallery of the ballroom. The space identical to the great hall and positioned opposite to it, the ballroom had been

finished, whereas the great hall had been left in the splendor of the stone walls and floors. With its polished inlaid walnut floor, the artful plaster reliefs on the tall white walls, and the rows of pillars lining the length of the room, it rivaled any of England's finest ballrooms.

Couples paired off, moving in front of Sloane onto the dance floor. Perfect. A moment of respite where she could quench her thirst.

As she walked along the border of the dance floor, she ran the tips of her fingers across the front of her lavender satin gown—split in the center front with artful draping of fine white India muslin. Just as she'd reached the nearest footman standing with a tray of madeira and took a glass, setting it to her lips, Lord Apton stepped in front of her.

"Lady Sloane, may I steal you away to the dance floor?" Sweet and far more spry than his aging years should have allowed, Lord Apton was one of the kindest men she'd met during her one season in London. He'd known her mother in her spirited youth and was full of stories of her. Sloane had already danced with him once this eve, but the London rules of limiting dances was eased considerably as they were far from town and she was to be married in the morning.

She finished a long sip of the wine and nodded, setting the glass back on the tray. "My steps with the waltz are suspect, at best."

He smiled, a twinkle in his grey, aging eyes. "I am willing to chance it." He held out his hand.

Just as she was reaching for it, Reiner stepped in front of her, half blocking Lord Apton. "Pardon me, Apton, as I have yet to dance with my intended this evening, I would kindly appreciate indulgence on that very score for this dance."

The twinkle in Lord Apton's eyes brightened. A man who understood the passions of youth. "Of course, your grace. She is yours." He leaned to the right to catch Sloane's gaze. "Do be sure to save a dance for me during tomorrow's ball, my lady."

"Of course, Lord Apton."

With an incline of his head, he walked away.

Reiner turned to her. His brown eyes heated into liquid gold as he took her hand in his and settled his other fingers lightly along her back. "Imagine that—the man thinking he could descend upon you for a second dance—and a waltz, nonetheless."

He took the first steps forward and her look dipped to his chest as she had to concentrate on the steps he'd taught her weeks ago in the library.

"Eyes up."

A grin cocked her cheek and her gaze lifted to meet his. Ridiculous that he expected her feet to move with any sense of grace when his golden brown eyes were that voracious on her.

Several turns passed and the steps finally felt natural enough that she could talk while he moved her about the ballroom. "Lord Apton is harmless. He was a dear friend of my mother's when she was young and he's old enough to be my father."

His mouth twisted half in disgust and half in a tease. "Which makes him young enough that all his parts still work and that lets him imagine he could sweep you away from me."

"Sweep me away from you?" She chuckled. "I didn't ken you were capable of jealousy."

"Watching you dance with every man in this ballroom has irked me to the pale." He shook his head, a mutter at his lips. "The waltz. Of all things. What was the man thinking? You reminded each and every gentleman you were to wed me on the morrow, didn't you?"

She shook her head, the grin not leaving her face. "There has not been a one that I've danced with that has not congratulated me on our upcoming nuptials. The people that are here consider it quite the triumph to be present for the Wolf Duke's wedding." The smile on her face widened. "Will that make me the Wolf Duchess? I rather like the epithet. Who would dare to cross me?"

He chuckled. "No one with any sense about them. I had to learn that the hard way."

She laughed, her look leaving him for a moment to glance about at the many couples around them. "This is so much more…free than during the season. I've been passed from one gentleman to another tonight without a blink in between—this is far more attention than I ever received in the ballrooms in London."

His bottom lip jutted up in a frown as he looked over her head at the men in the room. "Yes, the men are far bolder here than they are in the London. I'd never considered it before, but then, I never had to keep a wary eye on a wife and the attention she receives."

Her hand flipped up from his shoulder. "I am the novelty of the moment, that is all."

"And you are also gorgeous. That doesn't help to dissuade the wandering eyes of men. Nor does the dress you chose—the décolletage is too revealing and the lavender accentuates your eyes too well. And you smile far too easily with them. And I think I've seen you laugh with—"

"Reiner—stop." She squeezed the cusp of his shoulder. "You set me in this role as hostess, and I don't think scowling at your guests is what you intended for me to do. Besides, I do believe the majority of them mean to gain your ear through me and they think to use flattery to turn my head."

"Why do you think that?"

A shudder ran through her and she wrinkled her nose. "The amount of business schemes, and investments in merchant ships and in all manners of livestock—swine and sheep and bulls—that has been foisted upon me this eve is laughable. Llamas—one gentleman went on and on about llamas, for goodness' sake."

His eyebrows cocked.

"Yes, llamas. Just one topic of conversation. I barely even ken what the creature is. So I have either become the most sought after investment consultant in all of Lincolnshire, or each one of those gentleman is hoping I'll repeat to you verbatim all they think to fill my head with."

"Truly?" His head tilted to the side and his next step went further than intended, pressing his body against hers.

The jolt of energy that hit her when his chest met hers sent tingles along her spine and an aching into her core. She shouldn't be dancing—of all things, the waltz—with him if she intended to make it to her bedchamber alone tonight.

The earlier fire in his look reignited and for a breath that lasted ages, she stared at his eyes, transfixed, frozen in time.

A discordant screech from the bows against the strings of two violins peeled into the air above.

The shrill sound echoed in her ears and it took another breath to realize the music had abruptly stopped. A commotion at the far end of the ballroom swept in a wave toward them just as Reiner looked up from her, alarm in his eyes as his feet stopped.

Her hand dropped from his shoulder and she spun around, following his gaze.

From the main entrance of the ballroom, all the way toward them, people started shuffling, moving to the sides as they parted a path directly down the center of the dance floor.

With her shorter height, it took a moment before enough people cleared the space in front of her so she could see what was coming.

Ten burly, raging, swords-clanging Scots.

Men built for war, charging into the ballroom. Charging at her.

At the front of them, her brother.

Lachlan.

Furious.

Seething with every step.

His hard hazel eyes locked onto hers and his gait sped, a ball of fury storming toward her.

No.

No, no, no.

"Sloane, what the hell do you think you're doing here." Her brother's booming voice echoed into the high heavy beams of the ballroom. A command. Not a question.

Her jaw dropped, her face steaming with a rush of blood into her forehead. "Lachlan—"

Reiner stepped in front of her, cutting her words and blocking her view of the impending storm that was her older brother.

Reiner swept his hand out over the silent crush of guests. "Go."

A murmur snaked through the crowd, a few people making a half-hearted effort to leave the ballroom.

"Go." Reiner's voice thundered over the cluster.

Silently, people turned and disappeared out the various exits of the ballroom. Sloane shifted to stand adjacent to Reiner. It took minutes for all the people to amble to the exits while Reiner and Sloane and Lachlan and his band of nine men stood frozen in place, staring at each other.

The second the footman closed the last door of the ballroom, Lachlan stepped toward Sloane and reached for her arm. "I'm taking you out of here this instant." His rage had only swelled while people exited the room.

Reiner moved in front of her again, blocking her brother from grabbing her arm. "You're not taking Sloane anywhere."

Lachlan's head snapped back, his eyes narrowing as he scrutinized Reiner. "No?" He drew the one word out with lethal intent and then took another step forward.

Her brother was huge, but Reiner was just as tall. Just as deadly.

The two men stood, toe-to-toe, murder in their eyes.

Sloane jumped from behind Reiner and shoved an arm between the two men. "For the blasted devil's sake—you two are acting like deranged ogres."

"And you're planning to lie with the man that killed your brother." The bitter words fumed from Lachlan's mouth.

She shoved her body between them with a grunt, forcing each to take a step backward. She pinned her look on her brother. "We were misinformed. I was misinformed," she whispered in a hiss.

Lachlan didn't look down at her, his lethal stare above her head focused on Reiner. "You don't know what you're talking about, Sloane. I don't know what he did to get you here. To get you to agree to this, but you're not in your bloody well right mind and I'm taking you home."

"Dammit, Lachlan, no, you're not."

Lachlan grabbed her arm.

In a flash, Reiner had his dagger pulled, the tip pressed to Lachlan's neck.

The swoosh of drawing steel filled the air as the nine Scots standing behind Lachlan pulled their swords, lifting them.

Her screech piercing the air, Sloane shoved Reiner backward while twisting her arm free from her brother. "You blasted idiots. Stop. Just stop. Both of you."

She stepped to the side, glaring at the band of Scotsmen ready to battle. "Dom, go. I'm alive and well and not here under duress as you can obviously see. Get the men out of here." Her glare swung to her brother. "I want to talk to Lach alone."

Domnall nodded, sheathing his sword. "Aye, lass." He turned to the rest of the men and motioned toward the door. They all spun about, and with boots echoing against the wooden planks of the gleaming floor, filed out of the ballroom through the main entrance.

She waited until the heavy ancient oak doors were secured behind them before she turned back to Reiner. "You as well."

"Me? What?" Reiner shook his head. "If you think I'm going to leave you alone with him, you're mad, Sloane."

"He's my brother, Reiner. I will be fine. But you—you need to go as well."

The hard set of her husband's jaw told her he wasn't about to move an inch.

"Please, Reiner."

His glare lifted from her and the steel glint in his brown eyes found target on Lachlan. "You touch her again and you're a dead man."

"And you're a—"

"For blasted sake, Reiner—Lach—stop. You're both big and strong and can kill the other. We all bloody well understand it." Her hands flew up on either side of her, her palms to both of the men. "This is exactly why you can't be in the same room together."

Reiner's look dropped back to her. "Fine. I will be on just the other side of the door to the billiards room. No farther."

"Yes—thank you."

Reiner spun and stalked to a side entrance of the ballroom, through the door that led to the billiards room.

Lachlan didn't even wait until Reiner closed the door before stepping in front of her, his voice a roar. "So you think to now tell me I can't hate that bastard?"

Her hand went to her hips, squaring herself to him. "That's exactly what I'm telling you."

"If not him—then who? Who's the man that murdered Jacob? Who should I hate?"

"It was Falsted all along. We had it right to begin with. He was the one."

Lachlan's head swung back and forth, his hazel eyes frantic. "No. You saw the agreement for the purchase of the lands. And I confirmed it." His arm swung up to point at the side door Reiner had disappeared into, his words lifting into a deafening growl. "That's the blackguard that ordered Torrie's family land cleared."

"Reiner knew nothing of the fire, Lachlan. Didn't order anything." Her arms clasped in front of her ribcage. "Nothing. Nothing of the clearings."

"Lies he's apparently been feeding you."

"Not lies, Lach." Her forehead tilted down and her eyes turned up as she pierced him with her gaze, her words even against his raging. "You cannot hate him for it. Not when you don't ken the truth."

His eyebrows arched. "And you do?"

"He's my husband, Lachlan, so aye, I do ken the truth."

Lachlan shifted on his feet, his clenched fists banging into his thighs. "He's not your husband yet."

She held steady under his slicing gaze, taking a moment, just one second to breathe before she opened her mouth. "Actually he is. We were married in Scotland. The marriage tomorrow is a ruse meant to goad certain people in attendance into…action."

"Bloody hell, Sloane." His right arm flew high into the air and he advanced toward her, his forehead throbbing red. "Action? What the hell does that mean? What blasted idiocy has been going through your brain? No—don't even try to explain this lunacy to me. Not when you should be home at Vinehill where you are safe." His rapid words didn't cease, every word a shot barking into the air. "Because you obviously haven't been in London like you said you would be. Did you even go there? All this time and I thought you were safely ensconced in our townhouse and you've been tramping about the countryside—for what? And now you're married? You've always been too damn headstrong and this is reprehensible—marrying the damn man that did this to our family when you should be at home. Do you even ken what poor health Torrie is in—and you're down here getting married—married."

The last word thundered into the room, vibrating in her ears.

For all that Reiner had cleared the room, surely everyone in the castle had just heard Lachlan's latest tirade.

She waited seconds until he was merely skewering her with daggers in his eyes and not about to launch into another tirade.

She opened her mouth, her voice just above a whisper. "I went after him, Lach. I went after Reiner. I wanted to see him ruined just as much as you wanted to see him dead after what we learned from Falsted."

A long sigh seethed out his clenched teeth. "What did you even think you could do?"

"Falsted suggested I come and steal something from Reiner that would ruin him were it to ever see the light of day. I came to retrieve the item. To ruin him."

Lachlan's eyebrow cocked. "It doesn't matter, the man should die a slow death."

Finally.

The first words that her brother had spoken that weren't vibrating with rage. They lauded her husband's death, but at least they weren't spewed out of control. Small progress.

She moved forward and set her fingertips on the side of his arm, meeting his unyielding glare. "He didn't do it, Lachlan."

"Like hell he didn't." He jerked his arm from her touch. "He duped you."

"No, he didn't. The papers Falsted has from Reiner that order the clearing are false—a forgery of his name. Reiner bought the land, yes, but never with the stipulation that it be cleared. So place the blame back on Falsted if you need to hunt for blood, but you will leave my husband out of it."

"No." His lip curled. "Now I have two bloody Englishmen to hate. To ruin."

She stepped closer, her neck craned so she could be as close to him as possible. "You'll not touch Reiner, Lach."

His mouth tightened to a hard line and he refused to answer her.

"Lachlan—"

"A duel." He took a step backward, his head shaking. "For taking you unwittingly—that's what Milly said. He took you. And when in the hell were you in Scotland? Why didn't you come home?"

Her look narrowed at him. "I wasn't unwitting and you insult me with that comment."

"The man is going down, Sloane, one way or another."

"Or not at all. You do this and you are no brother to me. This is your bloody anger taking over all of the sane thoughts in your head again. You need to stop and listen." She grabbed his forearm, clamping her fingers around it. "Listen. Reiner is my husband. He didn't do this. If ever you were to trust me, now is the time, Lachlan."

"Sloane—"

"No. No more arguments—there is no stopping this, because it's already done." She squeezed his arm. "Aside from grandfather, it is just us now, Lach. I don't want to lose you over this, but if you go after Reiner, you are no brother to me."

Shock registered on his face, his eyes narrowing at her for a long breath. Seconds passed.

He exhaled. Long and tortured. "Aye. Your husband is safe from me. For now."

"Lach—"

"For now, Sloane. I'll promise no more than that. Now can be a very short amount of time. For the second he so much as sets a hair out of place on your head, he's mine."

"I expect no less of you." She smiled, warm and genuine. "Now I can be happy you're here and that my dear brother has travelled all this way to attend my wedding."

"We'll not be staying for this blasphemous event."

She twisted, tucking her arm into the crook of his elbow and tugging him toward the main doors of the ballroom. "Actually, you must stay now that you've appeared. It will cause quite the scandal if you left before the ceremony."

"I don't give a bloody damn about a scandal."

"That is clear for how you ruined the dancing for the evening." Her feet paused and she tugged him to a stop, looking up at him until he met her gaze. "But you care about me and I do give a bloody damn about not creating an even bigger scandal. So it is settled. You'll stay."

An incoherent grumble came from his lips.

Agreement. Or as close to it as Lachlan was able to give at the moment.

"Good. That's settled. I'll find Mrs. Flurten and she will find you and the Vinehill men chambers to retire to. The number of rooms in Wolfbridge is ridiculous and there are hallways and rooms I've never even seen." She leaned into his arm, smiling sweetly at him. "Plus there's a ball tomorrow evening you must stay through, so you may as well make yourself comfortable."

His feet stopped.

She tugged him forward, not giving him a chance to protest. "I am so happy you're here. I must tell you all of the mischief I've been in. Did you ken that Wolfbridge has the most excellent climbing vines?"

{ CHAPTER 18 }

Sloane walked along the dark corridor that led from the north wing where her brother and his men were assigned rooms. Sconces along the hallway were lit every twenty feet—enough to see, not enough to banish the many shadows. Rooms on this floor were mostly empty, reserved for the guests who would be arriving tomorrow for the grand ball.

She needed to find Reiner. He had been cornered by men in the billiards room when she and Lachlan were done conversing. Not wanting to extract him from his guests after the scene her brother had just caused in the ballroom, she sent a footman to relay to Reiner that all was well, and then went to find Mrs. Flurten to have her brother and the Vinehill men situated.

As she passed the second to last room before the staircase that led to the first floor, the door opened and Lord Falsted stepped out in front of her, blocking her path.

"Lady Sloane, it is good that I finally found a moment to speak with you."

Sloane glanced over her shoulder. Empty corridor behind her. Falsted in front. The last thing she wanted at the moment was to tackle this snake by herself.

Where were Claude and Lawrence? Reiner had had them discreetly shadowing Falsted's every move since he arrived at Wolfbridge.

Apparently, too discreetly.

She forced the edges of her lips into a tight smile. "As it was, I was just about to retire for the evening."

"Come now, my lady, surely you have a few minutes to spare for the man that knows exactly why you initially came to Wolfbridge?"

The smile at the corner of her lips wavered. "What is it you wish to say to me, Lord Falsted?"

He motioned to the open doorway of the room he'd been lurking within. "Come. I believe you would want this conversation to be just as private as I would."

Sloane bit her tongue. No matter what, the man mustn't know what she and Reiner were about.

She gave a furtive glance over her shoulder one last time. No Claude. No Lawrence. But she would have taken anyone. She just needed one person—any person—to walk into the corridor and she could remove herself from Falsted's tentacles.

Not a soul.

With a slight incline of her head, she moved into the dark room, positioning herself directly next to the door.

Falsted stepped into the room, his hand reaching to close the door.

"The door stays open, my lord," she whispered.

"As you wish." His head tilted to the side and he stared at her for long seconds. Then the side of his mouth curled into a sneer. "You're playing in much larger fields than you should be, little lamb."

"What are you insinuating?"

"You came here for one small purpose, which has morphed into something much, much larger than you realize. Be sure you know where your loyalties should lie, before you commit to one side."

Her head went down for breath as she smoothed the satin of her skirts, her heart thundering in her chest. She looked up at him with as much serenity as she could muster. "You speak of my future husband?"

"You should know you were useful at one point. But sleeping with the enemy will only get you killed in the end." His once distinguished face, now wrinkled with time, tilted to the side. "Or him killed."

"That sounds distinctly like a threat, my lord."

"Not a threat. A warning." His boney fingers slid along the lapel of his coat, creasing the fold line. Only a scant shaft of light fell through the doorway to illuminate his face and his colorless grey eyes. "Have you found the book?"

She blinked hard.

Hell. He didn't know.

He didn't know that she'd already found the book and left Wolfbridge with it. If he didn't know, then who were the men that were following her in Buchlyvie that knew she had the book?

Something wasn't quite right and the best she could do was play along. "I have yet to find the book and this"—her hand flitted in the air—"relationship with the duke went much farther than I intended it to. I was forced into it, but within it a unique opportunity has presented itself."

"The book is what is important, Lady Sloane. Not your own advancement."

"You think this has a thing to do with me actually wanting to marry the duke?"

"Explain." Even with the low light, the distrust in his dull grey eyes made her pause. Like he could crush her with one grind of his boot heel.

Her right hand swung out about her. "This. What better way to ruin the man than from the inside?"

"How?"

"The blasted fool fell in love with me." She lifted her gloved left arm. "And with my scarred arm I'm damaged goods and will never make a proper match. So why not take my pound of flesh directly from the duke? I become a duchess. Gain so much wealth and power none in society would dare look down their nose upon my scars. It gives me plenty of time to find the book. And when the time is right, I can give you the book and the man's downfall will be complete."

The corners of Falsted's mouth strained so low they almost reached his jawline. "Yet if he's ruined, your reputation will be as well."

"Do you think he would let it go that far?" She shook her head, maintaining the facade even as her tongue curdled over the words. "He's far too honorable for that. He adores me and he will take care of the matter himself long before he lets his ruin affect me or his niece."

"He'll off himself." The edges of his mouth curled up, salivating. "Conniving wench."

"Yes. And I'll be left with a sizeable estate and the power of the title." She smiled sweetly. "But you do not get to call me sour names, Lord Falsted. We may be at the same purpose where the duke is concerned, but that does not give you reign to speak on my person. I don't like to think of it as conniving. I much rather like to think of it as doling out due comeuppance."

His vulture eyes fixed on her for a long moment as his fingers ran up and down along the edge of his lapel. He nodded to himself. "You may just be far more valuable than I had given you credit for, Lady Sloane. Perhaps there's someone you should meet."

Her head tilted to the side as she pinned him with her stare. "Why?"

"He would be very interested in your plan and in your ability to sway the Wolfbridge investments. He's someone you would do well to ally yourself with." Falsted inclined his head, either threatening or confiding, she wasn't sure.

"Do not make presumptions about who I wish to ally myself with, Falsted." She forced another smile. "That said, is the man here at Wolfbridge?"

"Not yet. He'll arrive tomorrow."

She dipped her head toward him and started to move out of the room. "I assume you will find an opportunity to make introductions?"

"You may depend upon it."

Just as she stepped into the hallway, movement in the shadows of a doorway five paces away caught her eye. She started toward the movement, but then Falsted cleared his throat behind her.

"There is one more thing, my lady. So you are aware, the duke just made a deal with me tonight to purchase the remainder of the Swallowford lands that abut your grandfather's estate."

She spun back to Falsted. "He did what?"

"The duke is purchasing the lands. He requested they be cleared as the others were, so you would do well to advise your brother to encourage any remaining residents to vacate the lands."

She reeled backward, stunned, his words slicing her open from head to toe. Her shoulder blades banged into the opposite wall of the corridor.

Out.

She had to get away from the man before she crumpled.

With a gasp for a raw breath and a slight shake of her head, she veered toward the staircase, her entire body shaking.

Her legs moving on their own, she flew down the stairs, her feet slipping on the smooth edges of the steps. Only by luck did she make it down without falling and breaking her neck.

Blindly, she moved through the corridors, keeping a hand on the walls to stay upright, fighting the pain in her gut, vicious as it twisted deep into her body.

Reiner wouldn't have.

Wouldn't dare.

Couldn't have.

Could he?

~ ~ ~

"Here you are." Reiner walked past the tall hedge in the shadow of the night and the neatly trimmed evergreens brushed his shoulder and spilled a woodsy scent into the air. "Everyone has retired and you weren't in your room."

Sloane jerked, her body twisting in the moonlight toward him, her eyes wide.

Reiner walked around the bench Sloane sat on deep within the cove of perfectly manicured shrubbery. She'd been facing the fat moon sitting just above the tips of the evergreens, so big it filled the lower half of the sky. He'd been searching for her for the last half hour since he'd passed by her room and discovered she wasn't there.

She stayed seated and he stopped in front of her, looking down at her eyes, at her face, now in the dark of his shadow. There hadn't been even a hint of smile when she had seen him. Not the slightest curve along the edges of her mouth. Just the straight lines of her lips, almost as though she was wrestling them into submission.

It was the first time he hadn't seen a smile on her face when he approached since they were married in Scotland.

Something was amiss.

His mind raced. Had he told her he'd meet her and not shown? Slighted her at dinner somehow? Promised something else entirely that he'd long since forgotten about?

"You're unhappy."

She blinked, her lips pursing. "I'm not."

"You are if that decidedly cruel frown you're attempting to hide is any indication." His hands clasped behind his back. "What is it? Does it have to do with your brother? If so, I apologize for threatening him, but I cannot have the man thinking he can come into my home and pluck you out of it."

She shook her head and tightened the shawl about her shoulders. "No—no—that I understood. My brother does not possess tact or he wouldn't have charged in with swords

at the ready. When he gets angry he is not always the best at controlling it."

Reiner offered a pinched smile. "I saw that."

"You were right to not try to placate him—ferocity calls for ferocity in an instance like that with him. It is the only thing he'll respond to."

Reiner nodded. "So if it isn't your brother, what is it? Tomorrow? The rest of the guests should be arriving before the wedding in the morning."

Her look shifted off of him and she stared at the moon over his shoulder.

"Are you nervous about the ball? You shouldn't be. You've done splendidly as hostess thus far. You've even managed to charm the crotchety old hens that love the gossip."

"No, I'm not nervous—this was what I was raised to do." Her look whipped back to him, her stare intent on his face. "But yes, actually, who is it that will be arriving tomorrow morning?"

"Several more peers and their wives." Reiner shrugged. "A few men that arrange investments. One or two merchants."

"Tradesmen—they are welcome?"

"We're not in a London ballroom, so yes—one cannot imagine the amount of schemes and partnerships that are put in place during these house parties. People that wouldn't dare to even glance at each other on a Mayfair street are inseparable connivers at Wolfbridge. It is most difficult to keep all these ancestral titles and estates afloat without new funds and investments making their way into the coffers. And this is a place to do that."

Sloane nodded, a decided frown landing upon her face.

He reached down and grabbed her hands, tugging her to her feet. "So tell me what has put that sour look upon your face."

She shook her head, avoiding his gaze.

"I will keep you out here all night if I have to." He set his hands along her shoulders, his fingertips curling into her soft shawl. "And it will get chilly. These last few days have been unusually warm, but summer is gone. So tell me before your absence in the castle is noted by one of the gossipmongers and we have to marry under a cloud of scandal tomorrow."

Her look slowly made its way back to his face, her eyes slits, pinpricks focused solely on seeing into his soul. "Lord Falsted caught me in a room alone an hour ago."

His head snapped back. "Falsted? But I had Claude and Lawrence tailing him. He wasn't supposed to get within ten paces of you."

"Yes, well, he managed to slip away from them—if I recall, it's not such a difficult task."

Reiner shook his head, muttering under his breath. Imbeciles. The both of them. His gaze focused on Sloane. "He didn't touch you, did he? For if he—"

"No—no—he didn't do me any bodily harm."

Reiner's head angled to the side as he stared at her. "But he harmed your mind?"

She twisted her shoulders out of his grip and took a step to the side, backing three steps away from him. "He told me you agreed to purchase more Swallowford lands."

His breath caught in his throat.

What in the blasted hell had Falsted told her?

He stared at her. At her wide blue eyes glowing in the moonlight, begging him for an explanation.

To her core, she trusted him or she wouldn't even be asking the question—or at least she wanted to trust him.

Trust he better not squander with lies.

Reiner straightened, his chin dipping downward as his look went hard. "I did."

She took a deep breath, her jaw shifting back and forth. "And that you demanded the new lands be cleared of the tenants as well."

Dammit. Another test of loyalty. One he better not fail.

She seethed in a wicked breath, her arms wrapping about her ribcage. "So tell me, Reiner, tell me you didn't just do that. Tell me Falsted was lying. Lying to make sure I hate you. To make sure I hate you just as much as I did when I came here in the first."

His stance widening, he braced himself. "I did do it."

"What are you thinking?" She rushed him with a yell, her hands flying at his chest.

He caught her wrists in midair, stopping her in place before her body rammed into his. "Quiet your voice, Sloane." His words dipped to a whispered roar. "Falsted suggested the stipulation. I didn't want him to think I cared one way or the other. I don't need any more of the man's suspicion. I would never sign the actual agreement to do so. I just need him believing all is the same as always—I don't question him and he feeds off of that. It is just until he introduces me to the last man in the smuggling scheme. That's the target. That's the puppeteer that has caused countless lives."

"And what about the lives Falsted has taken? My brother's life? You say you won't sign a thing. But what will you do? How do I ken? How do I ken you haven't already signed the agreement?" She twisted, savage, trying to free her wrists. "How do I ken anything at all about you? I walked into a web of lies and I appear to still be caught in them."

He shook her wrists, tried to shake the suspicion free from her body. "You know the man you married—I married you in that baker's shop when we were covered in mud. That is the man you married—not this. Not this spectacle of people and parties and deals and schemes."

He yanked her toward him, their bodies colliding, his hot breath mingling with hers. "I am the man that taught you to dance the waltz. The man that held you against the terrors of your arm. The man that walked across a bog for you. The man that waits every morning to open his eyes and find your perfect, smiling face. The man that lives to hear your laugh. The man that took your naked body and made it mine—mine for all time. And if you dare to think I would betray all of that to be cruel to a few farmers on some measly strips of land, then maybe I had better be worried about your web of lies, Sloane."

Her body stiffened as her lip snarled. "I have told you everything—everything."

"Just as I have to you. The only difference being I have trusted you. Yet you—you still cannot trust me. Still."

"That's not fair."

"Fair?" His left hand dropped from her wrist, his hand going under her arm to the side of her ribcage as he dragged his thumb over her nipple. The nubbin hardened instantly under his touch. "I know this curve on your body, Sloane." His other hand released her wrist and he set his palm along the crook of her neck. "And this one."

His left hand moved off her breast and dipped along the curve of her waist and hip. "And this one. I know your body. And I know your mind. I know how your brain is already working, trying to figure out who is what. Suspicion on everyone, including me. But don't let the voices in your head take over what is in here." His right hand slid from her neck to cover her heart as his looked sliced into her, his voice a growl. "Don't let them take over what you know in your soul."

She held his stare for breath after breath. Not moving. Not blinking.

In one motion, her eyes closed and she inhaled, her chest rising under his palm. Her eyelids parted, the dark lashes fluttering, unable to decide on opening or closing. They closed, defeated, her words a whisper. "Don't destroy me, Reiner. Please. That is all I ask."

"Your destruction would be mine, Sloane." His words ripped from his throat, raw. "So no. I'll not let that happen."

{ CHAPTER 19 }

For how he parted with Sloane in the gardens, it was a feat of Roman proportions that he managed to walk halfway normal to his chambers. As much as he wanted to drag her deeper into that alcove and dive under her skirts, he also didn't want to risk the last moments of keeping her reputation somewhat intact.

He paused as he passed Sloane's already closed door. He'd given her ten minutes to reach her room before he left the gardens for his own chambers. He wasn't about to leave her alone outside with Falsted on the prowl.

His ear tilted toward the door. Her bare feet padded across the wooden planks of the floor. Drawers of a chest opening. Fabric rustling.

He moved on down the corridor.

Three steps before reaching his chambers, he heard a soft wail through the door he passed.

Vicky.

He knocked once, opening the door before there was an answer.

Vicky didn't cry. Ever.

His heart beating hard in his chest, he searched the dark corners of his niece's room only to find her sitting up in her tester bed. A little pixie in the enormity of what had been her mother's bed. The low light from the fireplace reflected off her face, sending sparkles onto the fat tears rolling down her face.

"Vicky, whatever is amiss?" Instantly at a loss, he glanced over his shoulder toward Sloane's room. She could handle tears. He was utterly inept at it.

"No." The word, strangled with tears but violent, burst from her lips.

He looked back to his niece. She was shaking—quivering with whatever was happening.

He approached the bed, his fingertips tapping on the edge of the peach coverlet. "Whatever it is, I'm sure Sloane can help."

"No." Vicky's head shook, fat curls swinging about her heart-shaped face. "Not Sloane—she cannot help."

"Why not?"

"It is her—it is about her. I thought I could forget—I thought I could sleep, but then I had a dream and it was so awful—so awful." Her voice petered into half-swallowed sobs.

With a deep breath Reiner sat on the edge of the bed, his hand awkwardly lifting to pat Vicky's arm. "Would you like to tell me of it?"

Her eyes went wide. "No. No, no, no—not if it will harm Sloane."

"Why would it hurt Sloane?"

Vicky shook her head, her hands gripping onto the edge of the coverlet and pushing the folds of fabric under her chin.

"Vicky, why would your dream harm Sloane?"

She shook her head again, curls swinging wide.

Reiner moved up on the bed, leaning in. "Vicky, you need to tell me whatever it is that has put the fear of the devil in you."

His niece bit back another sob. "You will not harm her?"

"Harm her—Vicky—I would never. But you need to tell me this instant what is happening."

"You swear it?"

"I do."

It took her four more breaths before she let the coverlet drop from her chin. "I heard her talking with a man and I don't believe it, but she said it. She said it, Uncle Reiner. I didn't want it to be true but she said it."

"Sloane? What did she say?"

"She's not who you think she is."

"What?"

"She didn't see me in the hallway. She was in a room in the north wing and she was talking with a man—I didn't see who he was. I only stopped and hid because I heard her voice and I thought to ask her to come to the kitchens with me for a tart. But then she started saying things—awful, awful, awful things."

"What did she say?" He attempted to shift his voice into calmness even as a rock was dropping to his stomach.

"She said you were a fool in love and that she wanted to ruin you. She said she wanted to take her pound of flesh from you. That she would use some book to undo you. That you fell in love with her and she would use that to destroy you. But that isn't the worst."

His lips stretched to a tight line. "What is?"

"She said you would never let your ruin affect me or her—that you would take care of the matter yourself—she meant you would kill yourself before letting harm come to us."

"Vicky—"

"No—she said it, Uncle Reiner—she said it and she meant it. You would kill yourself."

"I'm not going to kill myself, Vicky. You can be assured on that."

But he was about to murder someone.

Sloane had said nothing of this when she'd reported on her conversation with Falsted.

Nothing about how she was plotting his demise.

"You aren't? But what if you are ruined? Why would she do this? I thought—I thought she lov—"

"I'm not about to kill myself or be ruined, Vicky. I can assure you of both of those facts."

Her eyebrows lifted high on her forehead. "You can? But how?"

"I will take care of the matter, Vicky. That is all you need know."

Her eyes went impossibly round. "But you promised you wouldn't hurt her, Uncle Reiner."

Reiner eyed his niece. Even with all she'd heard, she was still protecting Sloane.

Damn that he had promised her.

He nodded, setting his tone to neutral. "I did. And I won't."

Vicky exhaled a sigh of relief.

"It is time to sleep." He stood and walked out of the room in silence.

Silence that belied the fury in each step he took.

He closed Vicky's door behind him and stilled.

To the right, his chambers and bottle of the finest 1810 Renault & Co cognac.

To his left, Sloane's room.

He spun to the left.

Just as his hand, vibrating with rage, reached the door handle to Sloane's room, two men stumbled around the corner of the hallway.

Blast it.

"Hey—stop there, ye bastard. You're not married to her yet or so you'd have us believe." Sloane's brother fumbled toward him, a full glass of spirits swinging in the air and sloshing drops onto the floor. One of his men, Domnall, followed at his heels.

Reiner's fingers dropped away from the door handle. "What would you know of it?"

"I ken she made the bloodiest stupid mistake of her life entangling with the likes of you. I ken about your—"he paused, searching for the word by swinging the tumbler clenched in his hand in the air—"escapade in Scotland."

Reiner crossed his arms across his chest, skewering Lachlan with his look. "You know nothing."

Lachlan's forefinger flung out from the glass, nearly touching Reiner's nose. "You're calling my sister a liar?"

"I'm questioning the truths your sister likes to live in."

Lachlan rushed in on him, his toes hitting Reiner's boots. "My sister doesn't lie, you bloody bastard."

Domnall reached around Lachlan, clamping his arm across his chest and yanking him backward.

It didn't slow Lachlan's words, his finger still jutting into the air with every word. "She is the most honorable one in the lot of us and if you harm one hair on her head I'll string yer cankerous maggot ass—yer moronic English innards from here to Glasgow."

Reiner didn't flinch. "You don't know your sister nearly as well as you think you do."

Domnall pulled Lachlan away, dragging him down the hall.

"She doesn't lie, ye bloody demon. And I'll be meeting you in hell if it's the last thing I do." Lachlan kept up the tirade until Domnall dragged him around the corner.

Reiner stood outside of Sloane's door, watching the corner, waiting for Lachlan to escape and rush back into the hallway.

Minutes passed.

No one.

He flexed his clenched hands, stretching his fingers as he let his arms drop to his sides and he turned toward Sloane's door.

An unmoving stone, he stood there, silent.

Unable to reach for the door handle. Unable to walk away.

Sloane was a liar.

But who was she lying to?

~ ~ ~

He married her with fury.

Fury in the rumble of his voice as he said, "I will."

Fury in his fingertips as he gripped her hand.

Fury in the edges of his golden brown eyes anytime they ventured near her face.

Not that he looked at her directly.

He hadn't done that since the night before in the garden.

The entire day, from the wedding, to the marriage breakfast, to the afternoon festivities, to the ball, he'd avoided looking at her directly.

Even as he took her in his arms for the opening dance of the ball, his fingers pressed into her flesh, pounding in anger with every heartbeat. He didn't look down at her, didn't so much as even acknowledge that she was now his wife twice over.

Aside from that one dance, she hadn't been near her husband, much less touched him in the last twenty hours. Not one private moment together, and it was all clearly of Reiner's machinations.

He'd shunned her all day and three hours into this blasted ball and she'd had enough of it. But even more importantly, she needed to know why.

When she had left him in the garden the previous night, he had barely been able to keep his lips off her neck, his hands off her bottom.

But something had happened between that moment and the morning when she joined him before the clergyman.

Sloane took the glass of cherry Ratafia that Lord Apton offered her and eyed her husband over the bobbing heads of the guests dancing, drifting away from the conversation with the crowd about her. Reiner stood at the south end of the ballroom deep in conversation with Falsted and another man she had not seen before today. Quite possibly the man Reiner had been waiting to be introduced to.

She smoothed the gold braided band high about her waist, an elaborate adornment against the rose pink of her silk gown that had twisted during her last dance. A dance not with Reiner.

As much as she wanted to stomp across the dance floor and drag her husband into an empty drawing room and pin him down until he told her what was amiss, she also didn't want to put his plan in danger. Whatever he was plotting with Falsted could be the key to putting this whole sordid mess behind them.

A life without lies. Without distrust. Without vengeance.

The gleam in Falsted's eye when she had told him she still planned to produce the book for him had sent bile up her throat. The man was determined to ruin her husband.

And she needed all of this danger—all of this intrigue—to end.

She wanted Reiner. She wanted Vicky. She wanted the three of them together in peace.

It was still an hour before the lavish dinner was to be served and she needed to get her husband alone before the meal or she wouldn't be able to swallow a bite.

Lord Falsted stepped away from her husband, leaving Reiner chatting with the other man. Sloane pounced.

She excused herself from Lord Apton and weaved her way through the crush of people that were thick along the outskirts of the dance floor. Wolfbridge held a healthy number of people, but she would venture to guess there was more than double the amount of people in attendance this evening over the last.

She managed to avoid getting sucked into several conversations along her route and was stepping up to Reiner within two minutes.

He saw her approach—she'd seen his sidelong glances in her direction—yet his attention stayed on the gentleman next to him. Slightly shorter than Reiner, the man had ghastly white skin set below the darkest hair—the whole of it lending him the appearance of a serious illness, even though his body appeared robust and trim.

She looked from the stranger to her husband.

Nothing.

With a distinct clearing of her throat, she looked back to the stranger.

Reiner's voice was tight as he motioned to the man. "Duchess, I present to you Lord Bockton. Lord Bockton, my wife."

"Ah, so this is the Scottish beauty you wed this morning." Lord Bockton bowed to Sloane. "I regret I only arrived this evening and missed the day's festivities."

Sloane smiled at the man. "We are just happy you have managed to delight us with your presence now, Lord Bockton."

"I have heard much of your charm, your grace, and I see it has not been exaggerated."

"My charm may suffer in a moment, Lord Bockton, as I must excuse myself and my husband from you as I need a private word with him."

"Of course." He inclined his head to Sloane, then turned to do the same to Reiner. "Your grace."

Lord Bockton exited into the throng of people along the wall with the French doors that led to the gardens.

Reiner kept his stare secured onto the back of Lord Bockton's pomade-thick hair.

"You aren't even going to look at me?" Her gaze on their guests, she whispered the words through a benign smile plastered on her face.

"To be honest, I don't know if I can, Sloane." The words were cold. Callous.

"Well, you can follow me without looking at me." She glanced up at him out of the corner of her eye. His jaw was set hard. So hard it was straining. Quivering. "So for our guests' comfort, I suggest you do so now before I explode in front of the lot of them."

Without waiting for a reply, she stepped around Reiner and exited through the wide south entrance and walked as fast as her feet would carry her up to her chamber. She stopped at the entrance, only to be yanked to the side as Reiner grabbed the back of her upper arm when he passed her.

"My room. It's the farthest from ears."

With his fingers digging into her arm, he walked them to the end of the hall, flinging open the door to his chambers and thrusting her into it.

His grasp gone, she stumbled a few steps before catching herself on the back of a plump wingback chair by the fireplace to her right.

She hadn't been in this room since she rifled through it to steal the red ledger book. Her gaze landed on the secretary that sat next to the window. The one she had to pop the lock on to unlatch the false bottom in the third drawer down on the left side.

Reiner slammed the door closed and turned toward her, his chest heaving, the full fury he had been suppressing all day unleashed. "I'm a bloody fool in love, Sloane?"

She pushed herself from the wingback chair, straightening her spine, her head shaking. "You are what?"

The gold in his brown eyes swirled in the cold rage of a hundred converging hurricanes. "Vicky told me everything—she heard everything of your damned conversation with Falsted."

The blood ran from her face, her cheeks tingling with loss of feeling. "She what?" Her head dropped forward, her mind in a flurry. "The shadow in the hall—it was her." Her look whipped up to meet his piercing glare. "No, stop. It's not what you think. Not at all."

His hands curled into fists at his sides. "And just what exactly am I supposed to think, Sloane?"

She took a step toward him. "You're supposed to trust me—that's first."

"Or am I to think that the bitch that I married wants to see me kill myself—but only after she revels in all my power and wealth?"

She reeled a step backward, his words said with such venom her stomach twisted into pain. Her palm tight against her belly, she forced her shoulders high and pulled them back. "Tell me you did not just mean those words."

"They weren't my words, Sloane."

"Yes—yes I said those words to Falsted—he cornered me and was demanding the book. He doesn't even ken I already have it, so those weren't his men in Buchlyvie. He was questioning me—he wanted to ken what I was doing marrying you, so I had to lie—had to say those things."

"Or are you lying now?" The malice in his voice sharpened. "You've gotten so good at it you cannot tell the difference?"

"No—you stop." She charged toward him, halting only a breath away. "Just last night you demanded I trust you—that the games you were playing with Falsted would not hurt me. But now you cannot do the same for me? Trust that whatever lies I told him were necessary to keep you safe—to keep me safe?"

His eyes narrowed at her, his breath still seething.

Her hands went to her hips. "Why do you get all my trust, while I get none of yours?"

She stared at him for a breath that she held for far too long.

Held, because she was either going to be destroyed or delivered by the time she exhaled it. This was the one moment to determine whether she was to have the husband she wanted above everything or have a broken marriage, every day from here till death torture.

He let loose a long, steaming sigh. "Why didn't you tell me?"

Her breath came out in a puff, her eyes closing. An opening. The smallest of gaps, but a chance.

It took her another five heartbeats before she could open her eyes and look at him. "I didn't think anything more on the lies I spoke once he told me of the Swallowford lands you agreed to purchase and have cleared. I was so angry it was all I could concentrate on. And I haven't been alone with you since last night in the gardens."

She dared to lift her hand and settle it on his chest. "The words I said were the most evil, the most vile thoughts I could think—the makings of my own worst nightmare." Her eyes closed, her words shaking. "I cannot lose you,

Reiner. Especially not to lies that never should have been spoken."

His lips against hers, hot, still seething, sent a jolt of disbelief down her spine.

He believed her.

And he wasn't too stubborn to admit it. Or at least, she hoped that's what his lips on hers meant. He could just as easily be kissing her goodbye.

His hands lifted, his palms capturing the sides of her face as he deepened the searing kiss. The heat of his body so overwhelming that her breath left her. He wanted her—fully and truly and completely—and she couldn't doubt it anymore.

She managed to wedge her head backward, breaking the kiss, her eyes searching his face. "With all of this, you married me anyway this morning?"

His lips brushed hers. "We were already wed."

"But you knew you could have petitioned for a divorce with our marriage in Scotland." Her hands crept up his chest, her fingers wrapping around his neck. "But you didn't—you still bound yourself to me—beyond all recourse—in that ceremony."

"You're mine, Sloane—come threats or lies or sunny skies. You're mine through it all—you have been since the moment I first kissed you. What this is between us—it cannot be denied. And if I have to trust you above all others for that"—he paused, taking a deep breath—"then I trust you above all others. You can tell me the moon is as pink as your gown, and I'll believe you. I may question you, but I'll believe you. And then I'll order some spectacles."

She laughed, pulling herself upward to find his lips once more. A kiss so deep, so full of promise and hope for the future that her toes curled, her body aching for him.

She jerked her lips away from his with a yelp, her face crumpling. "Wait—Vicky—oh, no. No, no—what she must be thinking of me. She must be so scared."

His right cheek pulled up in a slight smile. "She's still your champion—she didn't want to tell me. She was crying and I made her tell me what was wrong. And even when she did, she made me swear not to harm you."

Her bottom lip jutted upward. "I must go see her. This isn't right that she thinks this of me."

Reiner nodded. "I don't think she's been out of her room all day. We'll visit with her together." His fingers went to his forehead. "Except the dinner will be starting soon, so I must see the guests into the great hall for that. But you go to her directly."

"Oh, I don't want to fail my hostess duties my very first night as duchess. But Vicky…"

His fingers followed a lock of hair pulled into her upsweep. "Vicky is the most important thing at the moment. Join us when she is soothed. I will make excuses for your absence." He paused, cocking his head to the side as a mischievous grin lifted his mouth. "Or no excuses. This is our home and we get to do as we please. I'll see the guests into dinner and you will see to Vicky—tell her all."

Sloane smiled, so wide it hurt her cheeks. "I made a good choice when I dragged you in front of that baker."

He guffawed. "I think we both know it was me doing the dragging."

She stepped around him to open the door, glancing over her shoulder at him. "Maybe it was, maybe it wasn't."

Laughing, he swatted her backside on the way out the door.

CHAPTER 20

"Vicky?" Sloane knocked again on Vicky's door as she glanced to the right at the empty hallway. She'd searched all the nooks and crannies Vicky liked to hide in during parties—her new niece had shown her each spot proudly when Sloane had first stayed at Wolfbridge. Spots where she could watch and listen but no one would notice her.

But Vicky was not in any of them. So Sloane had reversed course and come to her room again. There had been no answer in it an hour ago, but maybe Vicky had slipped back up here while Sloane had been searching.

The cacophony of music and voices floating up from the dining in the great hall trickled through the air, but she could still hear rustling from inside the room. She knocked on the door again. Vicky could be stubborn and Sloane knew she was resisting opening the door for her.

"Vicky." She knocked. "Please, I must speak with you."

No answer.

Stubborn or not, Sloane needed to right this wrong with Vicky immediately.

She set her fingers onto the door handle and cracked the door to give Vicky time to prepare for the intrusion.

Flames flickered in the fireplace, lending plenty of light to the room. Vicky had to still be awake—or maybe she was pretending to be asleep.

Sloane pushed the door open a bit further, stepping into the chamber.

She wasn't fully into the room before a hand grabbed her wrist, yanking her forward and slamming the door closed behind her.

Vicky wasn't that strong.

Sloane found her footing before stumbling to the floor and she spun. Just to the left of the door waited Lord Bockton—and Vicky. Vicky stood next to him in her nightgown, shaking, with a white strip of cloth cutting tightly across her mouth. Her hands bound behind her, tears were streaming down her face as strangled whimpers smothered against the cloth on her tongue.

"What?" Sloane's hands flew outward to her niece and she rushed toward Vicky. "What are you doing?"

"Stop if you value your life, your grace." Lord Bockton flashed something silver through the air.

A pistol.

Hell.

Sloane skidded to a stop. Still too far away from Vicky. Too many steps to reach her.

She tore her gaze off the girl and looked to Bockton. "Please, Lord Bockton, what are you doing with my niece?"

He glanced at Vicky and then grabbed her arm and started to drag her toward the door.

"Stop." Sloane jumped in front of them, blocking the door while attempting to ignore the pistol aimed at her body. "Let her go. What do you think you're doing?"

Lord Bockton shoved Sloane to the left with the backside of his gun hand. "Ensuring safe passage out of England. The girl is my insurance against the duke stopping us."

Sloane flailed off balance for a step, then caught her feet, spinning to grab his wrist that held Vicky's arm, her words frantic. "No—stop, you can't take her. Take me."

He stilled, looking down at her, his pale skin glowing eerily in the light of the fire as a haunting chuckle rang from his throat. "I was hoping you would say that, little birdy. I'll take both of you."

Her eyes narrowed at him. "It was you—you are the one that Falsted wanted to introduce me to. You are the one that the duke wanted to find. He found out who you are, didn't he? He's going to see you hanged."

"So he did. The idiot Falsted told him. And now the intrigue is over. My only thought now is to remove myself from this land before that becomes a reality." He waved his pistol in Sloane's face. "And you two will ensure that happens."

"No." Sloane screamed the word, trying to wedge herself between him and Vicky. "You take me—not her. You take her with you and I will fight you every step of the way. Leave the girl and I'll happily go with you." She wedged both of her hands on the arm he held Vicky with and yanked at it. "Falsted told you of my plan—I ken he did. That I am waiting for the right moment to ruin the duke. Nothing has changed. I still want the man to suffer. You can escape this without taking the girl."

She took a sudden step backward, curbing the desperation in her voice. Desperation shrieked of lies. She couldn't have that. Not if she was to save Vicky.

She wasn't prepared to deal with a madman, but she didn't have a choice. And that's what Bockton was. Utterly mad.

And the only thing that madness responded to was more madness.

She steeled herself, setting her voice to cold disregard. "You see how the duke loves me. He'll do anything stupid for me. Like follow me into a death trap."

"Death?" Bockton's eyes flickered to her with a glimmer of interest.

She nodded. "I leave with you now, and it will give you time to arrange it. The duke disappears and you have nothing to worry about." She flicked a finger toward Vicky. "The girl he doesn't care for much at all. I doubt he'll even realize she is gone. But me—me, he will miss."

Vicky's eyes went wide, then shut tight with a tortured sob.

Sloane knew her words were killing Vicky, wounding her to the core, but there was no recourse for it. She had to get this madman out of Wolfbridge and away from Vicky— away from Reiner—any way she could.

Her look sliced into him. "Lord Bockton, you are beginning to bore me." She nodded to Vicky. "If you cannot grasp the fact that the girl will only hinder us as we get you to—where is it you plan to escape to?"

His head jerked back slightly. "I have one of my ships off the coast." Bockton's eyes narrowed, his words high and thin, just like his face. "I have heard Falsted's version, but tell me yourself what you have to gain with this." A command, not a question.

"You ken I wish the duke to be ruined?"

Bockton nodded.

Sloane shrugged. "If the duke comes after us to retrieve me from you, I win. Either he dies in an unfortunate

accident or he saves me and my plan to destroy him with
the ledger book and Falsted's help will continue. If he
doesn't come after me, I escape with you and start a new
life elsewhere—I'm positive you can accommodate that
in exchange for my assistance—and the duke has the
humiliation and scandal of a wife that abandoned him on
his wedding day to suffer. Whichever way it falls, I win, he
loses."

Another heaving sob shook Vicky.

For all Sloane wanted to wrap her arms around Vicky,
squirrel her away and hide her in a corner where her niece
would never get hurt, she held her arms solidly on her sides.
No emotion. Emotion would betray her.

A smile, slick with how it wormed its way onto his
mouth, stretched his thin skin tight. "We will have it your
way. You, not the girl."

Sloane flicked her head toward the bed. "Set her on
the bed, tie her foot to the rail. She'll be fine until morning
when the maid finds her."

Bockton's lifeless eyes skewered her. "You will come
willingly?"

"Absolutely." She nodded, biting back bile chasing up
her throat. "I have just as much to gain. And just as much
to lose."

~ ~ ~

Reiner's knuckles rapped on Vicky's door.

Sloane hadn't made it down to the dinner, which
meant her conversation with Vicky was taking much longer

than anticipated. Maybe all his niece needed was for him to assure her that Sloane was to be trusted.

Hell, Vicky probably already did trust Sloane more than him. A fact that would have made this all the more difficult for Vicky—not knowing who to turn to, to trust.

He knocked again on the wood, leaning his ear toward the door to listen below the strains of music and the buzz from the dancing that had resumed in the ballroom.

A small thud. Nothing more.

Another knock and he opened the door. His body froze.

Vicky sprawled on the bed, her hands bound behind her back, a gag tied about her mouth, and her foot tied to a bottom post of the bed. Her other foot swung in the air, thunking onto the wood post and making only the slightest sound.

Dammit. Not Vicky. Not the one person that couldn't defend herself. The one he was supposed to protect above all others. He swore it. Swore it to her mother.

Rage like he'd never known seared through his veins. He rushed to Vicky, his fingers franticly untying the rag across her mouth.

He tossed the strip of cloth onto the floor, his fingers furious on the knot binding her wrists awkwardly behind her back. "Vicky—blasted rope—what happened? Who did this to you? And where the devil is Sloane? She was supposed to be here—be in here."

A sob twisted into a cough in her throat and Vicky shrank away from his barked words. Angry, vicious words.

He had no place yelling at her. Not when she'd just been terrified so.

He coughed, trying to clear the rage from his throat, and reset his voice. "I didn't mean to yell, Vicky. I'm just horrified to find you like this—none of this is your fault." He ripped open the last thread of rope and freed her wrists. His hand on her back, he sat her up and then moved to the rope about her ankle at the foot of the bed.

He glanced up at her from the knots.

Stupefied and shaking, tears streamed down her cheeks. She'd been terrorized beyond comprehension.

But he needed answers from her. "Vicky, I know you're scared, but you need to find a way to talk to me right now. Fight through the tears to tell me what happened. Sob, cry, whatever it takes to get the words out, I need them. Tell me who did this to you."

A stuttered wail, and then words formed on Vicky's tongue. "She—she told him to tie me up like this."

Reiner's fingers stilled. His body froze as the blood in his veins turned to ice.

It took him several seconds to lift his gaze to his niece.

His words a tortured whisper, his look found her tear-stained face. "Who told who to tie you up? This is important, Vicky."

"Sl—Sloane did."

All air left his body, his heart stilling.

He didn't hear her right. He couldn't have.

"Sloane did what?"

She gasped a solid breath and words tumbled out of her lips, her tongue not fast enough to keep pace with the rush. "She told him to tie me to the bed before they left. He had come in here after I was done watching the dancing. He followed me and told me not to scream or he'd choke

me. And I believed him. And he tied me up—my arms and then shoved that rag in my mouth and tied it around my head and it hurt—it hurt so much, Uncle Reiner." Her face crumpled, tears flowing again.

Reiner let loose the last knot on her ankle and reached out, wrapping his arms around her, bringing her to his chest. She came willingly, happily—a safe haven in the middle of the maelstrom about her.

"Wait." He tugged slightly away from Vicky so he could look down at her face. "He had already tied your arms together before Sloane was in here?"

"He did. He had tied me up and was going to take me, but then Sloane came in the door."

"Did he say why he tied you up?"

Her head shook and then collapsed against his chest, her fingers tight on the lapels of his tailcoat. "No. Just that I better walk with him and better not scream or try to get away."

"Do you know his name?"

"Sloane called him Bockton."

He gasped, raging breath filling his lungs. "So he was planning on taking you out of here when Sloane came in?"

"Yes. And she said awful things again—awful, awful things. She said I wasn't worth as much—that you wouldn't care if he took me. That he should take her because it would destroy you if she left and I was nothing to you."

"So he decided to leave you here?"

"Sloane said I wasn't worth the trouble. That I wasn't worth anything." Her words cut out with a sob. "Then she left with him."

"Did he tie her up?"

Vicky shook her head. "No. She said you would either follow her and then meet with an unfortunate accident or if you saved her she could come back and ruin you as she had planned. She said either way she would win. She means that she wins when you die, Uncle Reiner, and I don't want you to die."

"I'm not going to die, Vicky." His hand clasped to the back of her head, smoothing her hair. "But I am going after Sloane."

"No." Her head jerked away from him. "You can't. She wants you dead and I'm scared and I don't want you to go. Why is she like this? I thought...I thought she loved us and now she wants you hurt or dead."

His mouth pulled to a tight line. "She doesn't have it in her, Vicky. Trust me."

Her hands tugged on his coat. "No, please, Uncle Reiner, she wants to ruin you—kill you—don't go."

"I have to, Vicky." He peeled her fingers away from his lapels and stood from the bed, picking up the rope and rag as he moved. "I'll send Miss Gregory in to sit with you tonight—every night until I am back. Mrs. Flurten and Claude and Lawrence will also always be around you. You are safe, do you understand?"

She nodded. "But what about you, Uncle Reiner? How will you be safe?"

"Sloane isn't about to hurt me, Vicky. And I cannot let anything happen to her either."

He turned from Vicky's distressed blue eyes and walked out of the room.

Vicky was wrong. Wrong about all of it. She had to be.

Sloane was probably downstairs at this very moment, chatting with their guests.

He was sure of it.

~ ~ ~

Reiner stood at the edge of the ballroom just inside the open French doors leading to the gardens. He searched the couples gliding across the dance floor, the melody of a waltz floating down from the minstrels' gallery along the north side of the room.

A waltz. Of course.

Every nook had been checked. Every face looked upon. Sloane was no longer at Wolfbridge.

His butler appeared next to him and Reiner couldn't quite yank his eyes away from the merriment of the dancers, willing his wife to appear in the arms of a random man—any man. It didn't matter who she was touching, just that she appeared.

He leaned sideways to Colton, his eyes focused forward, his voice low. "Anything?"

"No, your grace. Every room has been checked, one level at a time with watchers at all the stairs. There was no slipping past us. The same in the gardens."

As expected, but still a blow to his gut. "Where is her brother?"

"We checked with them first. All of the Scotsmen were in their rooms. They are preparing to leave Wolfbridge, your grace."

"Good riddance."

Reiner's eyes narrowed. Across the ballroom Falsted stepped out of the billiards room, smoothing the front of his tailcoat.

Reiner charged across the ballroom, cutting through the dance floor with no regard to the twirling couples stumbling in his wake.

Falsted jumped like the weasel he was just before Reiner wrapped his hand around Falsted's throat. He shoved him backward into the billiards room before he could consider what he was doing in front of an audience.

"Clear it." His yell thundered into the billiards room and all the men jumped, quickly scurrying through the doorways.

Footman closed the doors and Reiner spun Falsted to the nearest wall, slamming him back against the plaster as his fingers tightened about his throat. "Tell me where my wife is, Falsted."

Falsted's hands scrambled against Reiner's arm. "Why would I know that?"

Reiner loosened his hold for a second, then cracked Falsted's head against the wall again. "You know exactly what Bockton's plan is—he has been exposed and now he means to escape. And the bastard took my damn wife with him."

"I—I don't know anything."

His fingers gouged into the flesh of Falsted's neck. "He is not nearly the threat to you that I am, so tell me where in the hell he has taken my wife."

Falsted's head shook back and forth. "No—no, he wouldn't."

"He bloody well did. He took my wife to ensure his escape."

"I—I cannot—he'll kill me."

Reiner shoved his face in Falsted's, the fury of a thousand Roman warriors at his lips. "I know you're a sniveling coward when it comes to that bastard, but now you have someone even more deadly to worry about—me. So where in the blasted world is my wife?"

Reiner's hold around Falsted's neck cut his air and all the man could do was nod.

Reiner slightly eased his fingers from Falsted's neck. Just enough for air.

Falsted gasped, his fingers still clutching Reiner's arm, but too weak against Reiner's strength. "Fine." He coughed, his throat barely letting wheezed words through. "I shouldn't have told you of him. He's on his way to one of his ships to escape. The closest one is on the coast off of Butterwick. He means to get to the continent and still run his smuggling empire from there."

Reiner dropped his hand from Falsted's neck.

Hell and damnation.

At night Butterwick was only a six-hour carriage ride away. Four by fast horse. And then to navigate the salt marshes and lagoons, another two, possibly. And Bockton had left two hours—maybe more—ago.

He stormed out of the billiards room. Colton was standing just outside, waiting discreetly. Good man.

"Get her brother."

"I just received word that he has set out with his camp."

"In the middle of the night?"

Colton nodded.

"Where to?"

"I assume the northern route, your grace, but it has not been confirmed. They departed an hour past while we were searching for her grace."

Damn, her brother was now an hour in the wrong direction. An hour he couldn't spare.

"And Sloane wasn't with him—you are positive?"

"No. Not according to the two stable boys that helped pack their wagon. I did send a rider out to verify the information and their route."

Reiner stepped back inside the billiards room and looked at Falsted. The man still slumped against the wall, catching his breath. "It is you and I, Falsted. You know where the ship is so you're going to bring me to my wife and that heinous bastard." He stepped toward Falsted, his voice a growl. "And if you're wrong about this, may the devil take pity on your soul as I rip it from your body."

{ CHAPTER 21 }

Sloane gave one last glance over her shoulder before she stepped into one of the three skiffs set on the shore of the small cove of shifting sands.

No one.

Trees beyond the cove.

Sandy shoreline about her that lifted into a dune hugging the cove.

A tidal waterway surging inward at the crux of the three-quarter circle of sand.

And not a soul in the early morning light.

Not Reiner. Not her brother.

No one.

She had hoped against hope that someone would find Vicky before Bockton's carriage got too far from Wolfbridge. Vicky was safe from him. That was what had mattered. But once they were off Reiner's lands, she would have welcomed anyone to intervene and extract her from Bockton's clutches.

But for what she'd had to say about Vicky in order to get Bockton to leave her at Wolfbridge, she didn't expect her niece was about to encourage anyone to come after her.

Least of all Reiner.

Yet if her brother and Domnall knew—they would come for her. She didn't doubt that. But she'd left in such a storm of destruction with her words, she had to accept the fact that Reiner wouldn't tell her brother a thing. No one would be coming.

Not until it was too late.

"Get in the boat, Duchess." Bockton's nasally voice slid with mockery around the word "duchess."

Water sloshing about her feet, soaking her fine silk slippers, she lifted her leg and stepped into the rowboat in front of two disinterested sailors sitting at the oars. Unbalanced, the boat swayed with her movement and she flailed for a moment, falling until she grabbed onto the lip of the skiff to steady herself.

Within fifteen minutes, she was awkwardly ascending the ladder onto the smuggling ship waiting just offshore, attempting to keep the folds of her skirts tight to her legs so the two men beneath her didn't get a view.

She stepped off the ladder onto the main deck of the ship and glanced about. Deckhands were scurrying about, heavy coils of rope unfurling, a constant barrage of orders and blasphemies filling the air around her. Not a one looked at her. Not a one paused a step, other than to push past her as they hauled rope and canvas. Bockton stood across the deck, talking to a stout man with a thick beard and a faded blue coat—the captain, she presumed.

Leaving the captain, Bockton walked across the deck toward her, dodging the busy sailors running to and fro. He stopped at the side of the ship, setting his thin fingers on the railing and looking out to the land. The tips of his long fingernails tapped on the wood. "Take a last look, Duchess, for this isle will never be yours again. You realize you can never return."

"I can and I will. My family is here and I intend to return to them after some time." Her head tilted to the side as she stared at his profile, refusing to look toward the land.

The wide brim of his top hat sent a deep shadow across his ghostly skin. "But you—this is the last time you'll be able to see your home. You realize you will be hunted, far and wide, for your crimes."

"I don't worry upon that."

"Is it worth it? Your title will be stripped, your lands forfeit."

"It is. My estate in Belgium will surround me with the finest luxuries until my dying days. Or my estate in the West Indies will do the same, though the heat is not to my liking. Either one is a far better fate than the crumbling abbey and the bone dry coffers I inherited with my title."

Her lips pulled inward for a long moment. "You realize that the duke will find you, eventually. Even if you chose to be half a world away. He is not one to let a trespass slide."

Bockton looked down at her. "The problem with Wolfbridge is that I never had anything to leverage against him were he to find out my identity. No vices. No bastard children. No suspect investments. I looked far and wide for something after that idiot Falsted entangled him in my business. But there has been nothing he cares about, save for that niece of his—not that I ever got the impression he cared much for the girl."

Sloane winced. She'd said the very same thing to cover for how very important Vicky was, but to hear someone else speak the blasphemy cut her to the core. She knew how deeply Reiner loved Vicky. Like she was his own—because she was.

"But with you, Duchess—with you it's clear in his eyes. Any fool could see that he is besotted in a way that will be

most detrimental to him." A smirk curled the thin edges of his lips. "You are leverage, your grace. The best kind."

"What do you mean, leverage?" Her right eyebrow lifted. "I came with you willingly. I ensured your escape as I said I would. Your use of me is over and we will part ways on the continent."

"You can cease the farce, your grace." His right hand stayed on the smooth wooden railing as he turned fully to her. "I know you don't mean to ruin him—you never did. We are a long way from the continent and it will get tedious watching you maintain this charade of yours."

"You're wrong."

"I'm not." He shook his head, the line of the shadow bobbing along his chin. "You almost had me convinced. I thought to believe you for a few hours. But your actions since leaving Wolfbridge have failed you. Constant glances over your shoulder. The worry on your face." He exhaled an exaggerated sighed. "I should have taken the girl, as well, shouldn't I?"

Her lips pulled into a tight line. "Probably. Having Vicky would have ensured you of anything you wanted from the duke. A full pardon from the crown. Riches so plentiful you wouldn't ever have to scurry to the underbelly of the seas." The full truth, because it didn't matter now. The bastard was far away from Vicky and Wolfbridge. That was what mattered. "Though had you taken the girl he also would have hunted you down like the animal you are and killed you."

The next breath she took fell easily into her lungs. Relief. Finally.

An odd reprieve, free of should-haves and regrets. Free of the constant gnawing in her stomach over worry on Vicky and Reiner.

This ship was leaving as soon as the sails hoisted and there was nothing more she could do on it. By now, Reiner would have found Vicky and she would have told him what happened. What she had said. And he would never let her near him or Vicky again. Never.

Lord Bockton chuckled. "At last, we are at a shared understanding."

Sloane shook her head. "I don't ken that we are. You overestimate the leverage you think I am. For what I said about my niece, about my husband in her room—I am nothing to him now. A wife he will declare dead as soon as it is reasonable. A memory to be forgotten."

"Yet I still need something from him."

She stared at him for a long moment, her eyes narrowing. *Hell.* "The book?"

He inclined his head with a side smirk. "There are people in that ledger that I need to exonerate. To do that, I need the book destroyed."

Sloane chuckled. "You do realize you'll not get the book? Falsted wanted it as well to exonerate himself— maybe to ruin you with it for the sick games you two are playing with each other. But it will never be yours."

"No?" Bockton's mouth twisted in an odd line between a smirk and a frown. "Why not?"

"My husband doesn't have it."

"I know—I know you took it. My men sent a missive with that very message not but a day before they disappeared."

"Those were your men?"

"Yes." The slimy smile slithered back onto his face. "You think the dolt Falsted is smart enough to have you followed?" His long fingers tapped silently along the railing. "Tell me, how did my men disappear?"

"A bog ate them."

He stilled for a long breath, then nodded. "Fitting. They were not the smartest men. And you did not give the book back to the duke?"

She shook her head. "But I can get you the book." If this was how she was going to protect both Vicky and Reiner from Bockton ever setting designs on them again, she'd do it. She'd give him anything, including that blasted ledger.

"Hmm." He stroked his chin for a long moment. "Yet I will not need the book if I kill you. It will mold and rot away in whatever place you've stashed it—long past the time anyone will care what evidence is in it." He stepped closer, his thin fingers pulling along a rogue strand of hair at her temple that had fallen from her upsweep.

She jerked away from his touch.

"So what do you propose I do with you? A newly minted duchess, ripe for the taking. Why, you didn't even get a wedding night. That is a shame."

Bile snaked up her throat and she skewered him with all the hundreds of years of hatred her forefathers had borne upon Englishman such as him. "It doesn't matter what you think to do with me. You'll not hear me scream or cry or beg." Her chin lifted, her look unwavering on him. "But I will resist. Do you truly want to chance taking on a Scottish woman well trained with a dagger—or a fork, or a cut of glass, or a shard of wood? I'm not particular about my weapons and there are a thousand ways to kill you, Lord Bockton. All I need is one reason."

A strained chuckle flew from his thin throat. "Or simply, my dear, I kill you first. I do have need to keep you, though, at least until we reach the shore of the continent. Then, then I think I shall leave you to my men. Most of them haven't ever seen such a highborn lady—a duchess at that. Much less touched one." A serpent smirk slid across his face. "Oh, the tales they will tell."

She kept her chin high, belying the fact that her stomach had flipped and hardened into a churning rock threatening to make her heave.

"My lord—there be a skiff a'coming." The captain of the ship approached them, pointing past Bockton's shoulder to the water. "Did ye have more joinin' the party before we set sail? We are ready."

"A what?" Bockton's eyebrows drew together as he eyed the captain.

"Two men, rowing out." The captain pointed to the water between the ship and shore again.

Bockton spun to the water, his fingers gripping the railing.

Sloane followed suit, her look casual about the water until she saw the rowboat bob into view just past the stern of the ship.

Two men rowed with a fury, one on each oar with their backs to the ship.

The man on the left smaller. The one on the right, big, strong. Strong like…

Reiner.

A gasp flew from her lips and she gripped onto the railing, leaning out to see past the stern. The skiff was halfway to the ship. The man on the right glanced back over his shoulder.

Heaven to hell. It was Reiner.

Bockton chuckled next to her. "So he did come—you are the exact leverage I suspected you would be. But I think he'll be much more useful alive—alive and knowing I have you." He glanced to the captain. "Set sail."

Bockton's thin white cheek lifted as his look fell back down to the rowboat quickly skimming across the shallow waves. "Sails up before we have to kill him. I don't know what the fool thinks to accomplish boarding a ship full of men ready to skewer him at my command."

The sudden hope that had flared in her chest at seeing Reiner twisted, falling past the pit of her stomach. Reiner would be killed the second he set foot upon the deck.

Because of her.

She wasn't about to let that happen.

In that moment, her intentions crystallized into a needlepoint of focus. He wouldn't be killed. Not the man she loved. Not the man she would give up this earth for.

It took her less than a second to scan her surroundings and find a dagger hanging in a sheath off the waist of a deckhand six steps from her.

Without a sound, she turned and ran for him, yanking the dagger free as she knocked the two of them down. Arms and legs tangled, a litany of curses showered upon her as she found her feet.

One quick glance at Bockton. Amused, he chuckled at the scene.

Exactly as intended.

Let him think her a desperate, clumsy oaf.

Dagger in hand, hidden from his view, she stumbled a few steps on her feet facing the deckhand. Without looking over her shoulder, she slid the blade between her breasts, ripping downward through the bodice of her ball gown, tearing the fabric wide.

The deckhand's jaw went slack, the cursing silent as confusion registered in his eyes. Confusion she saw reflected on Bockton's face as she turned and ran toward the railing of the deck, ripping off her gown as she aimed for the railing.

Bockton saw her intention just as she set her hand upon the railing. Her gown only half off her body, it would have to do. She lifted herself over the railing just as Bockton lunged at her, his long fingernails scratching her arm. She flicked the blade in her hand outward, digging into his hand as she flew over the railing.

His scream pierced the air above her.

For one glorious second, she was free.

Just her and the air around her.

Free.

She hit the water hard, feet first. The shattering pain shooting up her legs stole her breath just as the sea swallowed her.

Her skirts heavy, pulling her downward, she sawed at the fabric pulling her away from the air. Away from the sunlight. Away from Reiner.

Now she had to survive.

~ ~ ~

"Row man. Row." Reiner's holler at Falsted cut above the churning of the sea with the furious pace he'd set with his own oar. "Faster. Faster. Faster." He looked over his shoulder at the ship. He could see Sloane's head above the top railing of the deck.

Sloane and Bockton.

A surge of fury poured through his veins and he pulled the oar with the strength of a hundred Vikings. "Faster, I said."

"I'm an old man."

"You'll be a bloody dead man if you don't keep pace. Faster."

Falsted looked over his shoulder at the ship they were closing in upon. "What?" He stopped rowing.

Reiner spun around.

Twisting backward just in time to see Sloane drop into the sea, feet first.

His world, his breath, his soul stopped.

One second passed. Two. Three.

She didn't resurface.

"She's gone," Falsted whispered. "That gown is dragging her to depths as we speak."

Falsted's voice yanked Reiner out of his shock.

He jumped to his feet, sending the small boat rocking. Yanking off his waistcoat, shirt and boots, he checked to make sure his dagger was secured with the strap about his calf so he could cut the dress free from her body. "She's not gone. And you better follow me and be ready to pull her from the water when I get her or this is your last day on earth, Falsted."

Falsted nodded, shifting to the center of the bench and taking both oars.

Reiner dove in.

His arms swung as brutally hard as they could through the water, his legs spiriting him fast along the waves. But not fast enough. His damn trousers were slowing him. In between strokes, he ripped free the false front, kicking out of them.

Closing in on the ship, he dove under the surface, the salt water stinging his eyes as he searched.

Up. Up for air.

Down. Down again, as far as his lungs would allow. Searching. Searching to where the sunlight dissipated into darkness.

Then he saw it. Pink. A flash of pink.

Pain seared his lungs, threatening to explode them as he went deeper. Stretching out. Pink fabric within his fingertips.

He yanked on the cloth. But it was free. Floating. No Sloane.

He spun. Spun in the water again and again, his eyes searching.

Sloane.

Sloane floating, suspended, her arms wide. Not sinking, not rising. Not moving.

Just as his lungs were about to burst, he reached her, grabbing her arm and stretching upward toward the light. Toward the air.

He broke free of the surface, his mouth open and gasping before he was into clear air. Yanking Sloane above the surface, he waited for her to choke in a breath.

Nothing.

His head swiveled, not seeing the rowboat.

Damn the bastard.

"Here. Here," Falsted called out from behind him.

Five hard strokes and Reiner dragged Sloane to the skiff.

Falsted dangled over the side, ready to grab Sloane's arms. With a heave, he pulled her dead weight upward, but her wet wrists slipped from his grasp. He lost his balance, falling into the boat, and her body fell back down onto Reiner.

"Grab her under her arms—yank her up hard," Reiner ordered.

Falsted scurried over the side again, setting his grip under her arms, and he jerked her upward with a grunt. But she slipped from Falsted's grasp again and he flew backward, landing hard on the bottom of the skiff. For a moment, her body teetered on the lip of the boat until the top of her slunk forward and she dropped hard, the edge of the boat kicking a straight line into her gut.

Blasted weakling. Not entirely successful—but successful enough that Sloane didn't fall back into the water. Reiner wrapped a hand along her thigh, holding the bulk of her weight up past the edge so she didn't slip down into the water again.

A cough.

Gagging.

Her body convulsed and water hurled from her lungs into the boat.

The sweetest sound Reiner had ever heard in his life.

He reached up and gripped the lip of the skiff and yanked himself upward. He had to see it, had to see her moving before he could do anything else.

Still draped over the side of the boat like a wet rag, her body writhed, expelling surge after surge of the sea from her lungs and stomach.

He glanced at Falsted, still on the bottom of the boat on the opposite side of them. "Stay there—counterbalance."

Falsted nodded and Reiner pulled himself up and over the edge of the boat. He sat on the front bench beside Sloane, his hand splaying on her back, almost afraid to touch her. Afraid if he moved her from the spot she was in all the water in her lungs would stay in place and drown her fully.

Six more heaves, and her body stilled, her breath panting.

Normal enough for him.

Reiner grabbed her fully, pulling her into the boat and onto his lap. His arms wrapped around her, tucking her under his chin, clutching her to him. Clutching her away from death and back to the living.

Falsted scrambled to the oars, sitting with his back to them as he worked them toward the shore.

Reiner looked past Falsted's head to the ship, noting the scrolled name adorning the rear of the ship. The *Minerva*. "Does Bockton look to come after us? Did any come down on boats in pursuit?"

"No. The sails have already caught wind." Falsted shook his head, not turning to look at Reiner. "He's more intent on making it out to sea before the Royal Navy catches the ship. If he doesn't get to the continent, he's done for."

Reiner grunted. For as much as he wanted to crush Bockton into the cold ground, he couldn't do a thing about it in his present state. That would have to wait until another day.

"You're naked." Sloane's voice, small and scratchy, wafted up to him.

He pulled his head back and looked down at her. Her blue eyes were wide and clear. A breath he didn't know he held escaped him. "And you're nearly naked in your chemise."

"I had to cut my gown away." She stretched backward against his arms, her limp fingers going to her stomach and rubbing at the thin fabric. Her eyes closed with a wince. "I got it mostly off, but then I had to saw it away from my legs. I started kicking, but then everything went black."

"It was enough." He kissed her forehead, her skin far too cold from the sea for his liking.

Her eyes popped open. "You saved me naked. Why did you save me naked?"

"My trousers were slowing me down."

She nodded, her eyes squinting at him in confusion for a long moment. Then a smile found its way to her lips. "That makes sense. But now we are both near to naked in a desolate cove."

"I'm positive Lord Falsted will scurry with haste to the cottage on the inland ridge and retrieve us proper enough clothes for the journey back to Wolfbridge."

"Falsted?" Her head swiveled to look at the back of Falsted.

To the man's credit, he kept his eyes forward, his pulls of the oars steady.

She looked up at Reiner. "You have some explaining to do."

A smile he couldn't quite control came to his face. "As do you."

{ CHAPTER 22 }

Reiner lifted her out of the boat after pulling it ashore. Off to fetch clothing, Falsted was already to the high edge of the cove, scrambling up the shifting sands that led from the beach.

Reiner held her for a moment in midair, clasping his warm body to hers as though the effort it took to leave her in the skiff at the water's edge as he pulled the boat in had crushed his very soul.

She didn't mind.

He'd put on his boots and his lawn shirt, and it hung low enough onto his thighs that it mostly covered what needed to be covered. He'd draped his waistcoat about her, which covered mostly what needed to be covered under her wet, transparent chemise.

Not that she minded him naked. Not at all. Not when she had just lived through moments where she'd thought she'd never see him again—and most certainly not in the nude.

He let her slide down his body, her toes burying into the sand.

"Ouch." Pain shot up her legs when her weight settled on her feet and she started to fall. "My feet."

He immediately picked her up again, his brow furrowed as he bent and set her backside onto the sand. "Both of your feet?"

"Yes." The sharp pangs shifted into swelling throbs rolling from her toes to her heels, one after another. She leaned back, her fingers curling into the sand. Her gloves had come off in the sea, and the tiny rough rocks of the shore rubbed into her left hand, a cool, odd relief against the itch of her scars.

Reiner dropped to his knees and lifted her right foot, examining it. Then he picked up her left, his fingers gentle across the skin.

"You went feet first into the water, you may have fractured them, but hopefully only bruised them." His low voice took on a hard edge. "Though if you hadn't, you could have died, Sloane—your body slamming into the water like that. It was too far a fall and you never should have jumped. You should have waited for me."

"I wasn't about to wait, Reiner." She stared at her feet, swallowing the sharp pangs of pain making her nauseous. "There wasn't any way I was going to let you board that ship. Not for me. You were headed for certain death."

"So your death was a better choice?" His voice notched up into a yell. "A damn idiotic idea."

Her look whipped up to him, her voice echoing his. "My death was preferable to your death, yes. So not so idiotic. But I also planned on living. I slit my dress on the deck—it was supposed to come off directly so I could swim."

His lip curled and he heaved in a breath. "Still a bloody foolish move."

Her fingers pointed to her chest, then to his. "I'm alive. You're alive. That is what matters."

He grunted a sigh. Not willing to agree with her, but not about to argue the point.

She'd take it.

He set her left foot gently down into the sand, then moved to sit next to her, pulling his bare knees upward and resting his forearms atop.

Sloane stared at his profile for a long moment. At the distinctive line of his jaw still flickering in anger, the slight dark scruff of a beard starting, his golden brown eyes staring out at the ship that was quickly disappearing from sight.

Her husband.

The man she never knew she wanted, but now needed like nothing else.

Her hand went to his cheek, her palm dragging across the dark scruff, pinpricks teasing her skin. "You believed in me. You came. You only knew where I was because you found Vicky. And she would have told you what I said."

His head dropped forward, his eyes closing for five long breaths. Her hand fell away from his jawline.

He lifted his forehead, his gaze pinning her. "I've always believed in you, Sloane. It's been my problem from the first."

She jerked back. "Your problem?"

"Yes. Absolutely and unequivocally. I believe in you over common sense and sanity. And it has taken a complete loss of control to keep you in my life. To keep you safe—alive. To trust."

"Oh." The blood drained from her face. "I didn't realize. I—I only said those vile things to Bockton because he was going to take Vicky. I had to make him take me and leave her and I was willing to do anything—to say anything to make that happen."

He nodded. "I suspected as much—no—I knew as much. You love her just as much as I do—probably more."

She nodded. "I do. I would do anything for her—for you. I protect my people. Vicky is my people. *You* are my people."

"Exactly—you know no bounds, Sloane. And I...I..." He paused, looking out to the sea, his head shaking slowly. "I had order—sanity before you fell into my life. And you are none of those things."

Her head dropped, the air rushing out of her, deflating her from scalp to throbbing toes.

His right hand slid under her chin and he lifted her head to look at him. "But I wouldn't have it any other way. I love you and you are worth it. Every second my heart has stopped because you were in danger. Every moment I wanted to throttle you for being so stubborn, so cantankerous. Every time you left me and I had to wrestle with the devil possibility of never seeing you again."

He clasped his left hand against her cheek, capturing her face in his palms. "Yet all of that is nothing compared to the moments I can hold you in my arms. Hear your laughter. Press my body into yours. Talk to you about nothing but the thickness of the vines growing on the castle. Bask in the light you bring into my world—into Vicky's world. You are the sun I—we—always needed."

Her body, her world slowed in that moment. Her heart shattering and building itself anew—stronger, without doubt of the past, without anger over what could never be changed. A heart never again to be haunted by demons of distrust.

An aching smile spread across her face. "If I am the sun, then you are my earth, Reiner. And you will always be so."

He pulled her close into a kiss so soft, so gentle from his lips it proved that for all the love in the world, they only needed the slightest touch. Something she'd always known, but never truly understood until that moment.

A cough from behind them interrupted their kiss.

Both of them craned their heads backward.

Falsted stood, holding a bundle of clothes in his arms, his face red with splotches and a sheen of perspiration glistening across his forehead. Apparently, the man didn't run very often.

"This clothing should do you well for the journey back to Wolfbridge."

Sloane's arm went across her breasts. She was covered enough by Reiner's waistcoat, but she wasn't about to take any chances where Falsted was concerned.

Reiner flicked a finger toward him. "Set it there and go. My horse is still on the other side of the cove?"

"It is."

"Have my men caught up with us yet?" He looked to Sloane. "Two horses went down in the salt marshes leading out here, so they were riding double."

Falsted shook his head. "Not as of yet." He set the pile of clothing on the ground, quickly turning to leave.

"Falsted, before you think to exit."

He turned back to them, his eyebrows lifting.

Reiner inclined his head toward Sloane. "Tell her."

Falsted's mouth opened and closed several times, looking at Reiner before his gaze shifted to Sloane. "I keep multiple copies of every contract I make with partners."

Her eyebrows drew together and she looked at Reiner.

Reiner's voice went hard. "The rest."

Falsted sighed. "The additional contracts are altered to cover any eventuality—reflect what I actually do. It appears as though my partners sign off on everything I do to fulfill the contracts."

"You mean…" She glanced from Falsted to Reiner.

"I never signed off on clearing the Swallowford lands," Reiner said. "Neither did my man. I had him triple check my copies with his staff."

Falsted nodded and quickly turned and started a retreat.

"Falsted." Reiner's voice echoed, bouncing along the sand dunes surrounding them.

Falsted slowed and half turned back to Reiner.

"You are not clear of this."

"No." Falsted shook his head. "But I do expect leniency, as you have your wife sitting, healthy and alive next to you."

No. Hell no.

In one quick motion, Sloane grabbed the dagger secured around Reiner's calf and twisted, scrambling to her toes even though the instant, vicious pain from her feet threatened to send her to her knees. "No, you bloody bastard. You don't get away that easily. Reiner may not see fit to gut you, but I am another matter."

Reiner chuckled and grabbed her wrist just before she was out of reach. He pulled her back, tugging her downward onto her knees.

The chuckle left his lips as he impaled Falsted with a fatal stare. "You've been warned, Falsted. Your next choices in life will determine what happens next. And that threat extends to any of the clearings you may have planned on

Scottish soil. Halt them now, for you don't want to make either my wife, or me, come after you looking for blood."

Falsted's jaw dropped. For a second, bitter chagrin overtook his face, but then he shook his head, a tight smile coming to his lips. He inclined his head to them. "Your grace." He turned and hastily started up the back edge of the sand.

On her knees, Sloane stared at the sniveling coward until he disappeared over the top line of the cove. She stuck the blade into the sand next to her and shifted onto her backside, facing her husband. "How could you let him go?"

Reiner shrugged. "I'm feeling generous?"

"But for all the blackguard set into motion."

"Plus I'm nearly naked—as are you." A grin on his face, his hand went along her shoulder, his fingers sliding under the loose locks of her wet hair as all the pins had long since been lost to the sea. "He sent you to me, even if the goal of it was my downfall. But were it not for him, I never would have met you."

She took a deep breath, filling her lungs, and then seethed it out. "That does not seem enough to wipe his sins clean."

"Don't worry, love, he will get his due." Reiner glanced to the rear of the cove. "Maybe not today, but a man like that will get his due. It is coming." He looked to her. "I thought you had given up vengeance."

"The man made me hate you—hate you, Reiner." She shook her head. "I am rethinking the thought that vengeance does have its place."

His hand curled around the back of her neck. "No, you were right."

"I was?"

"I'm sorry—it was my blasted need for vengeance that put you in danger. Vengeance that fed my bloody arrogance in that you and Vicky would be safe no matter what twisted minds were at Wolfbridge. And I was wrong. Vengeance obscured what I should have easily seen in front of me—the threat to you and Vicky."

"You couldn't have known Bockton was a lunatic."

"I should have." His head lowered between them.

She lifted her hands, sinking her fingers into his hair, tugging his look up to her. "You didn't fail me, Reiner. I wanted you to catch him. I wanted to help to unhinge the terror he and his partners have spread across the land. I wanted that peace for you."

His head leaned into her left hand, the scars brushing his cheek. "Vengeance is not a game I am willing to play any longer—not when I have the world sitting in front of me."

She inhaled, relief sinking into her lungs. "But what of Bockton?" She pointed out to the now empty sea, the waves lapping lazily on the shore.

"Falsted told me the name of the ship before we left Wolfbridge. I already sent word to the Royal Navy to pursue the *Minerva*. Wherever Bockton goes, the navy will be after him. And they are under direct orders to drag him back to England to stand for his crimes."

Her bottom lip jutted up in a frown. "Then let it be soon."

"Exactly." He leaned toward her, his lips brushing against hers. "But until then, it is not worth our worry. Not worth another breath of our time. Especially when I have a twice-made duchess to bed."

She laughed, pulling away for a second as she looked about them. Emptiness. Her gaze travelled back to him, a wicked smile on her lips. "Then what is stopping you?"

He gave a strangled groan, setting the length of her backward into the sand and hovering above her for a long breath, as though he were imprinting the picture of her body against the sand into his mind. "Absolutely nothing, my duchess. Absolutely nothing."

{ EPILOGUE }

The Wolf Duke was alone no more.

Far from it.

Especially not with his three-year-old son, Jacob, dangling from his neck, wedged onto the left side of his lap and making faces at his younger sister, Penelope, cradled in Reiner's right arm.

His body hadn't been his own since his son had started walking. The boy was always climbing atop him. Clearly born with his mother's love for scaling precariously tall objects.

But he wouldn't have it any other way.

From the settee, Reiner looked across the library at Sloane lifting their other twin girl, Priscilla, in her arms and set the babe's cherub face just above her shoulder. Priscilla gurgled up air, then smiled at him, her chubby cheeks expanding impossibly wide.

Both of his girls smiled far too much for their six months on earth. So much so, it was unnerving at times. Also a trait from their mother.

But he'd take that too.

Happily so.

Sloane leaned over the table, her look studying the seating chart Vicky had just created for the upcoming house party that would descend upon Wolfbridge in a few days. She shifted Priscilla tight into her bare left arm.

His look paused for a second on Sloane's scars. To see them now, he had to truly stare, for they had become just a

part of her—just as her eyes and her nose and her smile and her hair were.

She hadn't worn the glove in years—only out in public. She'd decided it was far too bothersome—and too often stained—after Jacob was born. And then the twins came, and there was no going back. Their lives were far too full for her to bother with constantly pulling the dratted glove on and off.

Sloane pointed with her right forefinger to a spot on the chart. "So well done, Vicky. It's perfect—and I never would have thought to seat Lady Harring next to Lady Thorew, but that is brilliant. Those two will feed off each other in a splendid way. You do have a knack for seeing how personalities play off one another."

Vicky beamed. She was looking more and more like her mother every day. "Thank you. Those two were the most difficult—what with how many people Lady Harring dislikes, and how Lady Thorew likes to talk endlessly about bee pollination."

Sloane's finger moved about the paper. "I just have one small change I would like to make. If we could maybe scoot Lord Apton to this location?"

Vicky's dark eyebrows lifted. "By Torrie?"

A mischievous smile curled onto Sloane's lips and she nodded.

"She's sat through a number of these dinners in the comfort of kind old dowagers cradling her. I think it is time she expand her conversation circle."

"But with Lord Apton?" Vicky asked.

"Yes. Lord Apton is harmless."

Reiner coughed a snort.

Sloane glanced back at him, shaking her head. She turned back to Vicky. "He's a very kind gentleman, quick witted, and he has a wide breadth of knowledge. He's older, but that has made him compassionate—he's no longer in the throes of the pomposity of youth. If any male can draw Torrie into conversation, it will be him."

Reiner heard the footsteps before Torrie walked into the room. The slight odd cadence of her boots on the floor. Torrie stepped into the library.

As he was the only one that noticed her arrival, Reiner cleared his throat pointedly, covering his wife's last words.

Sloane spun around, caught.

Torrie looked at Sloane's guilty face and her gaze went to Reiner, looking for the truth, as she knew she wouldn't get it from her cousin. "What did I interrupt?"

For all that Torrie was still bitter, still mad at the world, Reiner liked Torrie immensely. In the year she'd come to live with them at Wolfbridge, he could see how happy her presence made Sloane. They were as sisters, as Sloane had always said, and having Torrie back in her life had completed Sloane in a way he never could have imagined.

Anything—anyone—that made his wife happy, made him happy.

"Just your cousin's plotting for the upcoming house party," Reiner said as he wrapped an arm around Jacob's waist, tickling him. His boy squealed, giggling, falling away from Reiner on the cushions.

"Ah." Torrie looked to Sloane. "Matchmaking are we again? After your coup last time with Miss Dainers and Lord Newrun you are feeling confident?"

Sloane chuckled. "Something akin to that."

Torrie stepped to the settee, her hands ruffling Jacob's hair. "I was looking for this younger cousin of mine—he promised me he was going to take me to find the giant anthill he found in the woods."

"Ants, eh?" Reiner leaned over, getting one last tickle in before Jacob bolted. "Well then, you best get to it."

"I will come as well," Vicky said from across the library, jumping up from her chair at the table.

Still trying to avoid her Italian lesson, the scamp.

Sloane didn't remind her of the lesson. Conspirator.

Jacob already tugging on her right hand, Torrie held out her left fingers to Vicky. She ran across the room before Reiner could remind her of her lesson with Miss Gregory. For one second, Reiner thought to remind his niece of her lesson, but then he kept his mouth closed. Ants were important. Aside from the fact that not a one in the library would have backed him on the need for the lesson. Including his wife.

Always outnumbered.

A smile crept onto his face.

And that was a wonderful feeling. Exactly as it should be.

He was a lucky, lucky man.

~ About the Author ~

K.J. Jackson is the USA Today bestselling author of the
*Hold Your Breath, Lords of Fate, Lords of Action,
Revelry's Tempest, Valor of Vinehill,*
and *Flame Moon* series.

She specializes in historical and paranormal romance,
loves to travel (road trips are the best!), and is a sucker for a
good story in any genre. She lives in Minnesota with
her husband, two children, and a dog who
has taken the sport of bed-hogging
to new heights.

Visit her at www.kjjackson.com

~ Author's Note ~

Thank you for allowing my stories into your life
and time—it is an honor!

Be sure to check out all my historical romances
(each is a stand-alone story):
Stone Devil Duke, *Hold Your Breath*
Unmasking the Marquess, *Hold Your Breath*
My Captain, My Earl, *Hold Your Breath*
Worth of a Duke, *Lords of Fate*
Earl of Destiny, *Lords of Fate*
Marquess of Fortune, *Lords of Fate*
Vow, *Lords of Action*
Promise, *Lords of Action*
Oath, *Lords of Action*
Of Valor & Vice, *Revelry's Tempest*
Of Sin & Sanctuary, *Revelry's Tempest*
Of Risk & Redemption, *Revelry's Tempest*
To Capture a Rogue, *Logan's Legends, Revelry's Tempest*
To Capture a Warrior, *Logan's Legends, Revelry's Tempest*
The Devil in the Duke, *Revelry's Tempest*
The Iron Earl, *Valor of Vinehill*
The Wolf Duke, *Valor of Vinehill*

Never miss a new release or sale!
Be sure to sign up for my VIP Email List at
www.KJJackson.com

Interested in Paranormal Romance?
In the meantime, if you want to switch genres and check out my Flame
Moon paranormal romance series, **Flame Moon #1**, the first book in the
series, is currently free (ebook) at all stores. **Flame Moon** is a stand-alone
story, so no worries on getting sucked into a cliffhanger. But number two in
the series, **Triple Infinity**, ends with a fun cliff, so be forewarned. Number
three in the series, **Flux Flame**, ties up that portion of the series.

Connect with me!
www.KJJackson.com
kjk19jackson@gmail.com

Lightning Source UK Ltd.
Milton Keynes UK
UKHW040616281119
354396UK00002B/422/P